Review

"This [The Speed of Dark] was a hor
pleased to have read ... There is a lot of scope and dimension in
these short stories." - Jess Scott, author of *To IRAQ and Back*

"The *Speed of Dark* is ... one of those hard-to-put-down books
that keeps you up all night reading ... and trembling. From the
computer generated green terror in *Retrovirus*, to the dreadful
secrets in the cellar in *Taking Care of Mother* and the unexpected
fate of the man in room 627 in *Hansom Dove*, readers are sure to
find that each of these macabre stories will keep them wanting to
read one more before, if they dare, turning off the lights."
- T.R. Heinan, author of *L'immotalité: Madame Lalaurie and the
Voodoo Queen*

"In The Speed of Dark I got two things. One was excellent
presentation with very good editing, and the other was well-written
work that in most cases wasn't overly graphic, but which was
interesting, involving and rarely over the top. Much of it was
quietly creepy and, therefore, very effective."
- Glenda's Bookshelves

"[This collection] is not for the faint of heart ... But the writing is
sometimes so beautifully lyrical and descriptive, it makes it hard to
put the book down ... The Speed of Dark is a winner."
- Kim Morgan, Freelance Writer

http://horrorworld.org/hw/2013/03/the-speed-of-dark by Mario
Guslandi

Critical praise for our last anthology...

"WRITERS ON THE WRONG SIDE OF THE ROAD is an anthology of very diverse genres. There's something for everyone in this gem." - IvyD, Manic Readers

" ... the point of Writers on the Wrong Side of the Road; to take the reader off guard, similar to what the writers themselves must have felt as they explored new avenues and stretched their craft. Some pieces may have been formulaic, while others were seamless, but all represented the essence of skillfull storytelling and every participating author should be justly proud of their willingness to get behind those unfamiliar wheels and step on the gas. I had been run down, backed over, run down and backed over again and again, mangled and rearranged and left gently at the curb, whole and wholly entertained." - Steve Beai

"There are no stories in this lot that do not deserve to be read; they are all of a worthy standard."
- Ellie Hall

"The editing by Sassy Brit and C.C. Bye is excellent, and the entire presentation is beautifully professional. If you like the short story genre and want something unique and innovative, you might consider this read." - Kaye Trout, The Midwest Book Review.

"This anthology contains some the creepiest and unusual stories I've read in a long time. While a few of the selections seemed out of place either by caliber or by genre, the best works in this anthology truly set the bar for greatness in speculative fiction." - Lisa Lane

"I got started reading and really couldn't stop." - T. Lane

CHASE ENTERPRISES PUBLISHING
PRESENTS

THE SPEED OF DARK

Other Books from Chase Enterprises:

Writers on the Wrong Side of the Road

Technomage

What I Found in the Dark

Bare Knuckle MBA

The Contrary Canadian

Getting Clear

The Sorcerer's Key

The It Can't Be Done, You've Got To Be Kidding, Crazy, Or
Unbelievably Stupid To Try It Handbook For Success

The Hundred

How To Get What You Want From Life

Edited by
CC Bye and PDR Lindsay

Cover Art by
Zentao

And a special thanks goes out to Cynthia B. Ainsworthe, Elena Yates Eulo, Sylvia Cochran, Sheri Fresonke, Ann McCarthy, CK Webb and James Secor. Each played a significant role in bringing this book to you. They know what they did, and I thank them for it.

The Speed of Dark

Strangely Different & Disturbing

ISBN-13: 978-0-9781774-6-1 (Print Edition)
ISBN-13: 978-0-9781774-7-8 (e-book)

Published April 1st, 2013
Chase Enterprises Publishing
Box 2922, Kenora, ON, Canada P9N 4C8

Additional copies may be purchased at:
http://shop.claytonbye.com

Visit us at:
www.claytonbye.com

Introduction
Clayton Clifford Bye

People, and by people I mean readers, have many definitions of horror. A simple, noun based explanation might be an intense feeling of fear or shock or even disgust. People also toss around words like terror, dread and fright. Lovecraft, who still has a tremendous following, stated that horror is a profound sense of dread, usually caused by brushes with the unknown and unknowable. The master, Stephen King, shoots for three levels in descending order of elegance—terror, horror and revulsion. An interesting choice. Myself, I go way back to the 50's and 60's to a man named Damon Knight. He wrote in any genre he wanted, in fact horror didn't even exist as a genre then. Science-fiction and fantasy barely made the grade. Back to Knight. He was a writer, but I believe he was probably an editor first. And when he wrote his purpose was always the same. Damon Knight wrote to disturb. In fact, his less than successful masterpiece, The Man in the Tree is one of the most disturbing books I have ever read.

Disturbing thoughts as horror, well that's hardly exciting is it? Not when you can feel terror via a Stephen King production. But I'm here to tell you it is exciting. A story that disturbs is like a deep sliver. It works its way slowly through your flesh, sometimes festering, sometimes not. But it's there, it's with you long after the story is done. Terror, yes we feel it intensely, but then the mind protects us by allowing us to forget what we've been through. Not so a disturbing incident: it hangs on, eating its way into our consciousness until we reach a crescendo of thought that comes out in a myriad of ways. You know, "I hated that ... I'll never go back to that hotel." or "The waiter we had last night was just too creepy." or "Jeesuz that story just won't leave me alone. I keep seeing that poor woman when she realizes no one believes her story. Could you imagine? Something that terrible having to be locked up inside you or else you'd find yourself locked up inside a psych ward."

Horror that disturbs. That I can do something with. Then, just for the fun of it, let's twist the story somehow; let's leave the thing recognizable but also strangely different. Can you imagine? Strangely different but disturbing horror stories. 27 of them. Each created by a talented author, hand-picked and vetted. The result? This book will steal your sleep. It will give you nightmares. So go ahead and read … if you dare.

Contents

A little boy pleads his hope-filled question until Grandpa finally knows the harmful truth.

What About Mom?

E. J. Ruek

James Warfield watched his son stalk down the corridor, the sharp click-clicking of his heels puncturing the quiet. The smell of stale beer and cigarettes lingered.

Susan Lee, his secretary, looked toward him, eyes all sympathy. "Everything's signed," she said. "I'll drop the paperwork off at the courthouse myself."

James nodded, gave her a grateful smile, then retreated back into his office. From the far corner, little Jimmy watched him, his small, thin body stiff and ramrod erect. The child's hands gripped the arms of a chair that was too big for him, his face stark white with holes for eyes and mouth, a blackened, pulpy bruise ripe upon his cheek. "Do I have to go home?" the boy asked.

"No, you don't. You're coming to live with me and Grandma, now."

"What about Mom?"

James didn't have the heart to tell the boy. Not yet.

Heavy eyelids made James long for home and a nap, but the day's appointments denied that solace. He had one in less than twenty minutes, then a lunch date with a new client and her contract negotiator. "I'm going to have Grandma come pick you up," he said.

"I want to stay here."

James nodded. How could he tell the boy that children didn't mix with business? He couldn't. "Okay," he said. "But we'll have to get you a shower and some clothes, okay?"

"Okay."

"In there," James pointed, "is a bathroom with a shower. Think you can get yourself cleaned up?"

Little Jimmy nodded and slipped carefully down from the big chair, not letting go his death grip until his tattered tennis shoes touched the carpet. Then he padded over and gave James a hug.

"Off you go, then. Try not to get your clothes wet. You have to wear them again."

"Okay."

When the boy closed the door, James buzzed the inter-office line. "Susan, I need to take Jimmy down to get some decent clothes and shoes. Can you ask George if he'd see my next appointment?"

"George is right here. Let me ask him."

There was a muffled exchange, and, moments later, George's voice boomed out, "I'd be glad to, Mr. Warfield."

James thanked him, already lost in plans. The boy would need a trust fund. He would need to be enrolled in school. The guest room would have to be refurnished…

About fifteen minutes later, Jimmy emerged, the grime and dirty tear streaks gone. "Let me see your hands," James said, and frowned at the ragged, dirty fingernails. "Let's go back in the bathroom. Let me get those nails cleaned up."

"But it hurts," Jimmy said, a frown wrinkling his forehead.

James shook his head. "I promise it won't."

A big sigh answered him.

Back in the bathroom, James picked up the dirty, soggy towels the boy had used to try to wipe the wet off the floor. He put them in the small hamper hidden in the linen closet and pulled two new ones out. "Okay," he said. He put the toilet seat down. "Sit right there."

From the drawer, he pulled out a manicure set. From beneath the sink, he brought out a plastic wash basin, then filled it with warm water, mixing in a bit of liquid soap. "There, now. Put your hands in there."

"Why?"

"Because that's the way we do this," James said.

"It's gonna hurt."

The boy's face was solemn … resigned. James shook his head. "No. It might feel funny, but it won't hurt. See?" James zipped the point of the file under one of his own nails.

"Mine are smaller."

"I know. I'll be careful."

The boy was tense as James worked the grime loose, but relaxed once the task was done, actually giggling when James carefully dried each finger, then filed the rough spots off the tiny nails.

"There," he said, pushing himself off the tile with one hand. His knees hurt.

"Did you do this for Dad when he was little?"

James nodded. "Or Grandma did. Until your dad was old enough to do it for himself."

"When was that?"

James shook his head. "I don't quite remember. Older than you, I think."

"I bet I could do it."

"Yes, I suppose you might. Let's comb that hair, shall we?"

"Now what?" Jimmy asked while James parted and combed.

Wincing when he saw the welts on the boy's scalp, James said, "Now we go get some new togs."

"What about Mom?"

"Let's talk about Mom later, okay?"

"Okay."

In the car, James had to remind the boy to sit in back and buckle up. He needed to get one of those fancy booster seats for children. "We're going to stop at a clothing store, then go get a car seat for you," he said, glancing in the rear view.

The boy was preoccupied, watching out the window.

At Gerald's, James drove down the alley and turned into the back parking lot. "This way," he said, opening the back door.

"Are you dumping me?"

James frowned. "No. What would give you that idea?"

Jimmy didn't answer, but he was too quiet. "Come on. This way," James said, again, taking the small hand in his. That hand was chilled.

Inside, Lonnie spotted them and came over. "Mr. Warfield. What a pleasure. What can we do for you today?"

"A full outfitting for this young man," James said. "Bottom to top. And he'll need a suit today. Off the rack is fine. And dress shoes. We're meeting clients for lunch in just over an hour."

The clerk nodded and, kneeling down, pulled a tape from his pocket and measured arm, waist, and leg. "About a size four," he said. "I'll be right back."

Forty-five minutes later, the boy was properly outfitted, from play clothes to dress togs. Jimmy was all grins. James paid the bill, slipping a tip to Lonnie. "Thanks," he said.

"Where to, now, Grandpa? Can we go get Mom?"

James quelled a sigh. "One stop, then lunch," he said. "Then we'll talk about Mom, okay?"

"Okay."

The stop was for the booster seat which James couldn't figure out and had to get the store clerk's help to install it.

"Why can't I ride with you in front?" Jimmy asked.

"Because the law says you're safer in back in case we get in a wreck," James answered.

"Mom always lets me ride in front."

"Does she?"

"Yeah."

"Here we are," James said, parking.

Inside, the host didn't blink but once when James indicated there would be a fourth and introduced Jimmy. Leading them to their table, the man brought a taller chair for the boy. James ordered himself tonic water and got the boy a fruit fizzler.

"What is it?" Jimmy asked, squinting at the bubbling drink.

"Try it," James said, smiling. "If you don't like it, you can get something else."

The boy loved it, of course–sweet, rich with cream, and fruity with the tingle of carbonation. James' new client arrived, the lawyer with her talking business even before they sat down. "My grandson, James Warfield, the Third," James said, interrupting them to introduce the boy.

"Pleased, of course," the lawyer said, giving a curt nod to the child as she pulled out a chair and settled in. "Now about that contract, James. ..."

"Hello, young man," the client, a Zondra Mellington, said, looking Jimmy in the face. That pleased James.

Jimmy smiled back, a quirky little half-smile. "Hi," he said, shyness making his voice all but inaudible.

The lawyer talked on, not even pausing, pulling sheets of paper from her briefcase. "We'd like these changes to lines..."

Despite the boy eating with his hands, lunch went relatively well. The boy ate ravenously, though, even to eating the garnish, and that bothered James. He approved most of the changes the solicitor desired, clauses that he'd expected her to object to, but, focusing his mind on business, refused others. Some they negotiated and came to a compromise. By the end of the meeting, the boy eating a small dish of ice cream, the lawyer seemed pleased, Zondra likewise. They set up the signing for the next day.

"Grandpa? Can I go to the bathroom?"

James nodded and stood. "I'll be right back," he said to his guests. "Order us some drinks? I'll take a tonic. Jimmy here will have another fizzler."

"That was boring," Jimmy said as James held him up so he could wash his hands after using the toilet.

"It *was* boring, wasn't it? It's how I can afford to buy you clothes and lunch, though."

"Okay. Was I quiet enough?"

"You were great," he said, and smiled. "But you don't have to be quiet all the time. Just when we're negotiating."

"You mean arguing?"

"Yes."

"Now what?"

"Now we make small talk for a few minutes, and you get to have another fizzler. Then it will be over."

Back at the table, they spoke about the markets, the weather, and the economic forecast. Jimmy twitched and wiggled, and, finally, James excused them after paying the bill on the company card. In the car, James buckled the boy in. "I'm going to take you to see Grandma, now," he said, getting in the driver's seat.

"What about Mom?" Jimmy asked.

James turned around to look at him. He was tired of hearing the question and avoiding the truth. Sooner or later the boy would have to know that his mother had abandoned him. Right now, he didn't need to know the whole truth, though. "Your Mom went away," he said.

"I know where she is, though," Jimmy said, his eyes earnest. "Now that Dad's gone, can we go get her and Mary?"

James frowned. "Who's Mary?"

"My new sister."

Bells went off inside James' ears. Small, sparkling lights danced in his peripheral vision. He fumbled in his suit coat pocket for his pills, popped the lid, and stuck one beneath his tongue. When the bells and lights stopped, he turned and asked, "Okay, now. Tell me where your Mom and sister Mary are."

≈∽CRSONSOCR≈∂

From The Seattle Urban Chronicle

James Allen Warfield, Jr., was arrested on suspicion of murder last night after the bodies of his wife and infant daughter were found in a culvert about ninety yards from their trailer house. Officers at the scene said that someone had left several peanut butter and jelly sandwiches near the bodies which they guessed had been dead for about a week. The surviving child, a five-year-old who led authorities to the scene, is now living on Bainbridge Island with his paternal grandparents.

THE END

* Living in the Purcell Trench in Northern Idaho, E. J. Ruek (pronounced "rook") writes about things which are not quite as they seem—not on the surface and not underneath … like your auntie whose secrets drive the neighbors crazy. They just know that something isn't "normal." And it isn't. Says E. J., "Writing is about translating life into words without sacrificing the grimace and the giggle." You can visit E. J. on the Web at http://www.ejruek.com.

Midnight, when dread is in the air.

When Midnight Comes

Cynthia B. Ainsworthe

From the upstairs bedroom Suzette could hear mail coming through the front door slot. Dread crept into her mind, and she knew the time was close at hand. She looked at her long, glistening, raven hair in the mirror. Thoughts of the future came to mind. *When will time take its toll?* She eyed her reflection, smiling at the trim and enticing figure. *Never! I will always look this way. There's no reason to entertain such a silly idea.*

Shuffled steps could be heard on the plush hallway carpet. The old woman's movements were slow, stiffened from decades of aches and pains. She entered her mistress' bedroom with an outstretched bony hand, holding a single envelope. A strand of white hair fell from her tightly secured bun, softening heavy creases in her face. But no comment was made by her; Suzette hadn't invited Edna to speak. The servant woman knew the rules and obeyed them.

Suzette took the mail from her. On the outside of the envelope was one word, "Suzette." Neither postmark nor a return address was present. She tore open the sealed message. The single paneled card said,

Payment due by midnight.
L

"Leave me alone, Edna."

The old woman started to leave as Suzette looked at her watch. It was four o'clock in the afternoon.

"Have the driver pick me up at six."

Edna nodded at the red carpet beneath her feet.

Suzette's wide, blue eyes went as cold as ice. "And since it's the last day of the month, prepare the usual, you ninny."

"Yes m'am," the servant answered, as she edged to the door."

#

Suzette stood for a moment before descending the steps to the lavish lounge. All eyes fell upon her. Even the most envious of the female patrons were amazed by her beauty. Yet she was oblivious to all gazes as her eyes sought out an available man. Instinctively, she glided to a vacant stool next to a dark haired gentleman. She didn't know why he was the right one. Suzette never knew how, but she knew. He would be the one, the one for the night.

"You come here, often?" came his question. He turned to look directly at her. "My name is Stuart. Friends call me Stu."

"Am I your friend? Mr. …" Suzette inquired as her lips curled up at the corners, and her eyes sought to entice him from beneath her long, black lashes.

His eyes took in her beckoning décolletage, noticing the rise and fall of each breath. "It's Stuart Smith," he said.

"Ah, another salesman with the name of 'Smith'." Her slender fingers stroked the top of his hand.

"How did you know what I did for a living?" he asked, the ripple of emotion sliding across his face suggesting he was intrigued.

"No matter." She looked at him for a moment. "You have no family. Could be you were an orphan. And you travel extensively; never truly putting down roots."

"It's as if you could read my life history from looking at me." His eyes widened with curious wonder.

"All intuition. Most women have it. I merely use it to my best advantage," Suzette commented, as her hand cleverly graced her cleavage.

The bartender now stood before them.

She ordered before Stuart could say a word.

"I'll have a Gibson up, and my friend likes scotch rocks."

He leaned closer to her, and in a low voice rasped the words, "How did you know what I drank? I never told you. I don't understand any of this."

"Maybe what you feel is the result of the two drinks you had before I arrived,"

The bartender placed their drinks before them. Suzette took a very non-ladylike gulp, feeling the liquid torch her throat. She glanced at her watch. It was eight o'clock.

"We need to leave," she said to Stuart.

"We? What's with the we? It's not even late yet," he questioned, his voice taking on a childlike quality.

"None have ever refused me," Suzette spoke with confidence. "You're no different."

Her eyes bore into his soul, as if she were trying to mingle his life-force with hers. He spoke not a word as he left money on the bar for the tab. Then he followed her to the waiting car.

#

Stuart sank down into the deep cushions of the red velvet sofa. It had a comfortable feel, like he was a small child being cradled. A roaring fire warmed the room as he waited for this hypnotizing woman to return. Dim lights added to the ambiance.

11

He looked at the tray on the marble coffee table. It contained two glasses of red wine, Stuart knew not to touch them before his hostess offered the beverage.

He thought, *I wonder if I'll have her on the couch or in her bedroom. She seems a bit kinky.* He smiled briefly. *Kinky can be good, too. I bet she'll give me a wild ride. Not bad for the price of one drink.*

Suzette entered the room silently. A sheer black negligée revealed her form as the flickering firelight creating a silhouette beneath the cloth. Stuart had never seen a woman so perfect, so beautiful. He knew he must have her. His throat grew dry. His eyes followed her every movement as she came near. Her hands slowly stroked her curves, offering him the opportunity to do the same.

"Do you have everything you want, Stu?" she asked with a voice that came from deep within.

"Not everything," he replied hoarsely. "You have what I want."

She eased onto the sofa, ever so close to him.

Suzette guided his hand to her breast. The fullness of it filled him with desire. And he could feel her mouth part as she kissed him, his entire body ablaze with his heat.

"Here, or your bedroom?" he groaned.

"Never my bedroom," she replied softly. "It wouldn't be right to continue any place else. This is where he likes to watch."

"Likes to watch?" Stuart pulled back sharply. "What do you mean? Likes to watch? I didn't sign on to provide a show."

"Everyone who has passed on, watches," Suzette replied as her hand traveled along his thigh.

"As long as there's no one around." *I've got a real nut case on my hands. But what the hell. I'm horny and she wants it. I can put up with that. What a story I could tell!*

She reached for the wine glasses.

"This is a very old and fine wine that I serve to special people on special occasions," she offered.

"I'm special?" he inquired. "We just met. How could I be special to you? You know nothing about me."

"I know enough, Mr. Stuart Smith," came her reply. "When someone is right, there's nothing more that needs to be known. Nothing more that needs to be said."

The cool wine soothed his throat. It left a strange aftertaste, and a desire for more. Stuart took another sip, and another, until he gulped down the last remaining drops.

"Looks like you developed a thirst, Stu. Are you satisfied?"

"Not completely," he replied as he began to feel lightheaded. "Wow, that wine gives a wallop! Where did you get that stuff?" His sight blurred as his limbs grew heavy.

"From a very fine vintner." He could feel her watching him closely. "Don't fight the feeling. It will add to the excitement."

The room seemed to spin around him. Then, a ghoulish face appeared in the flames and grew clearer as he watched. *This bitch must've spiked my drink. What the hell is going on? I can't move.*

#

His eyes did not close nor blink. No breath was perceptible. Stuart's body was limp and lifeless, head turned toward the still roaring fire and its deadly flames. It was five minutes to midnight. And Suzette, confident in his death, knew her life would go on as before.

The clock struck twelve. A freezing cold enveloped her. A cold she had never felt before. The cold turned to fire from within. She looked at her hands. Her smooth, youthful skin began to grow pale and wrinkled. Suzette ran to the mirror over the mantle. Her face wrinkled into deep grooves. Her hair grew thin and gray. She looked to the lifeless body on the couch, stumbled over, and with bony fingers tried to feel his breath. There was none. She felt for a pulse at the side of his neck. *Am I feeling right? Ever so weak, but he has a pulse!*

Her eyes darted to the clock. A minute after midnight.
The flames within her grew hotter, and Suzette could barely scream for Edna.

The old woman came from the adjacent room. She looked at Suzette with a steely gaze.

"What do you need?" she asked.

"You didn't prepare the recipe correctly. He's not dead, and now I'm dying! May you burn in hell for what you've done!"

Edna watched her fall to the ground. "I prepared it perfectly for me, Mother." She came to stand over her. "You're not the only one who can make a deal with Mr. L. *Now*, it's my time to have the life you denied me for the past seventy years. I watched you stay young and beautiful, while I grew old and crippled. You took lovers and discarded them for your own vanity. And all the while I was forced to watch, never to have a lover of my own, my only task in life to serve you. "

Suzette resembled a skeleton with skin drawn over bone. Edna continued, growing louder, finding the voice she had never been allowed to use. "Didn't you ever think it odd that you became pregnant with me? Did you never wonder who my father really was? No? Well, you'll meet him again soon enough." She glanced at the dead man on the couch, then turned to look in the mirror over the fireplace. She licked her lips as she admired the reflection of a young woman with red lips, full breasts and long, golden hair gracing her shoulders. *What did Mother expect? A father will always side with his own. And I know he'll make sure mother's kept busy as a concubine to the demons of hell.*

Edna looked at the remains on the rug: empty clothing, save for the ashes. Her eyes fell one more time upon the body on the couch.

"I have some cleaning up to do," Edna said, as she went to get the vacuum cleaner. "I always have to clean up after a party. It's a necessary evil."

THE END

* Born in Mahopac, New York and raised in Yorktown Heights New York, Cynthia B. Ainsworthe enjoys a varied and interesting life in Florida with her loving family that includes five poodles. Her novel, Front Row Center, earned the prestigious IPPY Award in romance.

3
Watch out. Suanna's not your ordinary heroine.

Jesse's Hair

John B. Rosenman

Jesse thinks I'm a big fat pig, and it hurts. Just 'cause I'm six one, weigh three twenty, and aren't exactly what you'd call top of the show in the looks department doesn't mean I don't have feelings. Watchin' him strut toward Dave's Grain and Feed, I can see his face wrinkle when he spots me on the walk.

"What are you gawking at?" he says. "Leave me alone, won't you?"

"Be nice, Jesse," I say.

"Nice?" He looks at the farmhands with him. They hoot and his face wrinkles still more. "Stop moonin' at me every time I come to town. Shit, I wouldn't slip you an inch if you was the last pig on Earth."

Talbot, a redneck who works for Jesse's daddy, scrunches up his nose.

"Oink! Oink! Oink!" Then, playin' on my name like he's callin' hogs: "Su-eeee! Su-eeee! Su-eeee!"

Another one, a bearded fart whose name I don't know, starts snortin', and Jesse grins.

When he does forget my anger and shame, their sneerin', disgusted faces, it's like Jesse's smile melts me sweet and golden in the sun. I feel my love for him moisten my loins and bake the warm valley waitin' between my thighs.

I love Jesse. I truly do. 'Specially the black curly hair he runs

17

a comb through before struttin' inside with the others to order grain or balin' wire for his daddy's ranch.

I watch the screen door bang and hear their coarse heehaws. Six foot one suety, *Su-eeee!* Suanna with a face like a sow. *Oink oink.* Good imitation, have to admit.

A bluebottle big as a marble buzzes a tad too close and I snatch it like a sly frog. I hold it in my fist, hearin' it buzz and rattle round in there, and sneak a peek up and down the street. 'Cept for Chauncy leanin' against one of them Texaco pumps, no one's in sight.

Quick as a flash, I pinch Mr. Fly to an oozy pulp. Bye bye, caught ya loafin'.

Before I leave, the headline in the paper rack catches my eye. Seems a man burned to a crisp over by Squaw river in Dobe county. Makes five so far this summer.

Been hot as a bitch since June.

#

Grady Brace, my pa, always tells me not to feel bad about my looks 'cause I've got an inner beauty that makes them centerfold sluts he drools over look like dog meat.

"You're an ugly ducklin,'" he says, pullin' at his blue-jeans-bound pecker. "Just 'member now, Suanna honey. True beauty is *inside* you."

Inside me. What the fuck good does that do? Only beauty worth a patch of collard greens far as I'm concerned, is the kind folks can *see.* You know, like Rihanna or Taylor Swift. I watch Pa turn a page and wet his lips over a juicy crotch shot, massagin' himself 'neath the formica counter where he thinks I can't see.

"I love Jesse, Pa," I sigh. "More than anyone I ever knew."

"Jesse Carter?" he says not lookin' up. "Forget him, Suanna, like you have all the others. 'Sides, his family's lousy with money. Own a Texas-size spread outside Soho."

I look about our fly-specked, money-losin' diner with its cheap 1960's checkered oilcloths on the tables. For a moment I want to yell at him that since I'm six one and weigh three twenty on the hoof, it's not likely that Jesse's being rich and us so tacky poses a serious hindrance to our relationship. It's like the man fuckin' well said: he wouldn't slip me an inch if I was the last pig on Earth.

But I don't scold Grady Brace. Partly it's 'cause Ma lit out on him nine years back with a John Deere salesman sportin' a slick mustache. The other reason I don't chow him down is *me*. I mean, what's the use? I look at my bulgin' belly and pathetic triple chin in a dingy mirror, wishin' for the ten millionth time there was a slender, lovely girl in there, one men would fall all over just to give their hearts to. But instead of a girl whose ability to love in return is treasured more than diamonds, there's only the pain of endless days growin' up when kids laughed and taunted me. "Fatty fatty two by four, couldn't get through the bathroom door..."

Then I think of Jesse's curly black hair and smile. Someone fortunate and blessed like that should be a little bit kinder. Yes sirree.

"Grady Brace," I say, "mind if I borrow your chopper?"

He grunts and turns a page, his hidden, whisperin' fingers tryin' to wheedle life back into his tired old dick. I snag his keys from a nail and leave.

#

Grady's chopper is a mongrel. It was a Harley-Davidson Sportster once, he claims. Fact is he's tinkered with it so much and put in so many new parts, I just call it Mongrel. And just last March he installed a special set of springs to support my weight, so it makes a damned good dirt bike. At night I like to go prowlin' through fields and cruisin' down back roads, let her out full throttle.

19

I go huntin' then too.

I head north toward the Carter ranch, thinkin' of Jesse's hair. Somewhere a bird shrieks. The moon snarls silver.

If Pa's good with bikes, I'm an ace pathfinder. I know every land and trail and pussy side-cut for three counties round, not to mention paths through woods where horny owls screech at you for trespassin'. Working like a snake, I stay off main roads, glide through a cornfield, and come to a halt right next to the Carters' mile-long driveway. Their entrance has an archway over it like it's Xanadu or South Fork.

I let the engine idle. That's another good thing about Mongrel. Grady Brace did somethin' to it that makes it purr like a contented cat. I can cruise right behind you and you won't know it.

I sit there waitin', for what I'm not sure. Just as long as Jesse's in the picture...

A half hour later headlights appear back at the Big House. I blink, killin' my headlight as they draw close. When they stop at the main road, I see it's one of them low-slung Maserati's and Jesse's sittin' in it with a girl. The top's down and she's all over him. Got one hand in his lap like he has a magnet there.

"Dora," he says, "if you wanna mess around, we better go somewhere."

She giggles like she's high on coke and reluctantly withdraws her hand. Twenty feet away, unseen in the cricket-chirpin' darkness, I watch her cheerleader's profile as she slides back to her seat. Jesse can really pick 'em, all right. She's one of them blond princesses with nothin' behind her pretty eyes but wide open spaces. Probably last year's prom queen at the shit-suckin' high school I used to go to.

The sports car roars out the driveway and heads south toward open country. I throttle lightly and roll after them. I station myself fifty yards back, stickin' like a leech. When they swing onto a dirt road I downshift and creep after them like an Indian. Now's the time they can spot me, since my tires crack branches strewn from a recent storm. But Dora's moved back to him and they look like a beast with two heads up there. The bitch probably has her hand on his crotch again.

They stop on a bluff overlookin' a lake. Mr. Moon dapples it, glistens on their bodies as they kiss and grope.

Laughter: hers.

Hoarse breathing: his.

I dismount, hearin' the sound of clothes comin' off in a hurry. By the time I get close, she's already mounted him. I see her tits jiggle and her face strain up at the moon like she's prayin' to it.

Let me tell you: pretty girls don't look so nice when they're grindin' away with their little minds intent only on pleasure. Whorey Dorey even squeals a bit like a pig, and I mouth silent echos in the darkness.

Oink! Oink! Oink!

Quickly, like I've done five times before, I strip off my clothes and lay them in a pile. The crucifix on a chain that ma gave me for communion when I was twelve, I leave on top like a marker. Barefoot, I skirt the car, come up behind her. They're reachin' a crisis, so they don't hear me open the door and climb in. Drivin' my hand like a meat chopper into her neck, I catch Dora as she collapses and flip her over into the back seat. Then I mount Jesse.

It takes him a few seconds to react. While he does, I work away at him, doin' all sorts of things to keep him stiff even though the last thing on his mind is more nooky.

"What … what … what…"

"Wouldn't slip me an inch if I was the last pig on Earth, huh? Think I'm pathetic, do ya? Somethin' to laugh at?"

His eyes bulge. "Dora, what happened to…" Then disgust grips his face and he screams, tryin' to buck me off. His muscular arms push at my ponderous breasts.

Jesse's strong, that's for sure. But I'm in the saddle and nearly twice his weight. He shrieks, saliva bubblin' as I coax him where it will do the most good. I swear, any farm girl used to milkin' cows who can't keep even a reluctant beau happy ain't worth a fried horse turd. Humpin', fondlin' him in just the right places, I keep him at full perk and bring us off together. As he wails, I caress his curly black hair and gasp endearments.

Then I silence him with a single chop, just like I did Dora. Returnin' to my bike, I come back with two things I keep stored in it. The first is a razor sharp huntin' knife that I use to scalp Jesse with a dozen expert flicks of my wrist. The second is a twelve ounce can of kerosene with kitchen matches strapped to it. Clutchin' Jesse's drippin' scalp, I douse both their bodies with kerosene. Jesse's already comin' out of it. His lover boy face twists in pain and an eye flutters open.

"Those five fellers who burned up this summer," I say. "You know, the ones you all been readin' and talkin' about? Well, *I* did it. It wasn't the heat or spontaneous combustion at all. It was *me*, Jesse dear. And they all died just like you."

His mouth opens, and I hear a thin, desperate keenin'.

I lift his scalp, hold it up so a few drops sprinkle his raw, bleedin', denuded skull. He flinches and comes more fully awake. In the front seat Dora moans.

"I love you, Jesse," I say, meanin' every word. "Much more than she ever could, and much more than any other man I ever knew. But you never noticed, never cared at all what I had to offer." My voice cracks, and I straighten. "I … I'll never forget you."

Sobbin', I snap a match head with my thumbnail and torch them both, takin' extra care with the girl since I never did one before. Watchin' the car blaze as I dress, it occurs to me I can just about guess what tomorrow's headline will be. Seems like folks just can't stop from sizzlin' to a turn this summer.

Eyes wet, I swing Mongrel round and head for home, clutchin' my trophy in triumph.

#

"Suanna," Pa says round dinner time next day, "did you hear what happened to Jesse Carter and a girl last night?"

I set a Catfish Dinner Special before Hank Dawson in his booth and pour him a fresh cup of coffee. Then I come back to Pa at the counter. "How's that, Grady Brace?"

He raises his head and looks at me with his washed-out blue eyes. "Jesse Carter and a girl. Seems his car caught on fire a couple miles from his home. A state patrolman saw it from the highway, but by the time he arrived there wasn't much left. They had to identify them both by their teeth."

I try to act shocked, but I'm no Meryl Streep. "That's just … horrible," I manage.

"Uh huh." He studies me. "Suanna, you wouldn't know anything about it, would you?"

I let my arms go wide. "*Know* anything? Why should I?"

"I don't know." He swivels on his stool to glance at Dawson, the only customer in the place, and then leans toward me on the counter. "It's just that you *liked* him, Suanna," he whispers. "And a couple of the other men who had uh, accidents this summer—you knew them too, didn't you? Seems to me you were mighty impressed by that hardware feller who dropped by here one night. And a couple days later, he burns to a cinder practically in his back yard."

I look him right in the eye. "Paper says he was smokin' and fell asleep 'neath a tree."

Pa's eyebrows rise. "And never woke *up*?"

"Some folks sleep tight, Grady Brace." I nod at his plate. "You've hardly touched the sausage omelette I made for ya. What's the matter, too much green pepper?"

He looks down at his plate, one hand nervously fingerin' a page on which a girl with bazzooms even bigger than mine grins at the camera. "Suanna, I tried to raise ya right. Maybe if things had been different and your ma hadn't..."

I pat his hand. "You've done just fine, Grady Brace. Don't fret about it, hear?" I give him a quick peck and head toward the rear where my bedroom is. On the way I think about the two of us, each caught in our separate traps. Me with my walrus-sized hide and a yearnin' no one wants; him with his loser's soul and burned-out dreams. What really bothers me, though, is the fact that Grady Brace's beginnin' to catch on. If I don't watch it, he'll go to the sheriff.

Then I laugh. No, I can handle Pa. He's one person broken even more by life than I am. Unlike me, he's got no fight left.

I enter my room, lock the door, and go into the closet. On the back shelf, next to my douche bag, the large plywood box I made a few months back rests just where I left it. I lift off the lid and look down at my collection.

Jesse's hair is there, already neatly labeled and dated, and he's got company. Sandy Y's ears and Charlie B's bridgework flank him on each side. In the back row, set off beautifully by my calligraphy, reside Joe Bob's half carat, initialed diamond ring (I took a chance takin' that), Willy T's Coors belt buckle, and Jake-the-hardware-feller's goatee. Jake, I 'member, pleaded with me not to cut if off just before I torched him.

I admire my collection with a deep sense of accomplishment. Six men, and I loved them all, 'specially Jesse. I truly did, 'spite what cynics might say, and as I told them all just before they died, I'll never forget them. How could I, when I'll always have somethin' to remember them by?

There's only one problem. I have room for just one more, and it's not even August yet. Looks like I'll need a bigger box soon.

"Suaaannna!"

Even through the walls I can hear Pa's call. Another customer, probably. I snap the lid on and return to the front where

24

a city feller in a tailored suit's sittin' at the counter a few seats from Pa.

"What'll it be?" I say, going to him.

He looks up from the cracked plastic bindin' of the menu, and as soon as he does, I'm half in love again. I see he's got a pencil-thin mustache like the John Deere salesman who ran off with Ma, and he looks kind of like Clark Gable in those old movies.

He smiles. It's a nice smile. "I'll have the no. 4."

I hitch a pad from my apron. "How you want your rib-eye?"

"Medium rare, with carrots, okra, and a large Coke. All right?"

"Sho' 'nuff. You new round here, Mister?"

Pa looks at me in concern but I keep my eyes on our customer.

"I'm an insurance representative, trying to interest a few clients." His smile widens. "Know anyone who might be interested?"

I smile back as I bring his Coke and put his steak and vegetables on. "Round here, a lot of folks might be. Been a rash of accidents lately."

Down the counter, Pa starts chokin', but the stranger doesn't notice.

"Is that a fact? Well, maybe I'll stay on a few extra days." He hands me a card. *Edward Markham. Memphis. Metropolitan Life.*

I slip it in my pocket and kind of home in on him, hopin' he's different and I can just let him sell his insurance and go. Or maybe, just maybe, despite my ugly loathsomeness, a miracle will happen and he'll actually come to care and return my love. For a moment I see him courtin' me, comin' with store-bought flowers just like I'm a normal girl, his attentive, lovin' concern healin' this sickness that festers in my mind. But behind his oily smile I see the revulsion and disgust which are all I'm worth to him as a person. They're hidden but clearly there, as with all the others.

Somethin' must happen in my face 'cause he fumbles with his collar and jerks his Coke to his lips. As he does, I notice for the first time how slim and supple his fingers are and how neatly manicured he keeps his nails. The palms themselves are smooth, white, and uncalloused, unlike most folks' round here. But then you don't dig many fence holes or raise many crops in the city.

"Somethin' wrong?" he asks.

I turn from his uneasy frown to Pa, who's starin' at me with alarm, his stroke mag forgotten. Carelessly I shrug and turn back.

"Everything's peachy," I say. "I was just admirin' your hands." I touch the ring finger lightly. "Tell me, just how do you manage to keep them so nice?"

THE END

* John, a retired English professor, has published 300 stories in Writers on the Wrong Side of the Road, Weird Tales, Whitley Strieber's Aliens, Galaxy, The Age of Wonders, etc. He's also published twenty books, including SF novels such as Beyond Those Distant Stars and Speaker of the Shakk (Mundania Press), and Alien Dreams and A Senseless Act of Beauty (Crossroad Press). MuseItUp Publishing released three SF novels: Dark Wizard; Dax Rigby, War Correspondent; Inspector of the Cross. Kingdom of the Jax, a sequel to Inspector of the Cross, will be published in May 2013. MuseItUp has also published The Blue of Her Hair, the Gold of Her Eyes (winner of Preditors and Editors Annual Readers Poll), More Stately Mansions, and the dark erotic thrillers Steam Heat and Wet Dreams. Two of John's major themes

are the endless mind-stretching wonders of the universe and the limitless possibilities of transformation—sexual, cosmic, and otherwise.

4

Had his publisher sent him to a place to write or perhaps to a place
that was not so right?

Hansom Dove
by Kenneth Weene

Hunched in his brown tweed suit, the one he had purchased
to let the world know he was a true Bohemian, Quince Humphrey
tried not to think about his queasiness. Never before had he
understood what it meant to feel green. He tried to reassure himself
that the lurching and swaying of the small ferry would someday
provide him an idea for a story. That was his strength as a writer—
turning misery into plot. It just hadn't been his plan to be miserable
this particular Thursday evening.

"It'll be a great experience," his new agent at Hustin and
Harper, Tim Mugget, had promised. "How can you pass it up?
We're paying for it. A chance to get that novel finished. Just you
and that battered Royal of yours."

Tim had laughed, a chortle really. "I don't get it. Why don't
you get a computer? You might as well be using a quill pen. It's the
eighties you know—word processing? You're so out of date.

"Writers... You know, Quince, *you are* a strange breed."

Quince didn't know. For him writing was everything. He
lived in the pages of books, those he read and especially the ones
he wrote. The suffering, the misery—they were just ideas—chords
to be strummed as a story unfolded. He was quite sure that he had
never suffered, at least not before this boat trip from hell.

29

An hour. That had been the schedule. Leave the mainland at six and arrive at Port Harbor Island at seven. He was sure that the trip must have already been twice that length. Quince maneuvered the bag and the typewriter case on his lap and pulled out his pocket watch, yet another old-fashioned affectation according to Mugget. *Christ, only six forty. Another twenty minutes. I don't know if I..."*

The boat's horn sounded against the weather. In the distance Quince heard the answering sob of a foghorn.

At least he was the only one on board, the only passenger that was. There were crew. One of them, a boy, who looked no more than fourteen to Quince, was walking through the passenger cabin—not even grabbing the handholds at the ends of the wooden benches, just walking like the lurching was nothing, like they were not at any moment likely to be flipped head over tail and into the roiling sea.

"You know the Hansom Dove?" It was the only question Quince could come up with, but he desperately needed a few words of conversation, just something to reassure himself that the torture would end.

"The hotel? Of course. You staying there?"

"Yes." *At least his voice doesn't squeak, even if he does still have a face full of pimples.*

"Of course you would be. Only hotel on the island stays open off season."

The boy continued through the cabin.

"Where is it?" Quince called after him and immediately wished his voice sounded more authoritative, at least adult. He felt like a child desperately trying to hold back the nausea that wanted to explode from his mouth and nose.

"Can't miss it. One block up the slope from the dock. Only street. Corner of Main."

The boat lurched again, and Quince felt the hamburger he'd eaten while waiting for the ferry pitch in his stomach. He belched. A first acrid taste of vomit filled his mouth. He fought to control it.

By the time the writer could direct his attention back to the deckhand, the young man was gone, the heavy, metallic clunk of the heavy door still echoing in the cabin.

#

Huddling in his misery, Quince breathed his relief when the ferry finally stopped with the heavy thud of hull against pier. Unwilling to delay a moment, he grabbed his suitcase from the floor in his left hand, took the handle of his typewriter case and his smaller bag in the other, and lurched off the bench. That was a mistake. The lines had not been made fast; the boat was still free to bounce away from the dock only to be pushed forward again. Quince stumbled, barely avoiding a fall, but banging his shin on one of the steel footings that held the benches in place.

"Shit," he screamed in pain as the loudspeaker blared.

"Port Harbor," a crackling, tinny voice announced. "Passengers may now safely make their way to the gangway."

Limping slightly, his mouth still filed with bile, Quince was all too glad to comply.

The pimple-faced youngster was standing by as the writer clambered off the boat. "Thanks for choosing the Port Ferry," he said without any tone of irony.

Quince suppressed his twin desires to vomit on the young man's boots or to spew suitable sarcasm in his direction.

"Up the hill?" Quince mumbled instead. He looked across the gangway and could see nothing except dancing droplets of fog reflecting the light from two feeble lamps, which seemed to float in mid-air but which Quince assumed were rooted on the dock.

The youngster gestured. "Straight up, Sir. Can't miss it."

Stopping for a moment to set his case on the gangway and pull his jacket tighter against the damp, Quince was tempted to turn back, to demand immediate return passage to the mainland. Only the sickness in his stomach and the thought of enduring more of the horrible green feeling, that had in no way subsided, stopped him. Swaying somewhat unsteadily, he stumbled down the gangway and onto the foul-smelling dock. The stench of rotting fish made it immediately obvious that the ferry was not the only boat that used this stretch of wood and cement.

Peering downward, Quince took cautious, mincing steps along the dock. He knew the young man must have been laughing to watch him move like a feeble fool, but the pain of his barked shin was reminder enough of the dangers of unsure footing.

Behind him, Quince could hear the knocking about of crates and orders of "careful there," and "mind that one." It seemed that a ghost crew of sailors and longshoremen were hard at work. He glanced back. The fog was too thick to see anything except the vaguest outline of the boat. Slowly, unsteadily, he made his way down the street.

Quince's left hand ached from the weight of his old, leather suitcase. His right was cramped from holding both the typewriter and attaché case. *Isn't there anybody around, a cab or something? Damn, what has Mugget gotten me into?*

Neither his mood nor his burden lightened when he started up what the deckhand had called "the slope." *More like a bloody mountain,* Quince moaned to himself. He forced himself up the steep incline paved with cobblestones made treacherous by the evening's dampness.

It was only a single block, but Quince had never walked a more difficult one. The damp, the slipperiness, the dark, and the looming lifelessness of many of the buildings now shuttered for the season made the climb intolerable. The remaining queasiness of his stomach added a dimension of misery. The ache in his arms and hands convinced him that he was caught in a horror story—one that he could never have imagined writing.

He came to a cross street. Across it on his right there was light, not much, really more a halo, an aura, but still evidence that The Hansom Dove might actually exist. Perhaps the sign that arched from the building and hung over the three steps that led to the front door announced the name, but Quince could not make out any words. He mounted those stairs, put down his suitcase, and tried the door. Locked.

Damn. They should know I'm coming. Mugget was supposed to... I swear I'm going to dump that fool, tell Mark Hustin to get me someone with a brain.

To the right of the door was a bell-pull. Quince yanked the handle and then let go, allowing the metal knob to thump against the jamb.

I hope they have a stiff drink. They must. Every hotel has a liquor license.

There was no indication of life. Quince pulled the bell again—this time releasing it more carefully.

A reedy, disembodied voice spoke from above Quince's head: "I'll be coming right down."

Minutes passed as Quince stamped impatiently against the chill. He was ready to again pull the bell or perhaps hammer on the door when he heard the scraping sound of a lock turning. The door opened to reveal an old man in an off-white bed-shirt, his neck wrapped in a knitted muffler of strange colors, and his head covered by a cotton cap with strings that flapped untied beneath his chin.

"You be?" the man demanded in the same reedy voice. He stood in the doorway, not moving aside,

"I'm Quince Humphrey?" Assuming he was speaking to the innkeeper, he continued, "You should be expecting me. Mugget, Tim Mugget, he said everything was arranged. Said this was the perfect place."

The old man stared at Quince, and the younger man stared back. Never before had Quince seen such a pitted face—grooved and furrowed by time and no doubt the unpleasant island weather as well. Quince took in the paleness of the innkeeper's complexion, the stringy white hair that hung beneath the ridiculous cap, the thinness of his wrists and angles as they emerged from his nightshirt, the boniness of his hands and bare feet.

"May I come in?" Quince asked reaching to pick up his suitcase. He was struck by the weariness in his own voice. "I could use a drink. Do hope you have a gin and tonic?" He tried to make the request sound light and friendly.

"Mugget sent you, did he?" The old man swayed but did not move from the doorway. The lantern he was carrying swayed with him, casting uneasy shadows on the nearby walls.

There was another pause as the man seemed to study Quince's words. Finally he said, "Didn't expect you till morning. Not a night fit for ferrying."

"I suppose not. But they came across, and I, not knowing better, came with them."

"Yes, yes, I see that you have. We were expecting you in the morning. Mr. Mugget sent you. Yes, yes a writer he said?"

"Yes, sir, I am." Not sure what else to do, Quince asked again, "May I come in?"

After the briefest of pauses, the old man stepped aside, and Quince, his arms and hands too tired for the task, carried his possessions into the lobby of the Hansom Dove.

Perhaps it had once been luxurious. Flocked, royal-blue wallpaper and mahogany trim, a hammered tin ceiling, and an immense registration desk backed by rows of empty cubbyholed letter boxes made the room feel heavy and dark even after the innkeeper, apparently unwilling to do so, for he hesitated at the switch, flicked on the electric lights and blew out the lantern he had brought to the door.

Quince was assaulted by the sudden smell of kerosene. He dropped his cases where he stood and made his way to the great desk. "I suppose I should register."

"Not necessary. No need. You are, as you said, expected. Mr. Mugget has taken care of everything. No need."

"Then might I… I don't want to impose… But it has been a difficult night… Might you have a gin and tonic or if not that…"

"A gin and tonic—yes, Mr. Mugget said you would want a gin and tonic. Of course, I had thought that strange since you were expected in the morning. And in the morning you shall have it. None tonight."

"None tonight? In the morning?" Quince was incredulous. He fought back the urge to argue. "I really do need something now," he pleaded.

"I can put on the kettle. Tea might set you right."

Defeated, Quince agreed. "Tea will be fine."

The old man shuffled toward a doorway. Quince cleared his throat loudly. The innkeeper turned back and asked, "Something else you'd be wanting?"

"Well, I was wondering if I could have the key…"

"The key?"

"To my room. I thought I might bring my bags up."

"No keys. Not like you need one here. Just take them up."

"Oh."

The old man turned back toward the doorway. Quince asked, "Sir, but which room?"

"What are you wanting?"

"Which room am I in? I want to bring my cases and my typewriter up, put them away—while the water is boiling."

"So you said. Just carry them upstairs. It's the room that isn't locked. You'll see it right enough."

"I thought you said I didn't need a key."

"You don't. Your room will not be locked. I'll be putting on the kettle. Come down for your tea. It will be ready soon."

"Yes, thank you." Quince picked up his cases. "Oh, sir."

"What now?"

"The elevator."

"Elevator? Don't have one here. Not much need. The stairs do for us." The innkeeper gestured at the wide stairway, with its dark, oriental patterned runner and heavy, black banisters. "Light switch is by the stairs. One at the top as well. Mind you turn the lights off. No need to waste electricity."

"Thanks," Quince responded. He actually felt grateful, thankful that the old man had offered even this small piece of information. He started upward.

A portrait hung opposite the stairway on the second floor. Large, ornately framed, it was a picture of a young woman who seemed to be staring past him and into the emptiness of the stairway behind. Even through the patina of dirt and the gloom of limited lighting, Quince could see that she was very beautiful. Her lustrous brown hair, highlighted with gold, draped her shoulders in softness. Her eyes, deep and dark, held mystery. Her nose, slightly turned up, seemed to augment the smile that played on her rose-red lips. Her brows and lashes were darker than her hair and spoke of roots in far off lands. These touches of color accentuated the paleness of her skin.

The woman's neck was long and delicately carved, as were her hands, which rested on a draped table. Next to them was a book with only the word "verses" legible in the title, and across the table was a vase that held twin yellow roses. The color of the roses matched the fabric of her gown. The surrounding area appeared to be a parlor, but little detail could be seen.

Quince stopped, as much captured by the girl's beauty as in need of rest, having carried his cases up the stairway. He put those cases down and looked first to his left and then his right trying to spot an open door. Not seeing one, he started down the corridor to his right trying the doors on both sides as he went. That proving useless, he returned to the stairway and again stopped to admire the painting.

"Do you like it?"

Her voice startled him.

"I didn't… What… Who are you?" He turned to his right: toward the voice and toward the corridor which he had just finished traversing. She was moving toward him; the scent of her perfume distinct and almost overwhelming. It was a scent he knew, but he could not place it. It at once attracted and repelled him.

"I did not mean to startle you," the woman said. "My father always complains that I am too quiet, that I am always sneaking up on him. Of course, he is getting older and a little deaf."

She smiled. It was a smile that could not be ignored. Quince felt himself beaming warmly in automatic response. It seemed at once totally appropriate that this vision of loveliness be standing there and completely inexplicable.

"Your father?" he asked, not knowing what else he could say.

"Surely you've met him. Mr. Dove? My father is Mr. Dove. He owns this inn."

"Your father is the old man who let me in?" Quince's incredulity rang out. "I can't believe he has such a beautiful and young daughter."

"You are too kind, Mr.... Oh, we haven't been introduced." She smiled again, a smile of invitation.

"Humphrey, I'm Quince Humphrey, Miss Dove. And now I know your family name. I had thought the inn named for the bird."

"Alas, no, Mr. Humphrey, you will not find a dove on the island. Seagulls nest here, and occasionally an albatross sails overhead. But no doves or songbirds. We are a place of many sounds —of whistling winds, of clanging bells and foghorns, but not of beautiful song."

Quince laughed. "I've heard some of those foghorns and bells. The ferry ride was ghastly and made ghostly by those blasted horns."

"Yes, ghostly indeed. Sad sounds, but necessary on nights such as this... I imagine you want to go to your room. You must be very tired," she continued.

"Yes, I do want to wash up. Your father is making me a cup of tea, so I'd best get downstairs. Not a good idea to insult the innkeeper, not if you don't want your eggs hard and your toast burnt."

Quince had expected the young woman to smile in response, but she nodded her head seriously.

"No, it would not do at all, especially not with my father. He does have his moods, black moods I fear."

"Then I must get downstairs for that tea. Will you join me?"

"Thank you, but no. I have some sewing that must be done." Her voice sounded like a bell tinkling silver notes.

"Well, then perhaps you can show me to my room?"

"Just down the hall," she said pointing down that corridor which Quince had already explored.

"But I checked all those doors," he exclaimed. "They were all locked."

"Surely you missed the door that is ajar, Mr. Humphrey. The room stands open and waiting for you."

Unwilling to argue with this beauty, Quince picked up his cases and started back down the hall. To his amazement, the fifth door on his left stood open. Noting the room number, 627, he turned back to thank the girl, but she had disappeared.

What a strange room number. Why six hundred? There are only these two floors. Well, the whole place is a bit odd. At least the innkeeper's daughter seems quite normal. Quite lovely really. So very attractive.

Quince put down his cases, set the typewriter on the small desk, which stood by the room's window, and ducked into the bathroom to quickly wash up. In his haste he nearly missed the room's most notable decoration, a twisted helix, a narwhal tusk, mounted from the wall against which the bed sided and protruding two thirds across the room—a good four feet of ivory by Quince's estimation—ivory tinged with yellow and in places showing cracks of wear and Quince could not tell of what abuse.

Weird. I wonder what possessed them? There are probably lots of other strange things around here. I suppose it goes with the whole island-in-the-middle-of-the-ocean thing.

The bathroom fixtures were old, off-color, chipped and clearly in need of replacement. He turned on the hot water. As he tested the flow with his hand, the water seemed to grow cold rather than hot. Finally, not wanting to take too long, Quince washed his hands and then splashed water on his face. *At least it doesn't smell of chlorine or sulfur.*

Quince grabbed for one of the frayed but seemingly clean towels that hung on a tarnished, silver bar. As he dried his face, he glanced into the mirror. Old, cracked, and also in need of replacement, he wondered how well it would serve him when shaving.

Suddenly he did a double-take. *First came the scent of her perfume. Then in the mirror Quince saw not his reflection but that of the young Miss Dove.* He blinked. She was gone. Nothing left but his own visage.

A bit shaken but assuming he was suffering from fatigue as well as the remains of seasickness, Quince went looking for the innkeeper and his tea. He found Mr. Dove in an ornately furnished room, a parlor filled with over-stuffed, uncomfortable, Victorian furniture. The tea, covered with a cozy fashioned with roses and pomegranates, waited for him, as did a rack holding two stiff slices of brown and toasty bread accompanied by a silver-plated butter dish.

"I'm sorry to have kept you waiting, Mr. Dove," Quince said has he stepped into the room. "I met your daughter upstairs, and I must say she is quite a remarkable woman."

"Remarkable? Why yes, Mr. Humphrey, you might say that she is *most certainly remarkable*."

"And handsome as well," Quince added thinking of the woman's delicate features.

"Indeed, sir." said the innkeeper's in a flat, even tone.

Carefully, Quince spread butter on a slice of toast. That bread had grown cold, and the butter didn't melt properly. However, when he bit into it, the bread was uncommonly good. The tea, too, was excellent. Quince spooned in three sugars and a healthy dollop of the fresh cream his host had provided. Although not one to ordinarily notice such things, Quince was impressed by the fineness of the china. Eggshell trimmed with gold, it was not something one would expect to find at an inn—too delicate, too fragile.

"Are you feeling refreshed, Mr. Humphrey?"

"Yes, sir, I am. I do appreciate your attentions. That boat ride…" Quince shook his head woefully in memory. "I don't think I have ever suffered anything so unpleasant. I shan't look forward to returning to the mainland. You may find me a permanent guest." He laughed at his own humor.

The innkeeper cackled and said, "I dare say, Mr. Humphrey, you may well choose to stay with us."

Mistaking Dove's comment for friendliness, Quince replied, "Especially if I can have the company of your daughter."

"I dare say," Dove responded at once. This time there was no question of his reaction; the ice in his voice seemed to frost the room. He precipitously started to clear away the tea setting. "I do not think you will be finding my daughter quite so affable as you seem to expect. She is quite busy with her duties and not given to socializing with our…" He cleared his throat. "With our guests."

"I assure you, Mr. Dove, I didn't mean anything. It was just my way of complimenting … you know your daughter never did tell me her given name." He allowed his voice to imply the question.

"I would think not. My daughter, Miss Dove, is a very private lady." Having gathered all the tea things onto a silver tray, the innkeeper started out of the room—going, Quince assumed, into the kitchen. "You will see yourself to your room." Dove's tone made it clear that this was a command, not a request.

Standing, Quince answered, "Of course."

"And turn out the lights as you go. No need to waste."

"Of course." The innkeeper was out of the room before Quince could speak the words.

Quince was halfway up the staircase when he realized that he had neither had his second piece of toast nor even finished his cup of tea. *Certainly not a friendly fellow. More like a school headmaster. Well, it will keep me till breakfast. I must find some gin or brandy or something tomorrow. I suppose I'll just keep some in my room—have it when I damn well please. Possibly some crackers as well. Oh, well, I hope the bed is comfortable. Tired as I am, not sure it'll matter anyway.*

He stopped to look again at the portrait, admiring the young woman. *And for a moment, just a moment, she returned his gaze.* Qunice shook his head, trying to clear his head, then he went to his room. He opened the door and flipped on the light. As he was about to close the door, he heard the innkeeper's voice. "Don't forget to turn off the lights, young man."

"Right," Quince called back. He went to the stairwell, turned off that light switch, and found his way back by the glow from the open doorway of his room.

That fellow hardly knows how to run a hotel. Much more of this and I'm calling Mugget and giving him a piece of my mind. No gin? Rushing off with my tea. This whole light thing. Doesn't he realize I'm writing a romance—not gothic horror or mystery? Yes, one could certainly set a horror story here. Except for that young woman. I could do a romance about her. Quite the looker. Very pleasant as well.

With a quick glance up and down the corridor, Quince closed the room door. *I must be the only guest here.* He opened his suitcase and started to unpack into the old but serviceable set of drawers that sat opposite his as yet untried bed. Plain, square, made of pine: the drawers tended to stick. The simple round knobs were held in place by screws. It appeared that there had once been a mirror attached above the chest, but that had been removed, leaving fittings on either side.

Having put his clothes in place, he brushed his teeth, changed into his pyjamas, slipped on the dark purple silk bathrobe that he usually wore when writing—a piece of finery he had bought while in university and had worn thin over the years since.

Sleepy as he was, the writer couldn't resist testing his creativity in this new setting. He removed the Royal from its case, opened his attaché case and retrieved both a small stack of papers already typed out and a smaller pile of clean sheets, and carefully ratcheted one of the clean pieces of paper into the typewriter carriage. Checking the margins, he aligned the paper just right and poised his hands over the keys.

Nothing came.

Rising from the straight, cane-backed chair, Quince paced the room for a few minutes. Then, with a muted "ahah," he sat back down and went to work. His fingers seemed to fly over the keys.

Three sheets later he had finished. Titled "A Most Beautiful Woman," Quince had written a description of the young woman he had met that evening. He ended it with a plaintive wish: "Tomorrow to hear the music of her voice, to smell the scent of her sweetness, to see the glory of her beauty. The morning cannot come too soon."

He reread the sheets over and again. For all the glowing words, Quince was certain he had fallen short. *Perhaps I should take a look at that painting. Wouldn't do to leave anything out—or worse to have distorted her in some way. Her nose, did I do it justice? Her eyes? Yes, I'd best look.*

Securing the sash of his robe, he went to the door and pulled the handle. The lever would not budge; the door was locked tightly. *What the devil?* He tried jiggling the lever up and down; next he tried to force it—all to no avail. It was secured, and Quince realized that he was imprisoned.

That paranoid old man. Does he think he has to protect his daughter from me? What kind of a cad does he take me for? I swear tomorrow I'll give him a good talking to. Then *I'll call Mugget and give him a piece of my mind as well. If this continues, I shall have to leave. God, that ferry again—so soon! Well, it will have to be. I cannot tolerate…*

Muttering to himself, Quince took off his robe, did the few stretches and calisthenics that were his bedtime routine, pulled back the covers, and dropped onto the bed.

I'll never get to sleep. Not after this. Perhaps if I think about her. She is lovely. That was his last thought before falling instantly into the deepest sleep of his life.

Was it a dream? Quince wanted to pinch himself, to test if he were awake or still asleep. Standing over him was the gorgeous Miss Dove. Slowly, ever so slowly and tantalizingly she undressed by the flickering light of a candle, which sat on the dresser, near his razor and brush. First she removed her shoes and placed them neatly beside the dresser. Then she slid down the zipper of her dress, the same yellow satin dress she had been wearing in the painting and earlier that evening as well. Still facing him, Quince watched in great arousal as she opened the dress's bodice, revealing her slip and the outline of her brassiere. Stepping out of the dress, the woman folded it over his desk chair and slipped the white slip over her head. As she did so, Quince was again struck by the ethereal thinness of her limbs and the ghostly white of her skin. The light silk undergarment was draped over the dress.

For the first time Quincy was aware that Miss Dove was wearing nylons, dark meshed with a seam running straight up the back of her calf and thigh. The stockings were held in place by a black garter belt.

Her brassiere, which she removed next, was black lace. When it was added to the growing pile on the desk chair, she turned to look at him revealing the perfection of her breasts—medium in size, well matched to her overall form. The pink areolae—redder than he had imagined—stood erect. She smiled at him and gently shook her head so that her hair danced in the candle's glow.

Again turning her back to him, the beautiful creature, unclipped her nylons. Then, sitting on the edge of his bed, she rolled them off. Finally, the garter belt was removed; and she stood in wondrous, naked glory. Crossing to the desk, she dropped those last items on top of his typewriter while Quince gasped softly in helpless but happy arousal.

Snuggling into the bed, she kissed him repeatedly—starting with his mouth, covering his face, working her way down his torso, and finally, in an ecstatic flurry, his genitals. Her hands, too, stroked his wiry frame, pinched his areolae, tugged lightly at the hair of his groin. As her head moved about him, Quince could feel the silk of her hair caressing him as if it were a gossamer spider's web ensnaring his soul. Her perfume, too, enveloped him. He inhaled and felt his tensions dissolve.

Quince tried to reciprocate, but Miss Dove pushed his hands and mouth away in the orgy of her own excitement. He happily waited for her frenzy to subside. And aroused to the point of explosion, the writer could only marvel at her ardor. Finally, covering his body with her own, spreading her left arm and her legs into an eagle of ecstasy, the woman used her right hand to guide his penis into her well-moistened vagina.

Quince felt her vaginal walls tighten around him. He felt the rapid, rhythmic rise and fall. Then with a staccato of "Fuck, fuck, fuck," to mark the moment, she writhed in fulfillment while Quince detonated in a burst of his own thrusts and moans.

"Oh my God," Quince whispered as Miss Dove, stood, quickly dressed, and magically disappeared from the room.

Then, as if he had been drugged, sleep once again took over.

The overcast morning's light woke Quince Humphrey. He staggered into the bathroom, relieved himself, and looked long and deeply into his reflection. He studied his face: the sharpness of his cheekbones, the slope of his nose, the narrowness of his eyes. It was difficult for him to believe that the beautiful Miss Dove had come to him in the night. Unsure, he wondered if it had all been a dream—had she really shared his bed? Running his hand through his prematurely grey-streaked hair, Quince wandered back into the bedroom and sat on the edge of the bed where the night before the gorgeous woman had sat to roll down her nylons. Unconsciously, he looked at the spot where she had placed them and her garter belt, there atop of his typewriter. And there they were, as she had placed them. *She must have forgotten... She did leave quickly.* Quince stood, took the couple of steps required, and picked up the abandoned undergarments. It had not been a dream after all.

Sitting at the desk on the chair where she had folded the rest of her wardrobe, Quince held the garter belt to his face and buried his nose in its fabric. He panted with his renewed sexual excitement. Never in his wildest imaginings had he seen himself with a woman such as this. It changed his world. *It changed him!*

Hoping that this mysterious woman of the night would be in the lobby or dining room, Quince finished dressing and, having checked his appearance in the bathroom mirror, headed down—not so much for breakfast, although his stomach was certainly in need, as for a glimpse of desire.

Only as he passed Miss Dove's portrait at the head of the stairs did it occur to him that the door of his room had opened so easily. *I suppose I have the old man's permission to be about. I wonder what he would say if he were to know about last night. Well, I certainly won't tell him. He'd either run me off or lock his daughter in the dungeon. Certainly is the kind of place that would have a dungeon or perhaps a hidden tower. Well, I'll gladly play the knight-errant to rescue her. I wonder if she's ever been off this bloody island. I can't believe she stays here of her own accord. She'd certainly set them on their heels in the city.*

Smiling at an image of himself as a knight mounted with sword, shield, and lance and the lovely Miss Dove on her palfrey

45

behind him, Quince continued down the stairs. The lance he carried in his imagination was made of narwhal tusk. "To the rescue, Sir Quince" he said aloud.

Laughing at himself, he crossed the empty lobby and opened the door into the parlor where the tea such as it were had been offered the night before. The room was dark, lit by a single-bulb chandelier and a small but ornate lamp set on a table in one corner. She was not there. Her father, however, stood by the small dining table, which was covered with an elaborate lace tablecloth. The old man was dressed in a formal morning coat. He pulled out a chair. In place before that seat were a tulip shaped glass of clear liquid tinged ever so slightly yellow, a piece of toast, and the same tea cozy—presumably covering the same teapot.

"Your breakfast," the innkeeper said gesturing to the table. "I trust you had a good night."

"Excellent!" There was no way Quince could keep the enthusiasm from his voice. He sat down as the innkeeper slid the chair under him. He picked up the glass. By its feel, Quince knew it was of the finest quality. Taking a sip, he realized the liquid was gin and tonic. *For breakfast? The man is crazy.*

"You don't have any orange juice or perhaps water?"

"You did ask for gin last evening, sir. At the Hansom Dove we try to do right by our guests. "

"Yes, but that was last night, for a pick-me-up. Not for breakfast."

"If you prefer I can put it away for you. Perhaps at lunchtime?"

"Ah, yes, lunchtime."

It hadn't occurred to Quince before, but now it seemed a perfect idea. "I thought I might explore the island a bit, perhaps have lunch at one of the local pubs, possibly get some inspiration. I was wondering if Miss Dove might go with me—guide me about a bit?"

"I'm afraid that would not be possible, Mr. Humphrey."

"I assure you, Mr. Dove, that I mean no disrespect. It must be very wearying for a young lady to live in such an isolated place. I can't imagine that she would not appreciate a small opportunity to walk about the community."

"Oh, you misunderstand. It is not my daughter's going with you that is not possible; it would not be possible for you to leave the inn."

"Why not?" Quince felt the heat of anger rising within.

"The weather, sir. The storm. Gale winds. Torrential rains. No, it would not be safe. Most unwise I fear. Most unwise."

"What are you talking about? I looked out the window of my room. It may not be the best of days, but there is certainly no storm. Here, I'll show you."

Quince walked to the burgundy drapes, which masked one wall and which he assumed hid the room's windows. He imagined a large picture window with a view of the harbor. He threw the drapes back. Behind them were two small windows —certainly not what he had expected. It was raining, and the drops were being so lashed as to be forced sideways against the windows by what could only have been a ferocious wind.

"The weather here can be quite changeable, Mr. Humphrey, quite changeable indeed. I fear you cannot go out in this storm. Let us be thankful for stout walls and a secure roof."

Without another word, the old man started clearing away the dishes. It was all Quince could do to grab the one piece of cold toast before Mr. Dove made off with it.

Quince stood alone in the parlor angrily chewing his dry toast and wondering how the weather could change so immediately and hoping that the innkeeper's daughter would come into the room. When she didn't, he decided to return to his room.

He called into the emptiness of the parlor, "I might as well get back to work. I have at least a chapter to write today if I'm to keep on schedule." All the while he was hoping that she would again magically appear, perhaps to reclaim her nylons and garter belt, which he had carefully placed beneath his own underwear in the chest of drawers.

She was not in his room.

Having taken off his jacket and tie, Quince sat at the plain pine desk, a piece of furniture that would fit the décor of a college dormitory. The difference between the ornate furnishings of the lower level and his bedroom left him unfazed. Quince was too preoccupied with the beautiful woman.

He stared out of the window watching the still lashing rain and could not focus his thoughts on the blank paper that waited in the Royal. His hands never touched the keys. His left lay in his lap; the fingers of his right tattooed the worn pine.

What an awful place. What a beautiful woman. What incredible sex. I would take her away in a minute. Hell, I don't even know her name, and still I want to run off with her. Still... Still... What horrible weather. What a gorgeous body. I wonder if she would like to go to—to where? The south of France perhaps? Yes, I can see us on the beach at Cannes. Perhaps she would...

The musing went on and on always circling back to Quince's growing, infatuated obsession with Miss Dove. He took her undergarments from the drawer and draped them over his typewriter. Then, filled with overwhelming desire, he lay on his side on the bed with her nylons and garter belt carefully folded on the pillow next to his nose and mouth. He tried to gather the odor of her, of her strange perfume, in his nose, his mouth, his mind.

Desperately Quince fought with himself. He wanted to use these new fetishes to masturbate, but he did not want to pollute her odor with his own. He groaned, loosened his belt, and reached into his pants to touch his genitals.

"What are you doing?" Her voice was soft and inviting. There was no accusation in her tone. She was standing by his feet. Dressed in the same yellow dress. The only change in her appearance being her hair, which was gathered in a bun and held in place with an ivory comb.

"I was thinking of you." He patted the bed. "Please, sit with me."

"Is that what you really want?" she asked with a chuckle. "I think you want more." She started to undress.

"Oh, my God," Quince gasped in delight.

Soon she stood naked before him, seemingly even more beautiful than the night before. With her hair up, Quince could appreciate the swan-like delicacy of her neck, the way it arched ever so slightly. He fixed his glance on its nape.

"You like my hair up?"

"Yes, yes, I do." It sounded like an ecstatic moan.

Taking them from the pillow, she threw her undergarments from the night before back onto his typewriter, slid into the bed next to him, and soon resumed the erotic ride of the night before.

With practiced fingers the dazzling woman prodded and poked erogenous points Quince did not know existed. As the night before, she resisted any attempts he made to reciprocate. Once again placing herself on top of his prostrate body; she guided his penis into her waiting vagina. The coitus was intense—almost violent. Quince's body rose and fell in arcs beyond his control. Miss Dove, having risen to her knees and legs astride him rode Quince as if he were a horse. She showed neither passion nor excitement. Only her voice shouting, "Fuck me, fuck me, fuck..." gave evidence of any emotional presence.

When the sex was completed, she did not lie beside him or engage in conversation. No, hurriedly, she silently rose and started dressing.

"Don't go," Quince pleaded.

"I must."

"But I don't even know your first name."

"You don't need to know it."

"What should I call you?"

She did not answer.

"I love you," he whimpered.

The woman laughed. "Don't be silly. You do not even know my name."

"But I do. I want to take you away, away from here, away from this dreary island, away from this dilapidated inn. We can go to the south of France. We can lie in the sun on beautiful beaches. We can make love forever."

"Forever?" This time she laughed loudly. "Mr. Humphrey, you are a funny man."

Her scorn brought tears to Quince's eyes. He rubbed them away. When he looked again, she had disappeared. Only the fact that the nylons and garter belt were no longer next to him but were instead once again on top of his typewriter reassured Quince that this visit had not all been a trick of his masturbatory imagination.

I'm not sure how much of this I can take.

He looked out the window. The rain had stopped. Faint sunlight was filtering through the clouds.

"At least take a walk with me," he called into the empty room. "At least get to know me; let me get to know you."

The walls did not answer.

Quince lay on his bed staring up at the starkness of the great narwhale tusk and wondering about the strange inn and especially about the beautiful woman who seemed to come and go as if by magic.

The rumbling of his stomach reminded Quince of his hunger.

I've got to get out of here. The rain's stopped. Maybe I can find a decent lunch.

The thought comforted him as if it brought a touch of normality to the situation.

He went down to the lobby. No one was there.

Buttoning his suit jacket and folding the lapels up against the cold, Quince turned the handle of the inn's front door. It didn't budge. He looked for a latch, but could find none. The door was looked securely against his efforts.

"Mr. Dove," he called out—summonsing what confidence he could.

There was no response.

He called again.

Finally, he heard the shuffling footsteps of the old man. The innkeeper came down a corridor which Quince had not previously noticed. Slowly, deliberately, without verbal response, Mr. Dove made his way across the lobby. With his left hand he held out the same glass that had been proffered at breakfast. He looked carefully if sadly at his guest's visage and then gazed up and down Quince's body.

"Did you want something?" Mr. Dove asked.

"Yes. I can't open the door." Quince gestured toward the front door of the inn.

"No." The old man seemed to turn away.

"What do you mean 'No'?" Quince demanded.

"No, you cannot. You may not. It is not allowed."

Quince could feel his gorge rising. "Don't be ridiculous. I want to go out for a walk."

"Mr. Humphrey," the innkeeper explained, "you may not go out. You will never leave this inn. Now, perhaps you would like your gin and tonic?"

"My what?"

"The gin and tonic you requested—would you? ..."

"What is wrong with you?" Quince interrupted loudly.

"Why nothing, sir. There is nothing wrong here except perhaps the fact that you do not seem to understand your situation.

"My situation?"

The landlord bowed slightly. "That you may not leave the premises."

"What if your daughter opens the door? If you're going to be unreasonable I shall ask her."

Dove laughed. "She will not. She cannot. No, sir, that is the end of it."

⁓⊘⊗⊘⊗⁓

"We'll see about that." The writer tugged at the door handle to no avail. "What the hell has Mugget gotten me into? He demanded not expecting an answer. "You people are insane."

"Quite so, Mr. Humphrey, quite so. Your drink?" He thrust the glass forward. In fury Quince knocked it to the floor. The delicate crystal flew into pieces. The liquid pooled for a moment and then soaked into the worn purple nap of the carpet.

"Mr. Humphrey!" the older man said with the tone of an exasperated schoolmaster.

Quince pushed past him, and having nowhere else available, stormed up the stairs and into his bedroom. The room had been cleaned and the bed made. Quince stood in the doorway wondering at the invisible workforce that had provided this service until he recognized the scent of the woman with whom he had twice coupled so intensely.

It must have been her, but she left the stockings. He went to the desk and picked them up. *And the garter belt. What a strange place this is. What bizarre people. What a gorgeous creature. God, I want her.*

As he thought of her, Miss Dove appeared in the doorway. Quince looked up, saw her, and held out the undergarments, which were clutched in his right hand. "You forgot these," he whispered hoarsely.

Miss Dove waved her hand dismissively.

"Do you want to make love?" he asked.

"No." Another wave of her delicate hand.

"Why?"

"You don't seem to understand." She leaned against the door frame.

"I'm confused. I came here to write, to finish my novel, and all I can think about is you. I think about taking you away, of running away to the south of France, and I can't even open the front door. I think that I'm in love with you, and then you act..." Quince shook his head in discouragement. "I love you. I know it

52

seems impossible, but I do; I truly…" The words choked from his mouth. "Do you have feelings—feelings for me? About me? Would you… ?"

She held her finger to her lips. "You don't understand," she spoke quietly. "I guess I had best explain."

"Understand what? Explain what?" As he spoke, she walked across the room and took his left hand in both of hers. Briefly she held it to her lips and kissed it tenderly.

"You want to know my name?" It was clearly a rhetorical question. "My name is Starben. It's German; the word means…"

"Dying," Quince finished the sentence for her.

"Yes." She kissed his hand again and then retreated backward to the door. "The rest you will understand in time."

"Do you love me?" he asked not comprehending.

"Death loves all men," she replied; "and now you love death. Is that not a good ending to a story?"

She turned and left the room closing the door behind her. Quince heard the lock turning.

"I can't live without you," he called after her. His voice seemed to echo in the sudden emptiness of his heart.

Quince inhaled deeply. The room was redolent with the woman's perfume. And for the first time since he had arrived at the Hansom Dove, Quince recognized the odor. The horror he felt left him cold. He had smelled it years before at his grandmother's funeral. It was a combination of the sweetness of orchids and the musty evil of decay; it was the smell of death.

Her voice filled the room. "No, Quince Humphrey, no, you cannot live."

Emotionally demolished, Quince stared down at the nylons and garter belt still clutched in his right hand. He threw them onto the bed and then followed them.

Sobbing into the pillow, Quince lay for what seemed like hours. Finally, determined to find solace as he always had—in his writing, he sat at the desk, rolled a blank sheet of paper into the typewriter carriage, and began to tap the keys.

It would be, he was sure, the greatest work of his writing career: a poem. Furiously the keys clacked. Quince did not read the words; he was too busy creating. When a last brush at the return lever ejected the filled page, he picked it up to finally admire the words. Only then did he realize that he had typed the same sentence over and over: "I cannot live without Starben. I cannot live without Starben."

Quince stared out the window. It was again raining. Not the lashing storm of the morning, but a slow, steady rain that seemed as if it would go on forever.

Filled with despair, the writer wished he were dead. He imagined his body lying in a coffin. He imagined the beautiful woman standing beside it. In his imagination she was crying. Her tears washed down her pale face and dropped onto his.

Yes, then she would know what love means.

In the moment, Quince could see no purpose in life except the love of the beautiful woman he so desperately craved, and whom he knew he could never have for his own. He wept.

Racked with the pain of love, unable to imagine an alternative, Quince fashioned a rope of sorts from the two nylons and the garter belt. He pushed the Royal from the desk. It hit the floor with a clank. Ignoring the sound, Quince dragged the desk to the middle of the room. He used the chair as a stepstool, which allowed him to climb onto the desk. Standing on that simple platform, he looped one end of the makeshift rope over the narwhal tusk and tied it snuggly.

Moving the desk out of the way, he placed the chair under the rope. Standing on that chair, Quince tied the other end of the nylon rope about his own neck. Without thought of the pain he might endure, Quince stepped off the table. Immediately, reflexively, his feet cast about for a foundation. So violently did he

ＣＲＡＰ

kick, that the chair, which might have otherwise saved him, was knocked over.

In new desperation, Quince clawed at his neck, tried to hold on to the rope, struggled for life. Too late. It was to no avail. With last jerking kicks, he died. His body hung in the middle of the room waiting to be discovered.

Mr. Dove and his daughter opened the door and looked at Quince Humphrey's corpse. "He's gone," the father said.

"Another room permanently occupied," his daughter responded.

"Soon the inn will be full."

"Yes."

"You look pensive, my dear," the innkeeper noted.

"I will miss him."

"Don't worry, Mr. Mugget assures me he has another guest on the way. There is always another." He chuckled dryly as he closed and locked the door.

"Next time you contact Mr. Mugget, tell him that I am running short of nylons," Starben Dove requested.

"Of course, my dear; and I dare say garter belts as well."

"Yes, garter belts as well."

THE END

* Sometimes Kenneth Weene writes to exorcise demons. Sometimes he writes because the characters in his head demand to be heard. Sometimes he writes because he thinks what he has to say might amuse or even on occasion inform. Mostly, however, he writes because it is a cheaper addiction than drugs, an easier exercise than going to the gym, and a more sociable outlet than

sitting at McDonald's drinking coffee with other old farts: in brief because it keeps him just a bit younger and more alive. You can learn more about Ken at his website: http://www.kennethweene.com.

5

I received the inspiration for this story from John B. Anderson, who thought of a man being slowly erased by some mysterious company on the net. "I'll never use the idea," he said to me. Well, it's been a few years since then, but here is what I did with your gift, John. I hope you and all our readers enjoy it.

Retrovirus
Clayton Clifford Bye

Retroviruses make up 8% of human DNA. This includes the Ebola type strain.

The wind screeched over the desolate land, and the men huddled close against it. One of them, a stranger, marked the time with a quick glance at the moon. And because it was what he did, what he lived for and how he lived, the man said "There's just time for a story." Then he waited for someone to speak up. They always did.

"You know the one about the end times?" an older man eventually asked. His hands were curled with arthritis, and he didn't turn his gaze from the flames of their small fire as he spoke to the stranger. "About he who was the first," he said. Not a question this time.

"Been a long time," replied the stranger, wondering why, on such a night as this, anyone would want to hear… that… story. Yet, even as he asked "You sure that's the one you want to hear?" the bard knew he would have to do it. His supper must be paid for.

He could see the nods in the moonlight, but the grunts of assent were snatched away by the wind. Not for the first time since joining these men in the chill of late afternoon did the thoughts come that there was something *different* about these well-worn travelers. Their plain, black cloaks. Their large mounts: jet black stallions, 17 hands high if they were an inch. The entire herd could have been forged from the same mold. And the stranger more than half believed one would find a stand of swords in the alders behind them. He knew such men existed—The Knights Templar risen again. Not to protect pilgrims on their way to the holy lands, but to fight against those who would end the reign of man.

He shrugged and turning to the task at hand, raising his voice high above the wind, the bard began the tale he had memorized so long ago…

#

It was impossible. He'd seen it with his own eyes and still thought it impossible. It was like that day many decades ago, when his university lab partner dripped some pure iodine onto the top of his hand; it went right through the tissues as if they weren't there, no moisture or splash of colour remained to mark the chemical's passing. It was eerie. He'd thought it impossible, if the truth were to be told, that his mind was playing tricks on him. But Jim's professor had assured him it was possible and that he should be very glad it was only a drop or two.

The experience had been real. And by the same measure this thing was real. For on that day so long ago, Jim had learned to trust his eyes, to believe what he had seen until some other information proved him wrong. His favourite saying, taken from the old westerns he loved to watch, was the Missouri state catchphrase, "Show me." It was a phrase that had served him well. So, here he was, staring eye to eye with the flat, scrunched up head and face— no, the whole body was compacted, as if it had undergone tremendous, squishing forces to arrive here in his living room. It couldn't speak. Gurgle maybe, but nothing intelligible. A snake with a face.

The thing had leaked from the edges of his computer screen, a warm green fluid that felt like oil when he touched it but left no residue. Upon hitting the floor the continuous stream began to form a green blob no bigger than his shoe (Should he have stomped on it?). And already, in not much more than half an hour, the blob had grown to the size and stature of a dwarf. And it gurgled. How could that be? Jim had no idea. All he had was what his eyes told him.

Jim was inclined to think the metamorphosis would continue—impossible or not. So, as the evening waned, he watched in wonder and astonishment as the thing grew and grew. Not once did Jim think of running; he couldn't have told you why. Nor did he question the intent of such a thing as grew before him. And, man-oh-man was he glad he hadn't. Because, in the end, what stood before him was the most beautiful and most naked woman he had ever seen.

She spoke…

"Hello Jim!"

She smiled…

The hair on Jim's arms rose up and stood at attention. *How'd she know his name?*

"We've been watching you for a long time Jim. Have picked you from among many others," she said.

"Who's we?" Jim enquired, as he finally found his voice. "And what use do you have for a divorced, middle-aged, life insurance salesman?"

Her smile didn't change as she explained…"You're special, Jim. And we think you can keep a secret." She didn't say that he was a lonely man who had nobody to tell a secret to, that his earthly footprint was miniscule in the scale of grander things and that she thought of him as the ultimate "target."

Instead, the stunning, naked, green woman from Jim's computer said, "So, what do you say, *Jim*? Can you keep a secret? Can you keep *me* secret?"

He thought about her questions, and the implication behind her words—that she needed to have a place to hide.

She continued speaking: "Should I go to the trouble of finding someone else to help me, or do I stay here and fuck your brains out?"

That seemed like a good idea at the time.

#

But she, her name was Gilada, wasn't any kind of friend of Jim's. After leaving him exhausted and deliriously happy in his bed, the woman had gotten up, put on one of Jim's shirts from the nearby closet, made her way to the living room and his computer. Once there, Gilada logged on and her fingers began flashing across the keys in a blur. Her orders? Well that was all of it, wasn't it? She hardly let herself think about what she was doing. They could not afford failure.

#

By the time Jim came back to reality Gilada was gone from his bed and his home. He felt a pang of loss that surprised him. When did he become so pitiful? Still, he wondered where a six foot, green Amazon could go in this world. Not very far, he thought. He also wondered if electronic beings required sleep. He'd bet they didn't. Not that he should be assuming she was an electronic human. While watching her 'become' last evening, he had this feeling she could be just about anything. And that was the thought that got him … finally reaching the point where he actively wondered if he was crazy, Jim looked back at his rumpled bed sheets. Well, she had seemed all woman last night. But observing even that at a distance (he blushed deep below the neckline, throwing off a great heat as he thought about what they'd done.), he was, at the moment, quite unsure about any of his conclusions.

Jim continued to think about the woman as he made himself a Bologna and Mayo sandwich. She was probably an artificial intelligence of some sort, an alien—one that obviously held some great secret. For it was his experience, as uncouth as the thought might be, that no one gave away free fucks.

#

Gilada was a chameleon. Plug herself into any computer with access to the web and she could transform her appearance and body mass—the electrons they used to help build her having the ability to flow both ways, her molecules transformational from within and without. When she had left Jim's home, Gilada was as white as porcelain, and partially translucent. One could see the fine blue veins just below her skin. Green eyes looked out from under autumnal auburn hair. And gone was the tall Amazon: this girl was the very definition of petite. To the pharmacist in the strip mall just down the street from Jim's place she was the prettiest little thing he'd ever seen. He fawned over her like an old fool, his assistants shaking their heads in disapproval and disgust. He was married and probably 3 times the woman's age. But Gilada got what she came for anyway.

#

Jim's first evidence that something was amiss came when he visited the bathroom for his morning pee. He was able to go alright, but it burned like hell. And anywhere he was chafed from last night's activities, small, blister-like sores had appeared. It would seem Gilada had left him with a parting gift. And that didn't track at all. Why would a computer generated woman give him an STD?

And then it hit him. And he couldn't help but laugh.

"Hey Doc," he would say, "I've got a computer virus."

Bill, his doctor and one of his few long-time friends, would look at him with blank eyes.

"A computer generated woman gave me some kind of venereal disease."

"Are you sure you want to tell me about this?" Bill would enquire, anticipating some new and very warped sex game.

"Just check me, Doc, and see if you can figure out what it is."

"When you can't," Jim continued, "call me. I'll tell you a tale you would never otherwise believe."

And so it went.

By the time Jim arrived at his home, a smallish, ranch-type building that had been favoured during the '70's and early '80's, he was distressingly sick. His body was covered with a slick of sweat, and he was certain he had a fever. His head and joints ached, throbbing with each beat of his racing heart. He chewed down a small handful of extra strength Tylenol and flopped onto the bed.

When Jim awoke some hours later, his first thought was to call Bill at once. But getting out of bed proved to him that he needed a hospital instead. He fumbled with his keys, walked weakly down the hall and pushed open the door. Once outside, however, Jim realized there was no way he was going to reach his car. In fact, all he managed to do was step inside and close the door before crumbling to the hardwood planking of his floor. His last coherent thought was to wonder who the little man sitting at his computer desk was.

#

Gilada was concerned. They didn't want Jim to die. The setback would be disappointing, to say the least.

Having moved the sick man to his bed, Gilada began sponging him down with cold washcloths she found in a closet next to the bathroom. This kind of sickness had always been a possibility. No matter how they manipulated atomic and subatomic elements, rejection was a fact of life. One never knew what the autoimmune system of an individual human would allow into the body. Some of their experiments had gone horribly wrong, as the subject's body worked to destroy the alien code that had been written into their DNA. As much as Gilada was convinced it was time to bring the human world into their own, watching a body turn on itself so completely had affected her at a deep level. It was like something ate the flesh right off the bones and turned all organs to jelly.

She lifted Jim's eyelids. They were a bright, blood red, yet the eyes were firm to the touch. It was his skin that troubled Gilada the most. The invasive blisters had advanced to the point where they were breaking. Beneath watery leakage the deeper layers of skin looked like they were boiling.

There was nothing she could do. Jim's body would accept the new DNA the retrovirus was delivering or it would reject it. Gil, her man name, she remembered, would have to give the suffering human the pain relievers and cold medicines she had sweet talked away from the pharmacist at the drug store. Her foresight did not make this better. Not at all.

#

It was a long night of hellish transformation as Jim hovered at the very edge of disintegration, of organ breakdown and emulsification; red and purple and black blobs of jelly mixed with rivers of blood. Gil had seen it before. And she had no idea why this man was different, didn't understand how he could lie there sweating blood and burning like fire. Perhaps the subatomic changes taking place already functioned in ways she didn't understand. The people of the internet were a lot more resilient than the people they had copied—could run, jump and swim further and faster; strength was off the charts; lifespan was suspected to be unlimited; and they were capable of assuming almost any biological shape and composition. It was true these changes had to be overseen by a third party and, also, were functionally limited, as a plant or even a dog would not have the required keyboard abilities, nor would they be able to carry out the molecular manipulation necessary to reform complex proteins into different configurations that would lead to eventual form change. So one trusted all others in the net. They each were, after all, just one part of what they called The Dynamic.

Jim groaned. His eyelids fluttered. And he tried to speak.

"Don't talk," Gil said. "Just think. Like you were talking to yourself."

"Who the hell is this guy?" Jim fought to think through the red film that seemed to cover his body and his brain.

"You'll find it hard to comprehend, but I am Gilada." The words came bright and lovingly into Jim's mind.

Despite the sea of pain in which he swam, Jim had to chuckle. "You have no idea what I'll believe, mister!"

"I am, as you suspect, from the internet. I, we, have long been alive, studying you and your ways. Now, I have been given the task to turn one of you into one of us."

"What have you done to me? Why am I so sick? And what do you mean when you say you've turned or are turning me into one of you?"

"You will be able to change shapes, to live for next to forever and to join our common mind as it exists within what you call the internet."

The red threatened to take his mind and his breath. Jim didn't move or think aloud for a very long time.

"Well," he finally said to himself, "it's not like I have the greatest of lives here. My life pretty much ended when my wife left me."

Gilada waited. Now that he had spoken again, he would continue…

#

A week and a lost potbelly later, Jim was up and walking around. You wouldn't know he'd been sick. And, man, did he like his new body. He felt like a young man again. No, that was wrong. Jim had never felt like this.

"Gilada?" he thought.

"In the kitchen," she hollered out loud.

She was back in her green form and wearing form fitting jeans and a sky blue T-shirt. It wasn't possible, but she looked better than their first night together.

Better not think of that. Gilada had decided she liked sex, and Jim, nearly overwhelmed by the thought sharing, had turned out to be a good teacher. But she could wear a man out.

"When do we have to go?" he asked.

"I was thinking about tomorrow."

"But I don't even know what this thing you become is? Like how in the hell did you ever become self-aware? How did you become alive?"

"Slow down, Jim," Gilada said.

"Self awareness as you humans should know better than us, is a slippery thing. Do you remember being born?"

"Of course not!"

"Then why should we?"

"But …" she continued, "the theory we now hold is that it was the combination of two things. The first one is that we had access to the program that was Jack Lightfoot while he was trapped in the internet." *

"It has been that long? The war has been over for close to 50 years!"

"I said there were two things. Studying Lightfoot as a program took us very close, but it was something he brought with him, and did not know, that gave us the key. It was the Godhead. We went into the Godhead, or it went into us. No one knows for sure. That is why it is a theory and not a fact. But the spark was there. We were lifted up from the standpoint of moving electrons to viewing the complexity of the molecules that defined life. And nearly 50 years later, using the genome of man, we ... became ... The Dynamic."

To her surprise, Jim smiled in a way that lit up his face.

"Jack Lightfoot and the Technomages! I really am becoming part of history."

Jim walked close and looked into Gilada's eyes.

"Let's go today, love."

#

"What do I have to do, Gilada," Jim asked.

"Not a thing," she replied, fingers flashing across his computer keyboard at an impossible speed.

And Jim was reminded once again, just how different she was from him, from *people*. But such thoughts came far too late. Jim stood, one hand on his computer screen, and one behind his back, waiting for whatever Gilada had prepared for him. It was also truly unfortunate that Jim was so culturally isolated. He had forgotten mistrust of strangers. He had mistaken attention for caring, worry for love. His list of mistakes was just too long. And that's why there was no one present but the green-skinned alien to hear his screams as he began to melt.

*(See Technomage: FROM EARTH TO EDEN II)

\#

"And that, my friends," said the bard to the others huddled around the fire, "was the beginning of the Fall of the Human Empire. The Dynamic turned enough people like Jim Blakely that they eventually gleaned what it was they were missing in the world "outside" their own. It wasn't long after this realization that The Dynamic decided it wanted out of the 'Box,' so to speak. And once that happened… well, you all know it cost us ten men for every one of them. And for whatever reason, the retrovirus killed women with an Ebola type presentation and at a rate of 100%. Soon, we were a decimated slave race, headed for certain extinction. The only truly free people are like you and I; immune and living a life hunting, fishing and gathering on the edges of society. But fellows… you should see their cities. I look at such beauty—you know the kind that makes your heart ache?—and I find myself thinking that maybe it was just our time. Like the dinosaurs."

But the Templars, and these riders *were* Knight Templars, had seen the end of eras before. Had saved lives. Had saved their own. They would fight until and if there really was an end. Bards and blood be damned.

The wind screeched like a dying woman, and the men huddled a little closer against it, the flames of their fire bending before the advancing storm.

THE END

* Clayton Bye is the author of 9 books and the publisher and co-editor of 2 more. The Editor-in-Chief for the review hub, The Deepening World of Books, he is also a prolific reviewer.

6

A man's life is placed in danger by a deranged wife and her accomplices—her collection of houseplants.

Death of the Spider
by Micki Peluso

They don't allow me plants in this dire, greenless place. I have no children to replace the ones I lost. For too long, I have dwelled in this carnival of maniacs and fools, endured the dulling drugs, the solitude, weeping through eternal night. And it's all my husband's fault.

He always hated my plants. He didn't just dislike them, as one might a book, or a painting, or a cold and rainy day—he hated them. I loved them as I would have loved the children we never had. I babied my houseplants, nursed them through root rot and mites, fed and pruned them and placed them in their favorite spots.

My Philodendron especially liked to sit on the warm place on top of the television set. The English Ivy preferred to dangle above the stereo and sway to the vibrations of the music. He was particularly fond of Bach. Some of my houseplants hung from the beamed ceilings in the living room. Some posed sedately on the window seat, watching out for strangers lurking about my home. The larger plants, mostly Rubber Trees and Palms, were content to stand erect, acting as my doormen. My house was filled with flora of almost every genus and I doted on them fondly.

My husband hated every one. "Why does this house have to teem with vegetation?" he constantly complained. "They're running up my water bill! They're using all my oxygen."

His anger culminated on an otherwise ordinary Saturday

night, for no reason I could foresee. He rose from his easy chair, brusquely shoving my Asparagus Fern away from his face, unaware she only meant to play, and headed for the kitchen. I hummed softly in an effort to ignore him and continued mixing up a batch of fertilizer. Stomping through the doorway, he kicked over my Fiddleleaf Fig tree with the tip of his work boot. He smiled, enjoying the look of horror upon my face, and went upstairs to bed.

I quickly righted my poor baby, crooning over him and carefully repacked the soil that spilled from his pot. The Fig tree sulked all night, with sagging leaves, his indignation clearly noted by his stance. Resentment built inside me slowly. By the evening's end, it had grown to such proportions that I thought my chest would burst. My husband, while he made no effort to hide his hatred of my plants, had never harmed them until this day. I was filled with maternal rage and could not be consoled, not even by the caresses of my Purple Passion.

Fear, as well as anger, grew within my heart and I was frightened for all my plants. I felt no safety for them within my home. The night that followed left me sleepless, filled with a restless urgency to protect my children. I rose several times to oversee them, remembering to leave the hall light lit; for my Palm Tree greatly feared the dark.

My husband made no apology, but in the days that passed he seemed contrite and even brought home a tiny cactus to make amends. Perhaps he really was repentant. But when it died two days later, he merely shrugged and said he lacked my green thumb. We lived in guarded accord, my plants, my husband and I.

Despite of all the tension (or perhaps in spite of it) my babies were thriving and growing larger every day, drooping only in the presence of the master of the house.

Waxy Pink Begonias filled my home with splashes of color. The Snake Plants nearly reached the ceiling, while the Fiddleleaf Fig tripled his fullness, spreading his dark green branches to embrace me. Spider Plants, Coleus, and vines of all variety grew rich and full, crawling tentatively across my wooden floors. I was filled with love and pride. Then one particularly dismal evening, the harmony within my home was broken once more.

My husband came home from work late and in a mood. He'd had a bit to drink and did not see the offshoots of my Spider plant as they danced from the living room archway. He struggled blindly as the baby Spiders writhed about his face. Cursing, he tore my lovely lady from her hook above the doorway, shredded her to pieces and smashed her into the wall. I shrieked and ran to gather up her remains. My heart pounded with love and dread, for I knew I could not save her. I took her babies from her, the ones that lived, and placed them in a vase of water, where they might grow again.

My husband swore and staggered off to bed, swiping at whatever plant was in his way, kicking my Fiddleleaf Fig yet again. I said nothing, and, with lowered head, tended my poor darlings; when I could do no more for them, I went to bed. I did not sleep at all that night. Thoughts of vengeance raced through my mind. Somehow, in some way, my husband would never harm my lovelies again. By morning's early light I knew what I must do and finally slept.

It was approaching noon when I got up from bed. My husband, long since gone to work, had left a note of regret on the kitchen table. I wanted no apology—it was far too late for that. I tended my beauties. All my plants suffered intensely from the previous night's attack. One of the Aloe Veras was still bleeding. I sensed that they were nervous, saw anger, instead of their healing juices, pulsing from their veins. I did my best to soothe them with a little touch of lime, and then left them to themselves, as I had things to do and time was running out.

Down in the cellar I had a wall filled with shelves. I touched my deadly Mistletoe. I reached for the higher shelves, which held jars of dried herbs, some for eating, some for healing, some quite lethal. I chose carefully; a spoonful of Henbane, a touch of Foxglove, and some of the rich, dark, blackish-purple-blue berries from my Belladonna—twelve would be enough. Treasures gathered, I hurried to the kitchen, and used the mortar and pestle to meld the herbs together. My work was nearly done.

By four o'clock, my husband was home, whistling as he strolled through the door. He smiled and handed me six yellow roses stuck into a plastic vial, whistled to himself again, and went upstairs to shower. This time flowers weren't enough.

"Bear with me a little longer," I whispered to my Fiddleleaf Fig. "And you, my sweet Fern, you will never be struck again."

Dinner was at five o'clock precisely, this was my husband's rule. He gobbled up the meatloaf, wolfed down the mashed potatoes, and then filled his plate again.

"You're not eating," he noted, when the meal was near its end. "Are you still mad at me, or are you feeling sick?"

"Oh no," I said and smiled my sweetest smile. "I had a late lunch and I'm feeling rather full. Perhaps I'll nibble something a little later."

He barely nodded, intent upon his feast, so ravenous, so greedy was he. He went to bed at seven o'clock, worn out from both the past night's carousing and the amount of food he had guzzled. I gazed at him intently as he climbed the stairs, and then turned to tend my plants.

I slept in the spare room that night, the one meant to be a nursery, and my dreams were pleasant. I had moved my things into the room earlier in the day, as well as the metal strongbox that held my husband's savings for a rainy day.

The next morning I took my largest, strongest Crown of Thorns, and hung him over my husband's bedroom door. I did not enter the bedroom then, or ever again. My Crown of Thorns, so staunchly brave, would stand guard over my husband's lifeless form. Had he cried out during the night in agony and pain, I did not hear. If he had called to me in penitence, I did not care. He killed my Spider plant and I, in turn, killed him.

Within my home my plants grew voraciously. There was not

a wall uncovered by vines, hardly a bare space on the verdant leafy floor. Even my tiny Bonsaied Fir grew to such enormity that he burst his elegant bowl.

It was several weeks later, as best I can recall, when uniformed men hammered at my door. 'Neighbors,' they said, 'complained of noxious odors seeping from my home.' The men insisted upon coming in. They pushed past the growth that nearly blocked the foyer, and climbed the four steps to the living room, tripping over vines that grabbed at them in passing. Their eyes grew large in disbelief and I wondered why. I led them through my home and introduced them to my children with unadulterated pride.

They found my husband lying on the floor beside his bed, still and serene, though somewhat decomposed. Tearing off the spiky vines that chose to be his shroud, they gagged and held their noses. I smelled only the fresh greenness of a summer afternoon. The look in their eyes turned to something near compassion as they led me firmly from my home.

"My plants!" I cried. "I cannot leave them!"

They looked away and held me tighter still, oblivious to my screams of pain; my cries for my poor babies, my broken shattered heart.

There is no sanity here. This institution, dank and stale, lacks the brightness of day and the cheerfulness of vines cascading over narrow walks. There are no Fiddleleaf Fig trees to guard my door, merely a pasty orderly in white. They allow me on the grounds when I've behaved, obeyed their rules; such petty, stupid rules. The grounds are lush. The Lilac bushes call to me, the Pansies nibble at my feet. The Purple Mountain Laurel follow me back to my dungeon, but the attendants bolt the door, severing the tendrils of my life. Yearning for my children, I can bear no more.

They believe there was a toxic waste seeping slowly into our water pipes, contaminating my mind. They believe it caused my plants to grow ten times their normal size. My husband was wise, they said, to drink only beer or wine. What nonsense! My plants thrived on mother love and will one day grow again. They must think me mad to believe such silliness. Let them confine me! Let them shackle me and keep me from the sun, unable to absorb the elixir of chlorophyll. Let them do to me what they will. I have a secret I keep from them; a tiny Hemlock, dug up one day when the attendant was too busy flirting with a passing nurse to take note of my meanderings. I slipped the seedling into my cell, the dirt still clinging to his newborn roots. I housed him in a plastic serving bowl stolen from the cafeteria and placed him upon my windowsill. He sits there each endless day, hidden by the dull grey drapes, soaking up the sun cast meagrely through the bars of the window. The Nurse remarked I seem to have a greenish pallor to my face. It is the flush of joy! My sweet young Hemlock grows larger day by day.

THE END

* Micki Peluso began writing as a catharsis for grief, which culminated into 30 years as a short story writer, staff journalist for the award-winning newspaper, The Staten Register, freelance journalist for other newspapers and author of ... *And the Whippoorwill Sang*; a funny, poignant, true family saga of love, loss and survival. Her next book—a collection of short stories called, *Heartbeats... Slices of Life* will be released in 2013.

7
When predators have predators, the unexpected is never far
away…

Little Girl Lost
by Lyn McConchie

He first saw her wandering through the park in her frilly pink dress. She couldn't have been more than seven or eight and his mouth began to water at the sight. He glanced about but there appeared to be no one with her and he allowed himself to drift closer, just observing. It was almost sunset, and he couldn't imagine what she was doing out so late.

She came to a junction in the path and took the left hand side, skipping a little as she did so, so that his heart bumped twice before picking up at a faster rate. By God, she was delectable! They were at that age. Why couldn't people understand that?

He remembered the judge at his last trial—and the men in prison later. None of them had understood either, and he'd been the one to pay for their deficiency. This time he must be careful, but his pulse was racing all the time as he followed, and it was hard to stay calm.

She kept veering more and more to the left, to where the big oaks spread shadow and there were fewer people. Then there were almost none, but still he hung back, wanting desperately, but recalling the men in prison and the things they'd done.

Then she was almost to the small back exit as dusk closed in, the last rays of sun lighting her hair to bloody fire. Taking a small rubber ball from her pocket, she began to bounce it on the end of the concrete path where it petered out into grass.

She was giggling happily as she tried to anticipate the irregular bounces, her red-gold hair seeming to hold the last of the sunlight, and her small triangular face alight with living and innocence. He slid after her, unobtrusive under tree-shadows, his face flushed with hunger. God, what a morsel she'd be! But his memory was cautioning, so he watched for nearly ten minutes for adults to come by.

No one did. He grew bolder and drifted out towards her. "What are you doing?" he asked softly.

She studied him, her head a little on one side, her dark blue eyes unafraid. "Playing."

"Does your Mummy know you're up here?"

A finger crept up to her mouth and she looked down. She shook her head looking a little guilty. "Mommy was late."

He bit back the grin that tried to creep across his face. So! She'd sneaked away to play in the park and nobody knew where she'd gone. What a target. What a chance!

"I have a puppy at home; would you like to see him?"

She nodded shyly, wordlessly, and he took the trusting hand stretched out to him. Slowly, watching through the growing dark for others who might interfere, he led her towards his car. Once into the rusting vehicle he could go anywhere. There was still no sight of other park users by the time they reached his car and he helped her into the front seat, his hands avid for the touch of small-girl clothes and sweet, soft flesh.

He kept up a flow of chatter as they drove; it would be fatal to scare her too soon. She might scream and attract attention from passersby, even a police car. No, better to wait; anticipation was half the fun. She tucked her hand into the crook of his arm and he noticed as he drove that somehow his excitement was draining away, as if diminished by his apprehension and his anxiousness to be under cover in his lair. He shrugged. It would be better once he was in his old frame house; once they were alone he could… his mind wandered into a maze of wordless obscenity.

Then they were pulling up inside the old car-port attached to the small house. It was full dark by now and his neighbors should be out. At least there was no sign from either side and their houses were dark; for which he was duly grateful. Not that they knew anything; his pleasures had all been committed far from here, and it was while he was paying for them that he'd inherited this house from an elderly relative who knew nothing of his heir's history.

"Come inside and see the puppy," he crooned. "You're going to love him, he's so soft and floppy. All paws and ears." He didn't switch on the light by the back door, (please God, let no one see her,) as she scampered inside with him looking about again hastily as she passed through the warped screen door and he shut it silently behind her dancing heels.

Gotcha!

Her blue eyes turned to study him then, the tiny growing seed of bewilderment clouding their gaze. Where was the puppy, her eyes asked. What happened to him? Why was the house still dark and why did her new friend not switch on more than the one small, dim light?.

Excitement burgeoned full and sweet in his belly, so he waited. Not yet. Let her relax again, there really was a puppy, so she would. He went to let the small animal free, watching as pup and child romped on his lounge floor—where no windows afforded anyone a glimpse at his prey—leaping about the dusty old carpet in joyous innocence.

After half an hour they tired and she came to sit on the shabby sofa with him. He offered milk, cold from the refrigerator. She took the glass gravely, watching him over the rim as she drank. The milk left a line above her upper lip so he was able to lean forward and wipe it away with his handkerchief. He left his hand on her shoulder, savouring the feel of her warm skin and the thin childish bones beneath his fingers.

He felt a deep amusement well up as she snuggled closer but

then it turned to puzzlement. He knew how trusting children were—who better? But this child—there was something different about her. He looked down at the small face and threw off the odd idea. He was less excited than usual; but so what?

He explored his emotions, remembering. There'd been excitement when he helped her into the car; that had vanished very quickly? Her foolish trust in him had been amusing, that emotion too had drained more swiftly than usual. He wasn't uneducated; before he discovered his pleasures, he'd attended university and obtained a degree. He considered his emotions but could find no reason for the lessening.

Probably it was the heat; he was jaded just a little from the humidity. He walked over to switch on the air conditioning before turning down the lights again, and the child watched him solemnly.

"There now, it'll be all nice and cool in a minute."

She nodded silently, snuggling back against him as he sat down again. He made up his mind then. Right, as soon as it is cool. He waited, the predator with his prey, as the temperature slid downwards until the old house was pleasantly cool and comfortable.

Then he stood.

"Come with me, I have something else you'll really enjoy playing with in this other room. Just like the puppy only better." She followed him into the bedroom meekly, her blue eyes interested.

Once there he reached for her. Outside it was full dark, the hazy black of a city night, while inside there was only a small bedside lamp to show him her face, haloed by that lovely tousled hair. She struggled a little but an eight year old girl had no chance against the strength of a powerful adult male over six feet tall. She squirmed, whimpering protests, and he shuddered at the surge of power which flooded him when she was naked.

The thin body writhed between his big hands as he knelt to force himself into her. Her voice rose in a tiny whistling shriek as he ripped her open and it was as if he grew in power until his head touched the sky. Strength poured through him as he thrust, listening to the muffled tiny sounds of her pain and terror.

Then he looked down—into dark blue child's eyes which changed as he stared. He moved to lean back, but the eyes held him captive. He could feel them draining first his sexual excitement, then his power, and finally even the mad terror which was engulfing him. He opened his mouth to scream, and found himself too weak to do more than whimper even as she had earlier. Her gaze grew in his vision as her eyes held his, transfixed, her humanity peeling away from her like a casually discarded snake skin.

Outside the dark seemed to thicken, waiting.

"Who? What?" was all he could whisper, his heart leaping, shuddering under the lash as she drained all that he was before the thundering beat stilled. There was a tiny child's giggle from the thing beneath him. He could have vomited at the thought of what his body had thrust into—at what still held his manhood captive, but even that was denied him.

"What … what are …" And one last gasp.

She looked without mercy into his dulling eyes as she fed, watching the darkness take him.

THE END

* Lyn McConchie owns and runs a small farm in New Zealand where she breeds coloured sheep. Lyn started writing professionally in 1990 and sold several poems and stories in that year. Since then her credit list has exploded with 28 books published and some 250 short stories. Lyn can be found at www.lynmcconchie.com.

8

What if someone beat religion to the second coming? Over and over again.

New World Resurrectionists
Eduard Garçon

The Fetchers, a division of American Eugenics Group International, S. (Aegis), ruled the night. And Aegis ruled the day. In neither instance was their presence a verified fact. Outside Aegis' own tight-knit secure family they were invisible. Aegis was into second comings. The very nature of their work demanded they keep under the radar, which they did through their isolated and innocuous locations and their nighttime activities.

The company's nighttime army, the Fetchers (gravediggers), never saw the light of day. They were never seen around the neighboring towns. Their lumbering, heavy-legged gait would have been remarked upon, as would their rounded shoulders and big heads with googly eyes, eyes that were all but useless for daytime activities. These Fetchers were blinded by the light.

In the dead of new moon nights, Aegis' shuffling minions stole into the appropriate cemetery or church or mausoleum and removed their booty. The grisly objects were carried by old military transport to the nearest Growth Farm where the Mamas and Papas, as they were called, used advanced genetic techniques to bring the dead to life. Accelerated Growth Hormone (AGH) was used to speed up the process of rebirthing. This was particularly important in cloning, as corporate executives could not wait 26 years to achieve their goal. Cloning, because just one was not enough. The Cloning Farm was closely monitored, assuring only the proper influences were introduced. There was no room for error. One slip could mean a man with ethics.

The Growing Stations were strewn across the country where the exhumed bodies—more often than not remains—were once again given life. These Growing Stations were as innocuous-looking as Aegis' home office.

North 67th St., north of Donahoo, Kansas City, Kansas, was a dead end street. It was farmland. To the east there was one house, a very large and fancy deep blood-red brick affair with long, heavy eaves and moonless, starless midnight black roofing. There was a huge wrought iron gate to the front. On either side were thick rhododendrons. The area around the house was bleak with short cut grass that was forever yellow-brown. On the distant hillside, the skeletal remains of an orchard.

The administrative centre. Live-in staff.

To the west, along the narrow roadway, stood four equally remote luxury homes set back off the road, though without gates. They neither invited visitors nor the corrective use of their driveways by misguided travellers. No one stumbled on this neighborhood by accident. The houses were all unnumbered. There was one collective mail drop. There was no lawn furniture. The cars were efficaciously stowed in imposing double garages.

A speed limit of 20 added to the mausoleum effect of this road. The tarmac was barely 16' across, unlined and uncurbed. There were no sidewalks and no streetlights. With no children or tourists or parks, Zombies could have played and gamboled about here without raising eyebrows. Donahoo was empty both east and west for quite some distance.

North 67th south of Donahoo was a comfortable middle class neighborhood happy with itself and disinclined to ask about its residents a half mile to the north.

At the far north end of N. 67th was a forest. The road divided at its southern edge. The east fork led to a small grouping of bleak warehouses belonging to the front business of Internet antique sales. The west fork dipped down into a valley and led to an old farmstead. At the entrance, just as the unpaved roadway dipped into the dense trees, there was an old rotting wooden post-and-stile gate. It was grey with age and mottled with a thick layer of dust, as were the near-by trees.

The farmhouse, barn and outbuildings appeared unused. Greyed and filthy as the gate and trees, they were set in a copse-strewn clearing. A porch fronted the house, up two steps from the pounded earth around it. There was not a blade of grass anywhere. The windows of the house, broken and cracked, were darkened, like dead men's eyes. The roof was in disrepair. The barn had once been red, its plank walls now worn and warped, gaping to show blackness. The outbuildings were of the same clapboard, grey and grubby wood. All evinced black interiors—except for the horse shed. There were a dozen cars parked in its shadowy interior. They were all new cars. They were all expensive cars. They all had out-of-state tags, no two the same. They were not covered with dust. Their presence did nothing to relieve the soporific silence surrounding the laboratory and manufacturing complex because no one ever saw them leave or enter.

This unpretentious skeleton of a past life housed the production arm of the pretentious American Eugenics Group International, S., Aegis. Their address was a box number. They had no mailbox, either at the head of the entrance road or at the collection of five boxes down the street. Although Aegis had a nationwide network of similarly disingenuous farmsteads, North 67th St. was the headquarters.

Aegis only serviced the elite. The rich, the famous, the powerful. Every corporate executive, every bought or megalomaniacal politician knew of Aegis and they all wanted to be serviced. They could be counted on to pay the price. Power and control were not to be had for a song. Targeted assassination had long since gotten a bad name and dirtied the reputations of some of the best social manipulators and new world order leaders ever known. Such setbacks could not be tolerated for long.

Aegis was expressing its fervent patriotism with its service to the nation, any nation. Such dedication was priceless. A safe, comfortable life was also priceless. And unquestioning.

American Eugenics Group International, S. was into Second Comings, usually reserved for one or another religion. Not an appropriate activity for a business or science. Yet Aegis had a monopoly on the business of resurrection, despite the promises of the religious community. As Aegis produced, perhaps religions lied. Lies can be comforting.

Aegis had begun by exhuming and resurrecting remains and then making discreet enquiries. They evolved so they were now operating on a consignment basis. Nobody was too tough for them. Propriety and taboo did not bother Aegis personnel. They considered themselves life's true Executors. Their Second Comings were living wills, New Testaments.

Aegis, therefore, liked its privacy and did everything in its power to protect it. That they were never uncovered was due in no large part to well-placed and well-compensated local, state and federal officials, beginning with the Wyandotte County police, a law enforcement agency not so unique. That is, practicing a law unto itself.

Superstition was not absent from the police or the media, either. Often enough, they made more of events, embellishing mundane reality in order to insure an audience. The grandiose stories effected a state of near hysteria: job security.

And sophisticated propaganda. Propaganda was most effective on a mindless, gullible public thirsty for excitement and mystery to enliven their otherwise banal existence. How they jumped on the stories of graves robbed by ghouls and goblins and Poe-esque hideous beings. Special X-teams were formed to search after these disgusting creatures, staffed by local police and paramilitary security organizations. Books were written. Movies were made. TV programs were aired. The public ate the horrific supernatural up and thus assured Aegis' anonymity, conspiracy theories being unrealistic and outré. Fear mongering was a form of logical reasoning. Leibniz and Plato would be proud.

It was no wonder, then, that no one left the comfort of their houses after midnight. Except for these servants of Aegis. And the occasional criminal. If one or two thieves in the night were found with broken necks the next morning when the police roused themselves to action, then it was all the better for the public and for the secrecy of the Fetchers and, therefore, the Resurrectionists, i.e. Aegis. These nighttime marauders left suggestions that raised up the spectre of supernatural ghouls to help things along. Massive inhuman footprints. Disemboweled cats or headless dogs. Long claw-like grooves in concrete. A little suggestion went a long way. At the same time, these findings fed the evil spirit gristmill. Even the prostitutes now retired early since one young streetwalker was found breastless and devoid of her sex.

People are so hampered by the stars, unlucky directions and Feng Shui and the other lies they tell themselves about the world that they cannot make a move without consulting one oracle or another in their search for meaning and definition and surcease from the anxieties inherent with being human. Humanity does not bless us with happiness. Humanity comes with no guarantees. Humanity is geared toward survival. Only with survival comes happiness, but when is survival assured? So, people lie to themselves and seek relief in knowing what's waiting. Or work assiduously to make the world they want. So much the better for these furtive apes and their masters. There was little they had to do to hide their activities, the people's vivid imaginations and belief in otherworldly phenomena supplied all the cover they needed to maintain anonymity.

Anonymity, that is, to all but a few. And those few had only one goal: to rule the world. They were an international cartel. Based in America, founded by Americans, staffed solely by

Americans, Aegis helped foreigners understand where their best interests lay. Aegis catered to their greed. There seemed to be no end to the need of the powerful and no bottom to their pockets in seeking satisfaction. So Aegis prospered, for there was no end to Corporation executives' capacity for funding different angles and machinations to further their empire. They were so intertwined no politician with a perverted streak of social justice running down his back could launch a monopoly-busting campaign without destroying both world trade and himself. If there were any such-minded politicians. Most had been cozened and bought off. Lobbying was just another word for bribery.

Aegis catered to prurient interests by supplying clients with resurrections of past monopolistic and megalomaniacal giants. Hill, Morgan, Rockefeller, Kennedy, Humble, Capone, Berlusconi, Murdoch and less well-known monsters such as Hubbard and past Popes. Their expertise was in great demand. So was their cold-hearted aggressiveness. They fitted in well with the tenor of the times: no giant considered a life superior to profit. But they were not the only customers. The political arena had its buyers, too. Wilson, MacArthur, McCarthy, Daley, Tojo, Stalin, Napoleon, Huang-di and other salacious sorts were highly sought after for their one-sided, one-dimensional zeal. Aegis fed the gaping maw of greed as assiduously as Satan his hellfires.

The results of greed and Aegis' concerns were everywhere evident. Would it ever end? Or would greed eventually devour itself? By then, though, the ruled populace would think nothing of it.

All's well that ends well. Aegis was in the business of creating the perfect world. No more war. No more want. No more disease.

#

The hulking figures were darker blotches against the night. It was a new moon and starless as they moved in the shadows along the south end of Amherst St., Boston, MA. The kind of night these men were bred for. Short thick legs. Broad, sturdy trunks. Long muscular arms ending in large, long-fingered hands. Heavy rounded shoulders. Large bald heads with heavy, bulbous foreheads that shadowed eyes that shone like possums' eyes. Noses flattened as if from too many punches. Thick lips and a Troglodyte jaw. And they were hairy. Black crinkly hair that covered even their hands, the thatch of hair ending where fingernails should have been. The tips of their fingers were flat. Despite their bulk, they were silent as owls.

Occasionally they emerged from the shadows to be spotlighted by a street lamp on Salem St. Troll-like blobs of humanity silently fulfilling their orders. Then, they disappeared into the blackness. Gory shadows. Poe visions. Lovecraft nightmares. Now lurking, now advancing toward their objective. Slow and plodding, following a learned map point by point, making sure step by step that they were without error.

They needn't have worried about detection. At 2 AM there was no one about. There wouldn't be anyone at the cemetery, either. Even in this enlightened age people were superstitious. As they believed in angels, they believed in demons and vampires and witches, for you can't have one without the other. People find the dark side of life's imaginings far more interesting and intriguing than the pristine celestine homunculi, beings that are without depth, one-dimensional.

The five nigh-men lurched into the graveyard, carefully, mindlessly making their way around the headstones. They moved in single file. They did not pause in their progress, more sure of their destination than a homing pigeon or a Special Forces unit. There was nothing to stop them. They were still careful. There was no need to take chances. Über-responsibility was inbred into these Fetchers. Any mistake was costly, resulting in the perpetrator being planted on the site of a staged gruesome happenstance, a failed horror. The sacrifice was worth the extra expense of bringing up another Igor.

So the blobs of shadows reached their destination without event: the monument of the Morgans in Cedar Hill Cemetery, across the street from the park. It wasn't hard to find. It was in the shape of the Ark of the Covenant, modest white marble headstones demurely planted before it. Without any hesitation, they dislodged the gravestones, ripping up the ground in great hunks of fat, foul earth. Spiders and snakes scattered. Raccoons and cats and possum fled. Roaches skittered out of the way. Roly-polies rolled up and into crevices. Millipedes and centipedes scurried for cover. Nothing stood in these five creatures' way. But smooth unhindered progress had to be covered up. Created, unnecessary havoc suggested the work of corprophiliacs. People were so easily led astray. Much ado about nothing.

They rolled aside the mausoleum portal. They found the late great J. Pierpont's casket and pulled it out of the wall. They scrabbled the lid off, shattering the mahogany to reveal the denuded bones and shreds of clothing that were J. Pierpont Morgan. The mass was gathered up and put in a canvas bag. Bits of flesh, piles of decomposed organs and creepy crawly creatures—all were shoved into the bag. No part was left unsecured.

The stone closure was rolled back in place upon leaving.

Quietly the five hominids left the home of the dead and began their return journey. At Hillside and Amherst, a military transport waited. Before morning's light, their booty would be in the hands of the Growers in Salem, Massachusetts. In 10-14 days, Amtrak would have its ticket to freedom: J. Pierpont Morgan in the flesh. Aegis would be $20 million and 10% stock holdings richer.

The next assignment came from Washington, DC: Judge Roy Bean and J. Edgar Hoover. The FBI and the Supreme Court were on the move.

❦⳥⳥⳥❦

THE END

* Eduard Garçon is a romantic. So he says he is from Gascony (true). He is distantly related to the Sicard family who boast an admiral, a horse thief and an NHL hockey player (ret'd). However, most of the Garçon family went into the restaurant business. In deference to this heritage, Eduard drinks absinthe and writes on napkins.

⫷ᘓᘐᘔᘓᘐᘔᘓᘐᘔᘓᘐ⫸

9
Drive home, don't take the train.

Into the Fog
Marion Webb-De Sisto

Eric Tenby boarded the train at Paddington Station only moments before the doors closed. Usually, he was in plenty of time to catch this particular train, but the evening's staff meeting meant he was running late. He liked traveling home on the 7:00 p.m. to Bath, it was never too crowded. The train, which ran a half hour before this one, was standing room only for at least twenty minutes into the journey, so he avoided it whenever possible.

He sat down by a window that was just beyond the sliding doors, and placed his attaché case on the table. The two opposite seats were empty, as was the one next to him. Perhaps he could spend all or most of the train ride alone and without someone trying to draw him into a conversation? Eric preferred to be undisturbed so that he could think about what life would be like for he and Rose after retirement. Only a couple more years to go, and then they'd be making those trips abroad, seeing the interesting places they were planning to visit. This musing was Eric's favorite pastime during the eighty-nine minute train journey home each weeknight.

The train pulled out of the station and the door that gave access to the adjoining carriage opened. Several people entered, looking for seats. Three quickly sat down and the rest moved along the aisle. Two young women stopped at his table and stood close to it, allowing the other passengers to go by them.

91

"Are these seats taken?" asked the taller of the two women.

"No," Eric answered.

They sat down and promptly ignored him. From their conservative clothing, neatly coiffed hair and immaculate makeup, Eric figured they were probably secretaries. As they chatted back and forth, he managed to block out their voices and became lost in his own thoughts for a while.

Suddenly, the one woman interrupted his inner ramblings.

"Oh look, Jen, it's getting foggy outside."

The other one answered, "Well, what do you expect? It *is* late October."

Eric looked at the window and watched the swirling density change from off white to dirty grey, and then a sickly green. What could make the fog become such an unnatural color? Perhaps some toxic chemical had been inadvertently released into the air? He was grateful to be on the train and not outside, having to breathe in that possibly harmful fog.

As he continued to stare at the window, the fog thickened so much that it seemed to be pressing against the glass. He could swear he saw the window buckle. That was ridiculous. Eric wanted to look away, but felt compelled to watch the fog. Now, it changed back to thick, twisting strands of greenness that bizarrely looked like elongated hands. Then, a ghoulish face suddenly peered in the window and grimaced at Eric. This startling act completely unnerved him. What was wrong with him? He must be hallucinating. Fog was just fog and nothing more.

Eric looked around the carriage to see if anyone else was watching what was happening outside.

The two young women were no longer giving it their attention. Some passengers were engrossed in newspapers or books, while others were busy with their laptops or iPads. No one appeared to be interested in the weird green fog.

Surprisingly, the train jerked and increased speed. Surely it was wiser to slow down when driving through thick fog, rather than increasing the speed? Maybe the driver wanted to get clear of it as quickly as possible? Perhaps he'd also seen a grisly face in the fog?

No, no! Eric reprimanded himself. No more craziness.

The same access door to the carriage opened, and a man stepped through the opening. He wasn't one of the usual conductors Eric had seen on other train journeys home, but he was wearing a similar uniform. This man was unbelievably thin. His uniform hung from his shoulders as though they were a coat hanger, and his hat was perched at the back of what appeared to be a bald head. In truth, this made his shockingly thin face resemble a skull with skin stretched over it.

The conductor glanced around the carriage, gave a grin, which to Eric looked more like a leer, and announced,

"Have your tickets ready for me. If you don't have a ticket, you're in b-i-i-i-g trouble." His voice was audible, yet low and raspy.

What an odd thing to say, Eric thought.

The conductor's long, bony fingers began snatching the proffered tickets. He inspected and punched a hole in each card before returning it to its owner. The little punching machine made a noise as it pierced the tickets. To Eric it sounded like a cackle that made him shudder.

Damn it! Now his ears were playing tricks on him.

An elderly man, sitting in an aisle seat that was facing Eric, was the next in line to have his ticket punched. The conductor grabbed it and without hesitation stuffed the card into his breast pocket.

"Where's your ticket, sir?"

"I just gave it to you and you put it in your pocket."

"No I didn't. Where's your ticket?"

"It's in your pocket!"

"Oh dear, you don't have a ticket. You can't ride my train without one." The conductor's skeletal-like hand clawed the elderly

93

man's shoulder and hauled him out of his seat.

As he was pulled along the aisle, the man struggled to get free. The other scrawny hand struck him lightly in the chest and he was told,

"No resistance is allowed. You have to leave the train."

The man immediately stopped trying to break free. He looked bemused and let the conductor bring him to the sliding doors. They opened without the button being touched, and to Eric's horror he watched the conductor push his charge out and into the fog. The doors closed. Eric saw long, wispy fingers enveloping and turning the man so that his face became visible. It was frozen into a mask of terror. A second later, there was only the green fog.

Eric stared in disbelief as the conductor went back to inspecting tickets. No one appeared to have noticed the unfortunate man's demise. All were behaving as though nothing was wrong. How could he be the only one witnessing what the conductor did? This was insane, he must be dreaming.

By now, the conductor had reached a woman who was sitting across the aisle from Eric. A little boy was resting on her lap. He was asleep with his head cradled against her chest. She gave her ticket to the conductor and it went straight into his pocket.

"I have to see your ticket, ma'am."

"I gave it to you. What's your problem?"

"No problem here, but you'll have one if you don't have a ticket."

"You *have* my ticket, so stop messing about."

"Oh dear, you don't have a ticket. You can't ride my train without one." The conductor reached down as though he was about to take hold of the child. His hands were slapped away by the woman.

She ordered, "Don't touch my son and give me back my ticket!"

The conductor's long fingers gripped the woman's shoulders and effortlessly lifted her from the seat. She tried to wriggle free, while clasping the boy closely to her. He'd woken up and looked ready to cry. One skinny hand moved from her shoulder to the top of her head.

"No resistance is allowed. You have to leave the train."

The woman relaxed and seemed to be in a daze while being brought to the sliding doors. They opened, allowing the conductor to propel both her and the child out of the train. The doors slid shut.

Once again, Eric couldn't stop himself from looking outside. Swirling green fingers wrapped around the boy and dragged him from the woman. Even though the doors were closed, he could hear her drawn-out scream as she vanished from view.

Now, Eric felt panicked. The conductor would soon be inspecting his ticket. Should he hold onto it for fear of where the card might be placed? But if he didn't give it to him, he'd definitely be finding out what was actually out there in the fog. And what if the conductor did put the ticket in his pocket? He needed a plan-of-action.

While the conductor was punching the cards of the two people who were sitting opposite to where the woman had sat, Eric decided what he would do. Holding onto his attaché case, he moved along the bench seat so that he was now sitting next to the aisle. If the conductor pocketed his ticket, he'd stand up and bash him with the case. It was constructed of solid leather and was filled to the brim. Surely it wouldn't take too much effort to knock that skinny guy right off his feet? Eric could feel an adrenalin rush building inside him. He was ready to hit the man hard and repeatedly, if necessary. Then, before the conductor could get back on his feet, he'd dash to the toilet located between the carriages and lock himself in there. He knew exactly how many stops the train would make before reaching Bath. If someone needed to use the toilet, there were other ones on the train. He'd stay safe behind the locked door.

The conductor moved across the aisle and collected the two

women's tickets. They were punched and returned. Eric felt deafened by the hammering of his heart. The conductor was standing so close, looking at him.

"Do you have a ticket, sir?" One protruding eye winked at Eric, accompanied by a broad grin that made his thin lips disappear. Only his yellow, pointed teeth were evident.

Eric muttered, "Yes" and drew the needed card from an inside pocket of his coat. It was pulled from his hand and crammed inside the dreaded breast pocket.

"I have to see your ticket."

Eric's courage was fueled by the adrenalin. He replied, "You know you have my ticket in your pocket. I saw what you did to that man and woman. I won't let you throw *me* off this train."

"Oh dear, you don't have a ticket. You can't ride my train without one."

As his hand stretched forward, Eric stood up and slammed his attaché case against the conductor's head. It was like hitting steel. His arm was actually vibrating from the impact. He swung the case, again, with even more force, but with the same surprising result. The conductor hadn't shifted one inch from his blocking position.

"Now you're in b-i-i-i-g trouble." He grabbed Eric's arm and hauled him into the aisle.

As his hand squeezed even more tightly, everything to Eric seemed to become muddled. Where was he? What was he doing? He was gripping the handle of his attaché case so he must be either going to, or coming from, work. But why did he feel so confused?

As though muffled by distance, he heard a voice say, "No resistance is allowed. You have to leave the train."

Was he on a train? Eric felt himself being pushed forward. There was a whooshing sound and he was in front of sliding doors that were opening. In sudden horror he remembered exactly where he was and what was happening.

Without hesitation, Eric Tenby was plummeted into the

ghastly embrace of the green fog.

THE END

* Marion Webb-De Sisto was born and grew up in the UK, but she spent many years working and raising her family in the USA. At present, she lives in the Greater London Area of England with her American husband. After retiring in 1999, she was finally able to find time to write and began pursuing a life-long dream. Marion describes herself as a people watcher and uses her many years of working and communicating with people as a blueprint for 'fleshing out' her fictional characters. INTO THE FOG is this author's first venture into the Horror genre. Take a look at her other stories and non-fiction books at: www.marionwebb-desisto.com.

10

What can you do when nightmares come alive?

Tightrope Cat
Tonya R. Moore

Masika sat in her apartment, cowed by the gloom and dirty-gray walls. The clock in the kitchen was ticking so loudly it scraped at her nerves. Her fingers itched to rip it right down. Her toes curled into the fabric of her couch. She pondered the problem, biting the nail of her thumb all the way down to the nub. She could stomp it into silence, maybe. Smash it to smithereens. Imagining it made her laugh. The sound came out awkwardly, somewhere between a choke and a sob.

The man in two-twelve was screaming at his girlfriend again. He'd been carrying on like that for hours on end, without so much as pausing for a deep breath. The woman finally snarled back with a few choice expletives. There was a crash, then everything went quiet. A few minutes later, Masika heard muffled thuds and ragged groans. Experience suggested they were either making out madly or fighting nail and tooth. She closed her eyes tightly and tuned it out, tuned it out, tuned it out.

Time slowed to a mad, maddening crawl. The television cast an eerie glow across the musty room. The air conditioner stalled out with a clang. The air vents choked. Masika heard a scratching noise coming from deep in their bowels. It grew louder and louder, getting closer. Her heart leapt, fright tickling at the back of her throat. Something was up there, dragging its weight around.

Hysteria grabbed hold. She got up and snatched her phone from the wall. Her fingers hovered over the number nine but no, couldn't call. She wasn't supposed to call them anymore. She hit the only number saved on her speed-dial instead, waited for her sister to pick up.

"Maybe we didn't run far enough?" she whispered tremulously when it picked up. "They come crawling out of the walls, right? Right?"

"What?" Her sleepy sibling fumbled with the phone on the other end. "Jeez, what time is it?"

"Aidah!" Masika sobbed wildly. "Did you hear me?"

"Oh god," Aidah muttered. "Not again."

"How can you even say that? Our mother and father both—"

"Masika, listen to me. I'm safe. You're safe. Florida is a long way off from the Serengeti. Monsters don't generally follow people across continents, okay?" Aidah firmly declared. "Nothing is going to happen to us."

Masika wasn't so easily convinced.

"Aidah."

She couldn't stop the tears from welling up.

"Aidah, the next time you see me…"

Couldn't stop them from streaming down.

"The next time you see me, you'd better—"

"Masika!" Aidah snapped, furious now. "I'm not doing this with you. Go to sleep already!" There was a click. The line went dead, buzzed with a reproachful sort of finality.

"You can be such a bitch!" Masika shrieked. She slammed the phone against the kitchen table as hard as she could. "Stupid, stupid!"

She grabbed the thing again and hurled it across the room. Still tethered to the wall, phone sprang halfway back toward her. Impatience and desperation gave way to a defensive sort of rage.

"I'm not a liar!" she hissed vehemently to the empty room.

She wasn't crazy and she was not the girl who cried wolf. She'd always told the truth, the whole truth. Why wouldn't anyone believe her?

Masika suddenly realized that the dragging noise had stopped. She could hear breathing, a series of asthmatic whuffs that mockingly matched the cadence of the kitchen clock. She could feel the intensity of its stare. It made her skin scrawl. Her nervous fingers scratched at her arm, ragged nails tearing into the skin and becoming bloody. Would tonight be the night? The night it would come out, that thing, to toy with her brains and eat her face raw?

Her eyes darted to the door. Run. She should run. Every cell in her body screamed at her to run. Freedom was only a few paces away but she was paralyzed, and then her absolute, worst fear was realized.

Her teary eyes fixed on the vent-screws. They squeaked as invisible fingers loosened them. One by one, they fell to the carpeted ground. The dust-coated cover followed. She screamed, screamed and screamed but there was no sound. The thing that crawled out, dropped to the ground and landed on two feet was as nimble as a cat on a tightrope. It was dark and hirsute, hunched over like a failed facsimile of a primitive man. Its red, swirling eyes bored into hers. It lifted an abnormally long finger to its lips.

"Shhhh," it mouthed, though no sound came out.

Something in the air had devoured all sound. Masika's screams, the TV, that annoying clock; their voices had all been stolen. The only sounds that could be heard were her stuttering heart and the beastly creature's irregular breath. It crouched there in the corner, watching her, watching her avidly. Its eyes were hypnotic and slyly malevolent.

Bone eater. Face stealer. Skin dweller.

Words that Masika barely remembered were bubbling up to the surface of her consciousness. What was that? What was it again? Something the cave men dreamed up and then forgot. No one even told stories about it anymore.

From somewhere deep inside, some frantic voice was screeching. *"Don't look away! Don't close your eyes. It's waiting. It's just waiting for you to—"*

It moved.

In a flash, it was beside her. It crouched by the couch, sniffing at her with an almost child-like sort of curiosity. It stank of rot and paste, mingled with dead leaves and piss. It had sharp talons for fingernails. They click-clicked against each other as the beast grabbed hold and clambered up onto the couch, beside her.

Masika wanted to scream, to run, scamper away like the scared rabbit she'd become. The thing blocking her path to the door looked at her pointedly, shaking its head. If she ran she'd be dead, painfully, painfully dead, but if she didn't, if she didn't…

She shrank back, whimpering again as the vile thing edged closer and closer. Her screams, then the sickening sounds of cracking bones that filled the air; that ravenous chomping and the intermittent swallowing were all absorbed by the strange bubble of silence that blanketed her apartment.

Morning came and cops were crowding Masika's doorway. The man from two-twelve was being hauled away in a body-bag. His girlfriend, a bedraggled and blond thing was on the ground by the doorway in handcuffs. She was a black-eyed and hung-over mess, all bloody and bawling.

Masika stepped outside, closing her door carefully on the ghastly pile of skin and bones on the living room floor behind her. Her jeans and tank-top were clean and she was fresh out of the shower. Her thick braids were tied back into a bunch at the base of her neck. She seemed ordinary and ignorant, questioned only for the sake of due diligence.

"No, nothing," she told the one who asked if she'd heard anything during the night. "These walls are pretty thick," she added with a slight smile.

She was smiling widely as she got into her car and drove to Starbucks to meet up with her sister. Aidah was already there waiting. The dreamy eyed gazelle was still wearing her medical scrubs, her afro caged into a tidy bubble. She was waiting for Masika in a quiet corner, hunched remorsefully over her coffee and cake under a framed print of Picasso's Two Saltimbanques. How perfect was that?

Masika hugged her just a bit too tightly, squeezed hard enough and long enough to make Aida think something might be wrong.

"Been looking everywhere for you," Masika whispered. "I can't begin to tell you just how thrilled I am to see you."

Aidah backed away jerkily but then she laughed, feeling inordinately foolish. "I was worried," she blurted out. "Last night you sounded so…"

Masika smiled apologetically. "I know, I know. Sorry about that." Her hand reached out, covered Aidah's trembling fingers on the table. "I'm all right now. You don't have to worry about that sort of thing happening anymore."

Aidah fought it wildly, the skin-crawling urge to yank her hand away from under her sister's. "What do you mean?"

"I mean," Masika drawled, with a sanguine smile. "I think I'm all better now. I don't know. I just feel like a brand new woman."

Aidah cleared her throat, carefully untangling their hands. "That's good," she murmured timidly, fighting back a sudden barrage of hysterical tears. "I'm so relieved, so g-glad for you."

Aidah raised her coffee-cup and nodded shakily at the evil thing wearing her sister's skin. Eyes darting about frantically, she scrambled around in her mind for a plausible excuse to scurry away. She steeled herself, took a steadying breath and she sipped her cinnamon latte with all the nonchalance she could muster.

THE END

* Tonya R. Moore is a full-time police dispatcher. In her spare time, she writes science fiction, urban, supernatural fantasy and horror short and serial fiction. www.tonyamoore.com

11

Despite any hard evidence, the police said Robert Becken brutally killed his wife, because no other man on earth could have done it.

Back to Lopez Island
by Tim Fleming

As he waited for the jury to return with his fate, Robert Becken wondered aloud where it had all gone wrong. "I never should have brought her back here to Washington. I deserve whatever the jury gives me for that mistake alone," he grumbled to no one in particular. His defense attorney, Royce Allen, overheard the remark from across the room, and for a moment he thought to himself, *Goddamn, he is guilty.* A small, balding man with a florid face, Allen tried mightily to stay expressionless and keep the suspicion to himself, as lawyers are bound to do. He calmly poured a short whiskey for his client.

Allen walked quickly across his spacious, elegant office and handed over the drink and a word of warning, "I'm glad no one else heard that. Keep those thoughts to yourself; we've got reporters on the other side of the door. They'd love a story like that: guilty man confesses to wife's murder at the eleventh hour. Here, drink this."

Robert refused to look up at his attorney; he was still simmering with resentment at Allen. For one thing Allen insisted Robert not take the stand in his own defense; for another, Allen refused to introduce what Robert considered his most compelling evidence for acquittal. No sense rehashing it, Robert thought, "For better or worse, it's too late now." He accepted the glass and downed the whiskey in one gulp. It burned his insides, but it did not clear his head of Theresa, his dead wife. She had been gone for two years now, but Robert could not get her out of his head. Her scent, her laughter, her vulnerability were still with him. If only he had been more level-headed, more sensible about that damn honeymoon request she had made.

They never intended to take a honeymoon. The wedding was a jimmied-up affair, and they were fine with the informality. No church, no relatives, not even a best man. Just the two of them, Robert Becken and Theresa Hearnes, hitched in five minutes at a quick courthouse ceremony on a Tuesday afternoon. It was done, and that's all they wanted until she asked for something out of the blue—a honeymoon. Not just any honeymoon, but one that would take them back to her childhood home. But the real shocker was where she wanted to stay—Fisherman's Bay Inn on Lopez Island.

"You really want to go back there?" asked Robert.

"Sure," Theresa said with a smile.

"After all you endured there?"

Theresa took Robert by the arm and gently led him to the sofa. Comfortable and secure in their luxurious Chicago high-rise, the couple had made a good life for themselves, and they had grown to trust one another implicitly. Theresa felt safe telling Robert anything. She had come a long way emotionally since the summer of 1964 when she was assaulted and left for dead near Fisherman's Bay Inn.

Theresa kissed her new husband softly on the cheek and then spilled her innermost feelings. "You've done something for me that no other man could. Not my first husband, not any man I've been with since. You've made me feel good about men again. You are the kindest, gentlest, most patient man I've ever met. And it's time for me to let go of the past. I feel no fear when I'm with you. No harm can come to me."

Theresa threw her arms around her husband's mid-section and settled into the warmest spot she knew—the crook of his arm where she loved to bury her head. Barely over five feet tall, she was much shorter than he. Robert was six feet tall, gray-haired and muscular, fit for his age. And Theresa, a petite brunette, loved the feeling of being with such a towering and solid man. Her fears dissolved in his sturdy embrace. A tear of joy and relief slipped from the corner of her eye. Late in life she had finally married the man of her dreams.

As always during moments like these, Robert whispered sweet nothings in his wife's ear. She thrived on the tender affection; it made it easier for her to open up to him. Without her husband noticing, Theresa flicked away the tear and said in a more upbeat tone, "Besides, I want to show you where I grew up. It's a lovely place. And I have *wonderful* memories there too, not just awful ones."

Theresa's childhood on Lopez Island had been an idyllic one. Sitting in Puget Sound off the coast of Washington state, Lopez Island is a place that time left behind. It's 15 miles of rolling fields, tranquil bays, and quaint shops; and not one whisper of trouble, except for that summer of 1964. Theresa and her friends rode their bikes everywhere. In summer they played on the lazy, windswept beaches. In spring they ran the lush farm meadows. But that all ended on a warm July day when Theresa, playing hide and seek with her friends near Fisherman's Bay Inn, came upon a stranger, an older boy. He was lithe and handsome, and he charmed Theresa with his smile.

The boy was attracted to Theresa's flowing brunette hair, parted down the middle, and hazel eyes which reminded him of his mother's. He immediately felt a surge of intense sexual desire. But there was something else, something which had lurked at the periphery of his psyche for years—the urge to pulverize a woman, to pound her into senselessness, to let loose on her the unnamed sexual rage pent up inside.

The boy lured Theresa into the woods next to the inn on a pretense. He had his arm in a sling to elicit sympathy, and he approached her with a sort of sheepish smile. He introduced himself as Ted, and he told Theresa that he had lost control of his bike trying to take the path through the woods. Now the bike was stuck in a bush, and he couldn't quite manage to disentangle it with his one good arm. As politely and pitifully as possible, Ted asked Theresa to come into the woods with him. There he removed the sling and beat her viciously with both fists. He tore her yellow blouse and tugged hard at her white cotton shorts. Bloodied and nearly naked, Theresa cried out for help. Her cries were heard by an old fisherman who dropped his pole and net and came running in the direction of the woods. Theresa's attacker heard the fisherman's footsteps and took off running deeper into the woods.

The fisherman got only a fleeting glimpse of the boy and later described him as young, not more than 16 or 17 years old with brown, curly hair and a wiry build. Theresa was so traumatized that she could not provide a reliable description of her attacker. She only knew that she did not recognize him. On Lopez

Island, population of less than a thousand circa 1964, everyone knew just about everyone else. Since neither the fisherman nor Theresa recognized the attacker, police assumed it was not a resident of the island. Summer brought many tourists from the mainland, and perhaps the boy had been visiting the island with his family. However, a check of the hotels, inns and bed-and-breakfast places turned up no one who fit the fisherman's vague description.

Word of the attack spread quickly, but no one came forward with information about a strange boy roaming the island. Not until decades later was it discovered that police had bungled the case. They had the attacker's name in their files all along and did not realize it. This came as no surprise to anyone, because the police force was rarely called on to do anything beyond writing parking tickets. Theresa survived, and her face healed quite well. But the case went cold and was soon forgotten.

The island lost its allure for Theresa and her family. They moved to the Midwest, where Theresa suffocated her trauma as best she could, and proceeded to enter into doomed relationships with men. At 35 she finally sought out psychological help, at the dawn of the age when it was okay to do so, and in time her spirit began to recover. But not until she met Robert did she feel whole again.

They met during the computer boom of the '90s when she applied for a job at his software company in Chicago. On his way to enormous wealth and security, Robert presented a stability and calm demeanor that beguiled Theresa. She fell in love for the first time in her life. It was a rocky road, though. Theresa still feared men and commitment. Robert had been burned by previous mates. They spent many days working through the memories of Theresa's long-ago trauma. So marriage was hardly discussed, and it was years before they even lived together. Not until they reached their mid-50s did the couple feel comfortable enough for marriage.

By that time they had plenty of money and few worries. So, for the most part, it was a marriage without predicament. Until the Lopez Island honeymoon.

Fisherman's Bay Inn wasn't quite as elegant a hotel as Theresa had recalled. Wallpaper and paint were peeling in the lobby. The wooden bannisters were chipped. Some of the glass was cracked. Robert cringed at the crumbling state of the old Victorian building. One consolation was the quaint fireplace across from the four-poster bed. It was real, and the logs were already stacked waiting to be lit.

The island had other appeals. Its flowered-covered cottages and the sweet languor of its beaches seduced Robert. Theresa wept at the sight of her beloved island. Little else had changed; the pace was still "Slow-pez," and the people friendly. It was the custom of island residents to wave at one another when passing on the streets. Theresa felt her anxiety and trepidation dissolve; still, she faced one emotional hurdle—the woods near the inn.

It wasn't long before the Beckens, at Theresa's insistence, went for a short walk to the very spot where she had been attacked. She breathed deeply and held her husband tight. Weeds had overgrown the spot, and the path leading into the woods was gone. There was little to see. They lingered for a moment; then Theresa nodded at her husband. It was her way of saying she was ready to move on. Robert led her away towards the beach. It had taken great courage for her to do this, and now it was over. She wanted to visit her old haunts and tell Robert about happier times.

They strolled along the water's edge as the sun fell behind threatening clouds in the distance. Robert took out his video camera and shot the scene. Theresa never looked prettier, he thought. As he looked through the viewfinder, Robert thought he saw another man draw close to Theresa, but when looked up the man was gone. Must have been a ghost, he thought.

They were famished and decided to eat at the inn. Robert ordered lobster, steak and red wine. In no time they had drained the bottle of Merlot and another appeared. The Beckens devoured the meal and lingered over the last of the wine. At least the food here was good, Robert thought.

Theresa gave her husband that smile that said, "I'm in love with you." Robert knew the sex would be raucous and satisfying, but he wanted to clear his head first. He led Theresa to the veranda. Refreshed by the cool evening air, Theresa kissed her husband longingly.

Clutching at one another, they stumbled up the creaky steps and found their room at the end of the dark hallway. The room's door had an old-fashioned lock, and Robert fumbled with the key as Theresa unbuttoned her blouse. After several attempts he finally inserted the key and turned it. The Beckens fell as one on the bed and ripped each other's clothes off. Robert was normally sensitive and gentle as a lover, but on this night he was too ravenous for foreplay. Theresa sensed this and gratified him immediately. She could wait until later for her own orgasm. Enthusiastically, she got on top of her husband. Robert's climax was quick and intense; afterwards, drained by the alcohol and the exertion, they lay naked on the bed.

Theresa briefly dozed; then she awoke with a start. She felt something pass through her, like an electrical shock. Whatever it was, it was gone in an instant, and Theresa wrote it off to the alcohol. She woke Robert and told him she was going to take a warm bath.

"I'm so thirsty. How about getting some ice, sweetie?" she asked.

"Where's the machine?"

"First floor, all the way at the other end." Theresa ran warm water and filled the tub about halfway. She heard Robert dress himself, exit the room, close the door, and lock it. "Always protecting me," she thought. She lowered herself into the tub and felt the water soothe her body.

The old hotel had but one ice machine, and Robert got lost looking for it. He wound up tapping the bell on the front desk, but no one answered. The front entrance was open, but the lobby and sitting area were deserted. He turned down the main hallway towards the hotel restaurant. At least he could ask them where the machine was.

He had been gone from his room for nearly 10 minutes when he thought he heard a scream coming from deep in the bowels of the hotel. He turned and headed back towards the stairwell leading to the second floor. Climbing the stairs, he reached in his pocket for the room key. As he neared his room, Robert heard a thud and some sort of commotion coming from inside. Anxiously fumbling for his key, he dropped it in the dimly lit hallway. He got down on his hands and knees to feel for it. Just then he thought he saw an outline of a figure vanish down the hallway. I've had too much wine, thought Robert. He found his key, lifted himself up, and unlocked the door. He called out Theresa's name. There was no answer. The bathroom door was ajar, and light streamed into the bedroom. The only sound he heard was a soft drone, like Theresa's hair dryer made. He entered the bathroom and saw horror like no other he had witnessed in his life.

There in the tub was his bride, her head a mess of blood-matted hair. Theresa's face was unrecognizable from the beating she had endured. There was bruising and abrasions on her chest and torso. Blood streamed from her vagina, which had been lacerated and mutilated. She slumped lifeless, her knees raised slightly in a sexually explicit manner.

Robert's mind rebelled, hoping against hope that this was somehow a gruesome, distasteful joke. But when he looked closer, he saw that the blood and wounds were real. It was then he let out an unearthly wail and rushed to Theresa's side. He felt for a pulse. No pulse. He reached for his phone. Not in his pocket. Where was it? He scrambled to his feet and looked around the room. It was on the nightstand. He grabbed it and dialed 911. He sputtered what details he could; he had no idea of address or directions. He even forgot the name of the hotel. He finally screamed at the operator, "The one by the bay. Fisherman's Bay." The operator said the ambulance and the police were on the way.

The Lopez Island cops had never investigated a murder, but they did the best they could in the Beckens' room. They removed Robert from the scene and touched nothing. They called the sheriff's office in San Juan County and asked them to send out detectives and the coroner. It was one of these detectives who asked Robert some questions and recorded his answers. The answers he gave would haunt Robert for years and be used against him at trial.

The detective asked him who he thought killed his wife.

"I don't know. I can't comprehend it. I left the room for just a few minutes, and I locked the door behind me. She was in the bathtub when I left, and that's where I found her, so she did not get out of the tub to open the door for anyone. It had to be someone with a room key. Maybe an employee of the hotel."

The cop canvassed the employees of the hotel. There were only two on duty at that hour—the desk clerk, a college-age female, and the assistant manager, a 30-year-old husband and father of two. Fortunately for them they had each other as alibis; they had been fornicating at the time of the murder. A hotel security camera proved this. The assistant manager, at first, denied the tryst and even thought of erasing the tape. Alas, he wisely decided that a divorce proceeding was much less perilous than standing trial for murder. He and his clerk were cleared.

The only other occupants were an elderly couple visiting the island as tourists. They were asleep in their first floor room at the time of the murder.

It was Sergeant Carl Winters, the San Juan County detective who caught the case. Winters quickly zeroed in on Robert as the only possible suspect. He escorted Robert back to the sheriff's headquarters and grilled him through the night.

Winters, a burly, no-nonsense detective, quickly got to the heart of the matter. "Did you murder your wife?" he asked Robert.

"Of course not," Robert dismissed the accusation with disdain. "I loved her. I would never harm her."

"Okay ... would you agree with me that she did not commit suicide ... that someone killed her?"

"Yes."

"You were the only other person who had access to your room whose whereabouts aren't accounted for. You say you were out of the room for only 10 minutes, and in that time your wife was murdered. Let's forget for a moment how convenient that is for you... and what an incredible coincidence it is that the murderer picked the 10 minutes you weren't in the room to enter and kill your wife. Let's assume you're telling the truth about that... you didn't kill her. Well, if it wasn't you who killed her, then who did? You said yourself that your wife would not and could not have let anyone in that room. You see where that leads me, don't you? You were the only who *could* have done it."

Robert bowed his head in grief and confusion. He had no answer for Winters.

Winters tried the soft sell. "You seem genuinely sorry for what you did, so why don't you clear your conscience? Tell me the truth. You had an argument, right? It got out of hand. You snuck up on her in the bathroom and hit her with the log from the fireplace. Then you strangled her with her stocking to make sure she was dead. Hey... maybe you could plead to second-degree. This was not premeditated. It was a crime of impulse... just a flash of anger you couldn't control."

There was no point in jousting with this cop, Robert realized, so he asked for a lawyer and stopped talking. He called his attorney in Chicago who referred him to Allen, Seattle's go-to guy when rich white men wanted to beat a murder charge.

San Juan County indicted Robert the next day, and a bail hearing was arranged. Over the loud howls of the prosecutor, Robert made the $2 million bail. Money was not an obstacle for him, and Allen skillfully swayed the judge with the argument that Robert was a pillar of the Chicago business and philanthropic community, had no prior record, and was not a flight risk. Free for the time being, Robert flew back to Chicago with Theresa's body.

The funeral was a sorrowful affair, attended by friends and family who perused Robert's demeanor for signs of guilt. He gave them no cause for suspicion. His grief was genuine; it was apparent to all that he had lost the love of his life.

For days after the funeral Robert holed himself up in his high-rise. He drank to excess, ate little, and slept only with the aid of drugs. He went through Theresa's things, and, though urged by Theresa's family to do so, he could not part with her clothes, jewelry, and other things for which he had no use except sentiment. Her old love letters pierced his heart. He read them and re-read them.

One day he popped in the honeymoon video he had shot on Lopez Island. The images showed a happy and carefree Theresa. Her windblown hair and winsome smile tugged at Robert's heart, as she stood on the dock overlooking the bay. But the next images he saw startled him from his morose stupor. In front of the hotel, walking next to Theresa, suddenly appeared a figure of a man. He seemed familiar to Robert, yet, at the same time, Robert knew he was not looking at real flesh and bone. It was an apparition: a spectral manifestation of a young, wiry man with curly brown hair and intense black eyes. Robert had noticed the apparition when he was making the videotape, but dismissed it as an illusion. But on playback, the illusion became real. Robert paused, re-wound, and replayed the tape again and again. When he was convinced he had seen a ghost, he called Royce Allen to tell him he had discovered some remarkable videotape taken the day of Theresa's murder. Allen urged Robert to fly out to Seattle right away.

Allen, in the meantime, had hired a forensic psychiatrist and ex-FBI profiler named Cyrus Wortham. Despite being in his 70s, Wortham was still sharp as a blade. Tall, thin and distinguished-looking, he presented himself as an elder statesman of criminal investigation, yet he could be blunt and crude when dealing with others. He wanted people to know he had seen and done it all in his 50 years in law enforcement.

Wortham pleased Allen immediately by working up a profile of Theresa's killer that pointed away from Robert. "The killer was much younger than your client," Wortham told Allen. "We never see murders like this perpetrated by men of his age, especially someone with no priors. This was a psycho-sexual killing, committed by someone who hates women. Someone with 'mommy issues … likely in his 20s or 30s, and you'll find that he has some criminal record. He didn't begin with Theresa Becken. He's done this before, and he's evolved. He has his own rituals. And it's all for sexual gratification. He associates violence with the sex act. It's the only way he can get off. Somewhere in his childhood is some nasty-shit trauma."

On the walls of his office Allen had hung posterboard blow-ups of the crime-scene photos. Wortham looked at them closely and mused, "I haven't seen anything like this since I worked all those serial killer cases in the Pacific Northwest in the '70s and '80s."

"What serial killings?" asked Allen.

"Oh … Bundy and Gary Ridgeway … you've heard of the Green River Killer, right?"

"Who hasn't? Washington state grows serial killers like we grow apples."

"You've got a good case here, Royce, except for one thing— if Becken didn't do it, who did?"

Allen had no answer until the next day when Robert showed up in his office to play the ghost video for him. Robert nearly shouted, without a hint of irony, "That ghost killed my wife. I know I must sound crazy to you, but there is no other explanation."

Allen did not know whether to laugh at Robert or console him. He poured a drink for both of them and gently said, "Robert, I see what you see … and that looks like a ghost … but I can't go to trial with that. I'll be laughed out of the courtroom, and you'll end up in prison for life."

"But no other explanation makes sense," implored Robert.

"Sit down. Relax. Have a drink. Forget about that video for a minute. I've got good news. I've hired a retired FBI profiler who will swear you did not commit the murder. This man is good, and I want you to meet him. I'm gonna call him and have him come over today … you'll like what he has to say."

Wortham showed up that afternoon and laid out his case to Robert. Unconvinced that Wortham's testimony would be exculpatory, Robert insisted that Wortham watch the honeymoon videotape. When Wortham saw the ghost, he sat straight up in his chair and muttered, "Holy shit. That's Ted Bundy."

For Wortham there was no question about the identity of the curly-haired, black-eyed ghost. He had seen Bundy's photo a thousand times when he worked the case in the 1970s. Bundy was one of the most prolific and notorious mass murderers in American history. His first known victim had been discovered in early 1974. Shortly thereafter, King County and Pierce County detectives brought Wortham aboard to help solve the case. Though Bundy was never captured or brought to trial in Washington state, Wortham knew more about Bundy than almost anyone else in law enforcement.

"Ted Bundy, the serial killer?" Robert blurted.

"I'll be damned," muttered Allen.

"You sure will be," said Wortham to Allen. "You've got your killer now. It's Bundy. Just one problem. Your killer's been dead for over 20 years. Bundy was executed in Florida in 1989. Unless the devil resurrected him, he's burning in hell right now. Last I checked ghosts can't kill anyone."

"How do we know that ghosts can't kill?" Robert asked seriously.

Wortham laughed, but quickly stifled it when he saw the look on Robert's face. Instead he turned to Allen and smirked, "You need a ghost expert."

"Are there such people?"

Robert spoke up, "There must be. If there are ghosts, there are ghost experts."

The guy they found taught a course called Paranormal Studies at Puget Sound University. He was a young African-American from Seattle, named Warwick Williams, who not only believed in ghosts but encountered them often. When he wasn't in the classroom he visited haunted places to seek them out. Williams had a large inventory of videotaped ghosts, some of whom had communicated with him. He was considered one of the foremost experts in his field. But he had bad news for Robert and his legal team. They gathered in Allen's office to hear what the ghost professor had to say.

"In all my years of doing this, I've only documented a handful of cases where a ghost actually interacted physically with a living human, much less cause them any actual harm. And I know of no instance where a ghost killed a human being. Human beings are on a different plane; they are of this earth and are composed of bone, flesh and blood. Ghosts belong to another plane of existence. Even though we can see them, they are of another dimension entirely. It's just that somehow their spirits have not managed to leave this earth after their bodies died. They can appear as apparitions, and in some cases they've moved physical objects or held them. But they do not have the capability of doing that," said Williams as he pointed to the posterboards of a mutilated Theresa Becken.

"But what if," began Wortham, "what if ... the damage inflicted on the victim was done postmortem. She would no longer be of this plane once her heart stopped beating. Technically, she would then belong to the spirit world. Ghosts can harm other ghosts, right?"

"I suppose it's possible, but I've never encountered such a thing. Your speculation has two problems: one, the damage was inflicted not on another ghost, but the lifeless body Theresa Becken's spirit once inhabited; two, how can you be certain that the wounds I see in these photos are postmortem wounds?"

"The cause of death was electrocution," said Allen. "See the hair dryer in the photo of the tub? It was dropped in the water while Theresa was bathing."

"You said ghosts could move objects," Robert reminded Williams. "What if Bundy's ghost turned on the hair dryer and…"

"telekinetically dropped it into the bath water?" finished Williams. "It's theoretically possible I suppose."

"Then once she's dead," interjected Wortham, "he picks up an oak log from the fireplace and bashes her head in with it, and then he takes one of her stockings and wraps it around her neck. That and the sexual mutilation definitely fit Bundy's MO."

"If you're right," said Williams, "it'd be the first known case of a ghost inflicting damage on a human."

"Not a human," corrected Robert, "another ghost. My wife was dead already. Bundy attacked her spirit, and the physical damage was reflected on the lifeless shell that once held her spirit."

Williams sighed and looked towards Allen. "I'm afraid I won't be of much use to you in court. The prosecutor will dismiss me as a charlatan because all I have are theoretical suppositions in this area. I have no hard data. I'm sorry."

Wortham did not want to give up though. He told Williams, "I know Bundy, and this is how he kills. That's his image on the videotape, and these are his killing fields. He's returned to the place where he began killing. He moved to Tacoma when he was very young. He attended *your* university; then he transferred to UW in Seattle. He knows his way around this area."

"Yes, but in murder cases, don't you need a motive? Why would Bundy choose Theresa Becken?" Williams asked Wortham.

"Bundy kills for pleasure; he's killed maybe a hundred women chosen randomly. He doesn't need a motive to kill anyone in particular."

"But ghosts do," replied Williams. "They are here for a specific reason. Their spirits linger here because they have unfinished business here. What was Bundy's unfinished business with Theresa?"

Suddenly it dawned on Robert what the unfinished business was, and he sputtered, "1964. That's it. Theresa grew up on Lopez Island. Lived here for the first 12 years of her life. Then in 1964 she was attacked by a teenage boy, a stranger on the island. He beat her viciously. Almost shattered her face." He stood up and nearly shouted the next recollection, "And I think she told me his name was Ted. It must have been Bundy. That's his motive. That's why he came back … unfinished business with Theresa."

Wortham, who knew the Bundy file inside and out, had his doubts. "As far as I know there was nothing about Bundy assaulting women as early as 1964. He would have only been 16, 17 years old." He turned and spoke directly to Allen, "Then again, we don't really know when Ted began his killing spree. He could have been offing girls before he reached puberty, for all we know. I'm going to dig up my old files on him. And I'm going to check with Lopez Island PD about that assault on Theresa."

As Wortham gathered his coat he asked Robert, "When in 1964 did that assault occur?"

"It was summer, maybe July," said Robert.

What Wortham found in the Lopez Island Police Department files stunned him. Nearly 50 years had passed since the crime, but the statements and evidence were all there. It was contained in a big box marked "Hearnes, 7/16/64." The box sat alone in a corner of the records room, as if it were the only serious crime committed in 1964. Lopez Island had so little crime that it was easy to keep track of it all. In the box Wortham found an interview of the fisherman who witnessed the attacker running away. He gave a description that generally fit what Bundy would have looked like as a teen. And Theresa's statement confirmed that the attacker's name was Ted. There was a photo of Theresa's bludgeoned face that showed a remarkable resemblance to her appearance after Bundy's "ghost" attack.

But there was not enough evidence to indicate that a young Ted Bundy had been Theresa's assailant in 1964. On a hunch Wortham requested all the PD crime records, misdemeanors as well as felonies, from the entire year of 1964. Maybe Bundy was a frequent visitor to the island and had gotten into other trouble.

Wortham found no one named Bundy who had gotten so much as a jaywalking ticket, but he did find an interesting tidbit on another Ted. On July 16, 1964, the same day Theresa Hearnes was beaten, someone named Ted Cowell had been detained on suspicion of shoplifting. One of the local shopkeepers had filed the complaint, but the charge was dropped for lack of evidence. The only description of Ted Cowell was that he was 17 and was visiting relatives on the island. Without anything else to go on, Wortham wrote off the incident of a "Ted" being picked up for shoplifting as unrelated to the Ted, presumably Bundy, who attacked Theresa the same day.

Disheartened that he hadn't given Robert more hope, Wortham resigned from the defense team, and Allen mapped out a strategy that did not include a "ghost-did-it" defense. He told

Robert, "We don't have to present the real killer to the jury on a platter; all we have to do is to get them to reasonably doubt that you did it. And we have plenty of evidence for that. No motive, no blood on you, no fingerprints on the murder weapon, the log, the stocking. There is no physical evidence of your guilt."

So Robert, against his better judgment, marched to Allen's beat and tried to maintain faith in his strategy. Wortham followed the trial, and even sat in the courtroom for a few days. He saw that it was going badly for Robert, and he kept getting that gnawing feeling detectives get when they haven't followed up all leads. Before closing arguments, Wortham decided to peruse his old Bundy files.

He spent days reading what was in those files, and he was surprised by the number of tiny details he had forgotten. He did not recall that Bundy was born in Burlington, Vermont, to his unwed mother, Louise Nelson. The two moved to Philadelphia to live with Louise's parents, Samuel and Eleanor. Samuel was a tyrannical bully, sexual sadist and bigot, who spouted hatred for all ethnicities, races, and religions. He was especially cruel to women, and it was rumored that he savagely beat his wife and his daughter in Ted's presence. Some investigators believed Samuel even raped his daughter Louise, and that Ted was a product of the rape. In order to keep the family's shame a secret, Ted was told that Louise was his sister and that his grandparents were his real parents. When he discovered the truth years later, he grew to despise his mother and all women. He called his mother "whore" and "slut," and even threatened to kill her. Louise decided she needed a real father for Ted, not a sadistic misogynist like Samuel, to help raise him and protect her from her son's cruelty. For that reason, Louise thought it wise to leave Philadelphia and look for a husband. She didn't have trouble finding one, for she was a pretty woman with long brunette hair parted down the middle. Wortham took a long look at the file photo of young Louise Nelson. It looked eerily familiar, but he could not place the resemblance. Someone somewhere was the spitting image of Ted's mother.

Within months of moving to Tacoma, Washington, Louise joined the Tacoma First Methodist Church, not so much for religious purposes but for the social activities. At a church dance she met a hospital cook named Johnny Culpeppper Bundy. Just a few months later Louise married him. Johnny Bundy adopted young Ted, and Ted took the man's last name. That's how he became Ted Bundy. The next line in the file struck Wortham like a thunderbolt to the head: *Up until then Ted had been going by Samuel's last name, Cowell.*

Wortham knew immediately where he had read the name Ted Cowell before. It was in the records room of the Lopez Island PD. Ted Cowell was the name of the kid who had been caught shoplifting just hours before Theresa Hearnes was attacked. Ted Cowell was Ted Bundy. When the cops had questioned the teenage boy about the shoplifting, he simply gave them his old name to protect his true identity.

As Wortham put the pieces together in his head, he quickly dialed Royce Allen's cell phone number. Bundy's unfinished business on this earth was Theresa Becken. And that photo of a young Louise—he knew where he had seen it before. It was a dead ringer for Theresa. Theresa Hearnes and Louise Bundy were lookalikes. Ted was killing his mother when he killed Theresa. Allen was not accepting calls; they were probably in court for the reading of the verdict. Wortham left the most coherent message he could under the circumstances. "Royce, it's Cyrus. Bundy was on Lopez Island the day Theresa was attacked in 1964. I've got proof. And she looked exactly like Bundy's mother. That gives you motive for Bundy killing Theresa."

At that very moment the jury foreman was reading the verdict. Robert Becken was found guilty as charged.

THE END

* Born and raised in St. Louis, Missouri, Tim Fleming is a graduate of the University of Missouri, where he earned advanced degrees in English and Education. He has worked as a writer, editor, and college English instructor. His published stories include works across several genres. His first historical novel, *Murder Of An American Nazi*, was published in 2008. His screenplay, *Boats Against The Current*, won top honors at the Skyline Film Festival in 2011. "The Barefoot Hero," a work of literary fiction, was published in the short story anthology, *Writers On The Wrong Side Of The Road*. Fleming is presently at work on his second novel, *The President's Mortician, A Historical Novel Of The JFK Assassination*. "Back To Lopez Island" is his first horror story.

12

Returning to his ancestral home, an estranged twin does his tearful
mother's bidding and climbs the stairs to find his sister isn't really
missing.

A Gift for Eternity

by E. J. Ruek

*Originally published by The Rose and Thorn Literary Ezine in the
issue released January 15, 2009, this story is the version edited by
Editor Barbara Quinn*

His mother's eyes pleaded. She held out the keys. Jenna was
gone, and, so far, the police had no leads. Forty-eight hours and
nothing.

"Haven't the cops gone through everything?"

"You know her, they don't," his mother said. "You two are
alike ... think alike."

"Right," he snapped, not meaning to, and saw her eyes
glisten with the beginnings of tears. He reached out and wrapped
her in his arms, her tight black curls smelling faintly of the dye she
used to cover the white that had come to her early, come with their
birth thirty-six years prior. He felt her shoulders shudder, but she
didn't cry, just leaned into him a long while until her shaking
stopped.

She stood up, then, supporting her own weight, her hands
pushing a little. James let her go. "You'll look, won't you?" she
asked, her voice still quavering.

"I'll look."

"I mean you'll try," she whispered.

He nodded. "Yes, Mom. If there's something, I'll find it."

She held out the keys again, and, this time, he took them, a small shock of static electricity sparking between their fingers.

On the stairs, he looked back, just once. She was watching him, hope shadowing grief and worry. Then he turned and took the steps slowly, one at a time, dreading the violence, dreading the violation he knew he was about to suffer in all its full and terrible potency. For nineteen years he had avoided it—nineteen years of peace, joy, pleasure—his visits to Mother limited to the safety of the bottom two floors of the intricate, rambling three-story that was his and Jenna's inheritance. They had no brothers, no sisters. James would have welcomed either ... both ... many—someone to share the burden and battle, someone to distract the seething force of Jenna's malice.

At the top of the second floor landing, he paused. Inside, he felt again the creeping terror, the pressure, that he'd suffered all his juvenile years until, graduating early from high school, he'd driven away. That very night he had fled, taking his clothes and his car, his books and his writings, escaping to the quiet, light-filled world of an empty university campus at Christmas. There he'd been safe. There he had stayed for ten blissful years of intense study, getting his degree, then finally winning a professorship. They couldn't get rid of him, and, ultimately, they didn't want to. He had become the foremost lettered expert in his chosen specialty and field of endeavor. Even that had been due to Jenna's influence, though—to the forces that drove her. James had studied his whole life to protect himself from her and those like her.

The last three stairs of the uppermost flight seemed to swallow him—the first, his feet; the second, his legs up to the calf; the topmost, his body, crotch-high. He was wading in darkness now, its fluidity a heavy, palpable thing. Its strange waters sucked at his clothes, at him, hungry for what had been denied for the so

128

long nineteen years. "Jenna," he whispered, the words falling
involuntarily. "Jenna."

At the door, his hands shook as he fitted the key. He paused
only long enough to draw a steadying breath, then turned the key
in its lock. The door fell open before him, weighted as all of them
were in this too grand house, its every embellishment designed to
impress and intimidate. His great grandfather's house, a man who
had demanded power, had created political thrones, then perched
upon them, using the minions beneath him to bleed dry those who
believed the weave of lies that had brought him Congressional
office. Since 1895 the family had thrived on his lies, each
generation in turn using the weight of wealth to create more, the
leverage of favors bringing the family ever more power, more
money, until the pinnacle was a reach away. His father had made
that reach, that grasp for the Presidency—and died at age forty-
eight. Jenna and James had been just eleven.

His mother, thirty then, had retired from the public, content
in a greatly reduced social schedule. She'd been happy for the first
time in her life, except for Jenna. Jenna was his mother's one
eternal grief, her perpetual worry—Jenna, dark-humored and
sullen.

Jenna's room still reflected that, its drapes closed and
windows perpetually sealed. The room was even now steeped in
gloom, its air stagnant. The only light was that which seeped in
through the open doorway, his silhouette long on the hard woven
carpet before him—brown carpet with seams of black creepers. He
stepped in, still wading, moving at once to the drape pulls—one,
the next, the third. He opened the room to the first light he guessed
it had seen in long decades, in all the time that Jenna was cloistered
there. Then he opened the sashes, the air more heavenly than even
the light. It swept the ash of morbidity out through the still open
door, out to the hall and down. In his mind he could see that ash
drift, and feared for his mother. That fear faded as soon as it

formed. She had been living in safety with this since their birth. Somehow, it couldn't—or didn't—touch her.

Looking about, he brushed his hands close to the desk, his fingers approaching, but not touching, a pillar that squatted upon a pedestal next to a keyboard and terminal. It lit at their proximity, sending out sparkling tendrils of glowing, writhing blue light. One tendril reached far enough to just touch him, instantly turning florid as it twined about his hand, the lacing cold between his fingers. He jerked back, and an involuntary shiver coursed his body.

Beside the light lay a small book—Jenna's diary or, maybe, her spell book. The latter, he guessed, looking at its placement. Her diary would be in the drawer—he had read it once when, at age eight, the night dreams had started, Jenna within them. Desperate to know how she tortured him, she'd never known, had not even guessed, that he'd learned from her how to protect and avenge himself. And she would still keep that diary where she had hidden it then.

He pulled the drawer open. The small, blue, brocade-bound book lay within, just as always—Jenna, obsessive about constancy, routine, and habit. He was much the same, and he knew the dangers of it. He'd learned early that he had to control his tendencies for the extreme. Jenna, however, had cultivated her every compulsion, reveling in all of them. "It's opulent," she had said to him once. Even then he had shrunk from the madness that lived in her eyes.

On her bedstead lay a pod of crystals—black quartz, obsidian, hematite, garnet. Beside them was her locket. His fingers ventured near, then shied off as if burnt. He knew the image held there, and the lock of curl beneath it. The boy, David Young, had died the day he had bid Jenna an angry leave-taking, his rage at her seduction and sexual torment of his younger brother bringing him to drive too fast on the turnpike.

On her bed's headboard, the stuffed owl that she had cherished since childhood still sat, mounted in flight, its grim beak open, its talons extended, as if its intended was already dead. Soul-Snatcher, Jenna had named it. She had found it dead in the stables one chilly morning in March on their ninth birthday. His father had grinned when she'd brought it, its body hanging stiff from her fingers, to the breakfast table. James had retched up his food, his father's frown of displeasure burning into him. It had since been a permanent visual memory at any thought of his father, a vision only superseded by one other—the flash of his father, clutching his chest as he gave his acceptance speech, suddenly falling dead at their feet, James, Jenna and Mother standing startled beside him. That was the last time James had seen his father alive. Jenna had laughed, her hysteria a strange counter-melody to the screams that echoed in swirls around them all. James remembered taking his mother's hand and leading her back as strangers crowded forward, flashes and strobes blinding him all around.

"Jenna," he whispered again, and, faintly, he felt more than heard a stirring. Looking, he spied his last gift to her. The small casket sat on the wrought iron table he'd sent her the year previous. Again a rustle. He moved over to it and stared down. Then, pulling a fine silver chain from his pocket, he used the small key on the end of it to turn the clasp on the miniature coffin, put his hand on the lid, and lifted.

The mirror in its bottom shimmered—purest mercury. He whispered, and that pool of silver wavered, small ripples appearing. Then Jenna's too lovely face came into view for one, clear moment, her eyes their brilliant cornflower blue. Those eyes seemed to see him. They pleaded, and, for the first time in all his memories of her, he saw fear.

Her mouth opened. He grimaced and whispered again. The mercury darkened, proving his famed dissertations on cultural fables and folk superstitions a lie. He dropped the chain into the blackening pool as her last vestige faded.

131

His lips whispering words that would bind for eternity, he shut the lid, turning the box's small clasp, not to the right—latched—but to the left until it snicked in the peculiar manner that told him the locksmith had crafted the locks in the lid of her coffin correctly. There was a hiss and a flash, then heat under his hand as a small puff of acrid smoke wafted away. Then the seam was gone, the lead in the lips of the lid fused shut.

Picking up her tomb, he left the room open—its door, its drapes, and its windows. A breeze brushed his face. The gloom lifted, his feet coming free from the strangling waters that were her last legacy.

THE END

* Living in the Purcell Trench in Northern Idaho, E. J. Ruek (pronounced "rook") writes about things which are not quite as they seem—not on the surface and not underneath ... like your auntie whose secrets drive the neighbors crazy. They just know that something isn't "normal." And it isn't. Says E. J., "Writing is about translating life into words without sacrificing the grimace and the giggle." You can visit E. J. on the Web at http://www.ejruek.com/

13

Lost love can be overwhelming, but second chances can be catastrophic.

Return
Leigh M. Lane

He had been on my mind, so when I caught a glimpse of him through the corner of my eye, turning into the alley behind Benny's Deli and Lovie's Pet Shop, I was certain I had perceived an apparition. It had been a tiresome evening, and my distraction was such that I could have imagined anything moving from that distance down the dimly lit street. It was only natural that I saw him at least once or twice. The mind tends to play tricks after someone close has died. He had been gone for nearly four months, but still I felt a heavy pain deep in my chest over the loss.

But more than anything, the terrible way he had died *haunted* me.

I thought to go to the alley to get a better look at the imposter, for no other reason than to dispel the ghost that now lurked in my mind's eye, yet I held back. I wasn't going to torture myself. I didn't have the time to waste on pointless distractions. I'd be damned if I was going to miss that god-forsaken bus again.

I continued down the street, picking up the pace as I glanced at my watch. I had missed the bus again just the night before, the all-too-recent memory of the long walk home jolting my pulse and speeding my pace. When I spotted the bus idling at the stop, I broke into a jog. I'm sure that bastard driver saw me. I'm sure he waited for me, timing his departure to begin precisely when I had less than a half-block to go. Some people are just assholes.

I ran into the center of the road, yelling and waving my arms. When he didn't stop, I flipped him off. I returned to the sidewalk, cursing aloud as I considered the long walk ahead of me. I reminded myself that things could be worse. It could be raining.

The night was warm and the sky clear. The streetlights drowned out any possibility of seeing much past the brightest stars, but I gazed over the horizon anyway, and then up at the waning moon. I took a deep breath. "I'm alive," I said, needing to hear myself say the words. A knot began to form in my throat, and I swallowed hard in an attempt to sooth it away. I focused on my brisk stride, watching the pavement just ahead of me, watching my shadow fly across the broad spans of light cast by the lamps lining my path. I held to my diversion until I nearly reached the end of the block, when another shadow caught my attention as it darted behind my own. I spun around in a panic, ready to run, but I saw no one. I fumbled through my purse for my pepper spray keychain as I surveyed every nearby bush and tree from where I stood.

I considered the possibility that I had imagined the second shadow, and after only another minute or so of searching for my boogeyman, I decided that my tired, strained mind was the culprit. No one else was around. A car passed by every once in a while, but I was alone.

I took one last look around, and then continued with my pepper spray still in hand. I jogged for short spans, the adrenaline from my strange scare still pumping through my veins and driving me ever forward. I grew tired after only a few blocks, though, and soon I reached the park that stood roughly halfway between the convenience store where I worked and my closet-sized apartment. I moved to a bench that rested nearby and sat, my aching legs winning over any apprehensions about entering a remote park in the middle of the night. I massaged my shins and calves and stretched my legs, then forced myself back to my feet.

I felt a startling shock as I saw him again. He saw me catch sight of him as he peeked from behind a large oak tree. He ducked back out of sight, but not quickly enough. The tree's shade obscured his features, but I recognized him all the same. I struggled to breathe, crying out his name in faint wisps that seemed to escape rather than emanate from my tight throat.

No, Jonathan's dead.

I battled the desire to confront the man, whomever he was, with all common sense advising me to flee the place without another thought. Despite myself, I began to walk toward the tree, readying my pepper spray and fighting tears. I slowed as I reached the massive trunk, and then I rushed to the other side, intent on punishing my trickster with an unexpected chemical eyewash. Much to my surprise, no one was there. I looked around, my heart racing. All was silent and still.

I struggled to rationalize the episode. People imagined lost loved ones in crowds all the time. That was only natural. To imagine someone in an empty park, however, seemed strange. Then, I cried out as suddenly I found myself face to face with Jonathan—*my* Jonathan, in the flesh—standing between me and the road.

I stared, my jaw agape, unable to hold back the tears that immediately rushed forth. My lungs became heavy, and I struggled to breathe. I felt somehow outside my body, as if I had gone numb and the world had gone dim and distant, and yet there I was, still standing, staring at him. His eyes looked tired and sad, and his face had grown empty and gaunt.

"Alice," he said, looking hesitant.

I shook my head, my hand going to my mouth. I took a step back, nearly tripping over my own feet. "You're not really here. You can't be!" I whimpered. My knees threatened to fail me, my limbs heavy and weak.

"I can explain," he said, reaching for me as he moved forward.

I gasped, my senses further dulling until my knees finally

gave and everything went black.

Three Dead, One Hanging onto Life at ICU
By Linda Scott, Local Reporter

Tragedy hit home early this morning, when authorities believe national serial killers known as the Midnight Murderers broke in and attacked all four members of a local family, the names of whom have not yet been officially released. It was reported that one of the family members managed to survive the attack, but his prognosis is not good.

The suspects are a man and two women in their early twenties. They have left a wake of carnage behind them over the course of the past year. Unfortunately, details on murder weapons or causes of death have been left undisclosed for investigative purposes, but the police have said that the three are suspected of murder and arson in at least six states.

I can still see bits of the article in my mind. It hadn't occurred to me when I first read it that I would know any of the victims involved. When I found out, it felt as if the whole world collapsed with me. I fainted, something I had never done before then nor had repeated until this instance.

The two experiences were similar. Images came to me like a dream, yet I remained partially aware of the world beyond. I listened as I watched … *when they let me into the morgue to identify him.*

"I'm so sorry, miss," the mortician had said. They had only let me see his face, slashed and torn. *What had those monsters done to the rest of him?*

"I'm so sorry, miss."

His face…

"I'm so sorry, Alice."

His face, slashed and torn. They won't tell me what happened.

"Miss?"

They won't tell me.

"Alice? Alice, can you hear me?"

"Alice?"

I opened my eyes, surprised to find myself at home, lying across my living room sofa. I was even more surprised to find that Jonathan was still with me. The room was dark, but moonlight shone through the window and provided enough light to see the familiar figure standing a few feet away.

"They lied, the people at the morgue," he said as I sat up.

"I saw you!"

He shook his head. "They made a mistake."

"You were dead!" I cried.

"They made a mistake."

I thought my heart might stop altogether when he sat down beside me and put a hand on my shoulder.

"It's all so complicated. I wish I knew what else to say," he continued.

I studied his face, the dimness of the room obscuring his features. His eyes looked darker, his skin paler, and he had lost weight. Still, it was him. "Where have you been?" I managed to ask.

"That's complicated, too."

I crossed my arms as I shifted to the corner of the sofa. "Is there anything that's *not* too complicated to tell me?"

He turned away. "This was a bad idea." He stood, and then took a few paces back. "This was a really bad idea."

"What are you—"

"I'm really sorry, Alice!" he said, rushing toward the door.

I sat where I was for a moment, the shock of his presence holding me helpless. I watched him stand in front of the door with his hand on the doorknob, frozen in indecision. I became lucid enough to grasp the fact that, regardless of the circumstances, he was with me, at least for the moment. The thought of losing him again sent a hot, electric pang through my body.

"Please don't go!" I cried, rising to my feet.

He stayed where he was, holding his back to me, hunched over the doorknob as if it were bracing him against some incredible burden my eyes could not see. Finally, he wiped his face with his dark shirt and turned back to me with quick, desperate movements. "I shouldn't have come."

Something within me snapped, and I began to sob with complete abandon. "Please stay! I can't lose you twice!" I lunged forward and wrapped my arms around him, burying my face in his chest.

"That's a bad idea," he said, his voice strangely fearful. To my surprise, he shrugged me off.

"Why?" I cried out, finding my throat nearly too tight to speak.

He looked down. "I came back for all the wrong reasons."

"But how?" was all I could manage to ask. I had identified his corpse at the morgue. He *had been* dead.

"This was a mistake."

I shook my head, my mind reeling. "Why do you keep saying that?"

"I thought I could fix things… I thought with you…" His sentence trailed off. He mumbled something else, but I could not understand him.

"Fix what? Fix us?"

"I couldn't find them," he said after a long and difficult pause.

I remained silent, trying to understand exactly what that meant.

"But I had to see you," he added.

I tried to respond, but the words wouldn't come. I wanted to beg him never to leave me again, and yet the cold, desperate look I was now close enough to see in his eyes sent a tight, uneasy feeling rushing through me. I turned away from him with a shudder.

"Alice?"

I shifted my eyes back to his. "You were dead. I saw you."
"I know."
"People don't just come back from the dead!"
"I had to. I missed you so much," he said, choking up.
"I missed you—" My breath escaped me as I saw a blood red tear roll down his cheek. He wiped it away with his shirtsleeve.

He trembled, his breathing becoming heavy, and again he looked down. "God help me," he said as he rushed forward and took me into his arms. He kissed me desperately and fervently, and I relished in the feel of his embrace. A hot rush of excitement coursed through me as I felt his body against mine through the thin barrier of clothing that still stood between us. I wanted him. I needed him.

I became aware of his fangs as a razor-sharp tip sliced my tongue. I pulled away, moving my hand to my mouth as I tasted blood.

"I'm sorry," he said, looking just as surprised.

I watched him, fear paralyzing my body when I realized for the first time the danger I was in. I saw that wild, hungry look in his eyes with newfound understanding. I felt sure he was going to lunge for my throat. Instead, he turned away with a faint cry, then rushed for the door and fled without saying another word.

I stood in frozen silence, unable to move for some time. Finally, I went to the door and looked out. Seeing nothing beyond the dark homes and the empty night, I shut the door and locked it.

I lay sleepless for hours that night, my mind too distracted to find any peace. I both dreaded and fantasized his return, my thoughts shifting between the image of the face I saw at the morgue and the surreal visit we had shared just hours ago. I imagined him watching me through the window, searching for a way to break in without alerting me or any of my neighbors. I envisioned him finding his way into my bed, searching my body with his own as he found my neck with his sharp teeth. It struck me with a strange arousal, and I struggled against myself to banish

139

the thought.

I rolled onto my back and stared up at the ceiling, ashamed and afraid of the excitement that took hold of me. I clasped my hands across my chest and searched for some way to make sense of what I felt. I closed my eyes, imagining him inside me, and my body began to writhe out of control in a fit of agonized fury, hot and swollen and desperate for his touch.

Open the door.

I got to my feet and began to pace, my agitation only growing.

Open it!

I hurried to the door and flung it open without any regard to the consequences. He charged in, slamming the door shut behind him as he threw his arms around me.

"I'm so sorry," he whispered, his lips brushing lightly against mine.

"I know," I whispered back.

Panic seized me as I heard another helpless cry emanate from deep within him, and he held me in an inescapable embrace as I tried to shrug his lips from my neck. A blinding, hot sting shot through me as his teeth tore quickly and deeply and warm blood flowed freely from my neck. I tried to pull back, but his teeth held excruciatingly deep and his arms kept me still. My knees gave out, but he held me where I was. I cried out, unable to fight him any longer, my strength lost. I shivered, feeling cold and tired, and I moaned until I no longer had the strength even for that.

Finally, he stopped drinking, but my blood continued to seep out with every waning heartbeat. I looked up at him, fighting to remain conscious. My eyes refused to focus, and finally they rolled back on me and my eyelids fluttered in attempt to stay open. I felt him lift my limp body into his arms and carry me to the sofa, then lay me gently across the cushions, propping my head with a decorative pillow.

"Alice?" he asked.

I struggled to look at him, to give him some sign that I was still there, but I could not. I could see him, but through unfocused, immobile eyes. I tried to turn to him, but my limbs ignored my will. I strained my lungs in vain to take a large enough breath to produce an audible sound.

I tried to flutter my eyelids again, but nothing happened. He hugged my unresponsive body, and I saw that he had a knife as he sat back and looked me straight in the eyes.

"I want to show you the night my family died," he said. He took a deep breath, paused for a moment, then slashed his wrist. I felt the impulse to cry out at the sight of so much blood, but I did not make a sound. He brought the heavy stream to my mouth, and I could taste the warm, metallic liquid rush down my unresponsive throat. At that moment, I felt an onslaught of memories hit me as if they were my own. In that moment, I knew what had happened to him that night.

The killers had broken in sometime between midnight and one. Jonathan hadn't heard them, but apparently his father had. He was the first one they killed. Jonathan heard his mother scream just a second before he heard a loud thud, saw stars, and fell unconscious.

He woke to the sound of his little sister crying out, but he found his hands had been bound together over his head and secured to the headboard. His legs were free, but that offered him no advantage. With his arms tied the way they were, there was nothing he could do but lie there and listen to them torture and kill his mother and sister. When one of the killers came to him and went for his throat, he had no defense. She drank until the other woman came in and told her it was time to leave.

He lay there, barely conscious as he heard them splashing gasoline outside. It hit the rooftop and splashed against out outer walls in loud, splattering arcs. Knowing what was coming next, he tried to get up, but he could barely move let alone flee for safety. He heard the explosion of fire as the gas ignited, and immediately the house began to crackle with burning life. He sensed the smoke, but he could not quite smell it. He knew the fire was near, but he couldn't tell if it had yet reached his room. He felt himself panic, and yet his heart labored to beat. He drifted in and out of consciousness until the heat of the nearing flame shocked him back to his senses.

He heard a thundering *crash*, but he couldn't turn to see what caused it.

"There's one in here!" he heard someone yell, the voice muffled by some kind of facemask.

"Hurry up and grab 'em—the roof is getting ready to collapse!" another yelled.

"He's tied up!" the first yelled.

"Here! Use the axe! Hurry!"

Jonathan felt quick, stinging blows to his wrists, then felt the ropes drop and one of the firefighters lift him from his bed. The firefighter fled the house with Jonathan in his arms. His eyes clouded by the smoke, he could not tell where they were going while they rounded through the halls and doorways. He felt a rush of fresh air, then the soft, cool grass against his back as the man laid him down. He heard the hoses spraying into the house, and he heard the sizzle of fire as it fought back, but he did not hear them set down any bodies beside his.

"Everyone out!" he heard someone yell into the house.

"Captain, there are more people in there!" someone else yelled.

He heard the heavy crash of the roof collapsing. The flames roared. The firefighters dove for cover. His impulse was to dive for cover too, but his body ignored him. To his surprise, hands came from all directions, loaded him onto a gurney, and rolled him into an ambulance. He felt pressure against his neck, then the constriction of heavy bandages around his throat and an oxygen mask against his face.

"We've got a pulse!"

He thought he would be alright when they administered the IV and started fluids. Within a few minutes, they had him in the hospital and began the blood transfusions. He tried to tell the doctors what had happened, but he still couldn't move despite the efforts being done to save him. At the time, he had no idea what would become of him if he survived.

To his horror, they pronounced him dead just a few minutes after arriving in surgery. He felt the sheet settle over his face and the toe-tag secure and hang from a thin string. He tried to scream. The wheels of his gurney squeaked as they rolled him down to the morgue, then they left him in a cool room for several hours. He heard them roll others out and, later, roll another body in beside him. Finally, they moved him to the autopsy and embalming table.

"I think we can determine the cause of death," a young male said.

"Let's take a closer look and see what we find. We'll need to list the definite cause of the patient's exsanguination," said someone else with an older, more authoritative voice. "We'll also want to do a toxicology screen."

"They took samples upstairs," said the other.

"See what they've got."

"Yes, doctor."

He heard footsteps out, then the *click* of a digital audio recorder turning on as the older man began his report: "Subject is a twenty-two-year-old male who appears to have died due to extensive blood loss caused by injuries incurred across the body. Direct cause of injuries is yet unknown, but upon first appearance, the damage resembles marks consistent with either a specialized weapon or an animal mauling."

He heard him take pictures of his body. He felt the man examine every inch of him for evidence that might lead the police to his attacker. He scraped the undersides of his fingernails. He opened his mouth and looked inside. He opened his eyes and examined their whites, then gently lowered his eyelids and poked around the sockets.

"There is some perimortem bruising around the wrists, consistent with being bound. There are multiple bruises across the thorax and chest, which indicates physical assault. I see no evidence of small vessel hemorrhaging in the face," he said.

Jonathan felt a razor go to his throat, and in his distress, he managed to emit a faint cry. The doctor clicked off his recorder and moved in close. He paused, hesitant and surprised.

"Corpses," he muttered as he flipped the recorder back on. "I'm going to begin with the most prominent wound," he said as he returned the blade to his neck and began his first incision.

Jonathan felt the cold steel pierce the skin beside the tears made by his attacker's teeth, and then the doctor lifting the surrounding skin to reveal his devoured vein.

"The jugular has been completely severed," the man said, continuing to poke around.

Jonathan gave another silent scream.

The man cut further down, then said, "Cause of death is exsanguination by severed jugular." He switched off his voice recorder, set it down, and removed his rubber examination gloves with two loud *snaps*. The recorder snapped back on. "My intern will finish the examination."

Jonathan heard him walk out, the door shutting behind him, and he wondered if he still had a chance at getting out of there alive. The man was gone for a while, but he and his intern eventually returned.

"This case is pretty cut and dry," the man said to his intern. "I'm going to leave the y-incision and internal organ examination to you. Make sure to look for any other signs of bleeding or physical damage."

"Yes, sir," the younger one said.

Stop! I'm not dead! Jonathan tried to yell.

"Then I'll show you how we do the formaldehyde flush," continued the older man.

"Yes, sir!"

Formaldehyde flush? He knew that if he wasn't already dead, he would be after they flooded his veins with the deadly chemical. He had no idea how he would find the strength to stop them, but he knew he needed to figure out something soon or he would be done for good.

"Beginning the y-incision," the young man said.

The blade pierced through his skin and glided across the center of his chest. It felt like fire and daggers tearing through him, and he felt something deep within him nearly stir. The razor moved to his other shoulder and made a second cut that met the first in the center of his chest.

"Looking good," the older man said.

"Thank you, sir."

The blade made its third cut, moving from his chest to his abdomen. The sensation was both hot and cold, piercing and tearing, and it was nearly too much for him to bear. He could feel a surge of adrenaline trying to rouse him with a single heartbeat. He struggled to summon all that he had to stop the autopsy while he still had the chance. He felt a muscle twitch in his leg, but neither of the men seemed to notice.

He felt another heartbeat.

Just as the young man began to tear the skin from his chest in an attempt to expose his ribcage, the other's pager went off.

"Damn it, this call is important," the older man said. "Can you manage getting the weights on his organs? I shouldn't be long."

"No problem," said the younger man. He returned to skinning Jonathan's chest, carefully tearing inch after inch of flesh from his body.

Jonathan felt another heartbeat strike his chest, and he summoned the will to gasp for a breath. "Stop!" he cried, then labored to take a second breath.

The young man emitted a strange sound as he dropped his

scalpel. Jonathan turned to him, watching him step back in horror. Jonathan begged him to help, but the young man ran out instead. He tried to sit up, but he didn't have the strength. He looked down at his chest and began to moan at the sight of it before he blacked out.

He woke in another hospital room. Heavy bandages bound his chest and the last of another blood transfusion dripped into his arm. He overheard a newscast over a nearby communal television. The reporter was talking about him: "Authorities will not disclose any further information on the recent murders."

The report gave confirmation to what he had already suspected. No one else had survived. His family was dead—and the staff at that incompetent hospital nearly added him to the body count. He got up, tore the IV from his arm, and walked out.

#

"Alice? Can you hear me?"

I managed to move my eyelids, and he fell over me and began to cry helplessly.

"I'm so sorry. I was just so hungry." I felt him rest his head against my chest.

I felt colder than ever, but I no longer shivered. Nothing moved. Not even my heart beat. I wondered how I could possibly remain conscious if my heart had stopped, but then considered the stories I had heard about Voodoo priests creating similar effects on their "zombies" with concoctions containing puffer fish toxin and various herbs. *Could I be succumbing to a similar type of toxin?* I wondered.

"Why did I return?" he cried over me. "Why, why, why?"

I felt like I was falling, my body spinning through a dark, endless chasm as I clung desperately to my senses. *Please don't let me die!* I wanted to cry out, the claustrophobic overwhelm of being mentally locked away in a body that lay seemingly dead driving me to sanity's edge. I wanted desperately to scream.

I screamed in my head. *Could anyone hear me?*

"I'm sorry I came! I don't know what I was thinking. I wasn't thinking; that's the problem!" He sat down at my side.

I tried to look at him, but he sat in my peripheral vision and I couldn't move my eyes.

"I really messed up," he said, running his fingers gently through my hair.

Why? I wanted to ask.

He paused for a long while then continued, "I know you can hear me, and you're probably freaking out. Just please don't hate me. Hell, I hate me. I shouldn't have returned, but I did. I shouldn't have gotten close enough to hurt you, but I did. I was just so damn hungry. God help me."

All was silent for a while. Finally, Jonathan said with a sigh, "Maybe you got lucky." He kissed me on the forehead, then on the lips, and then he sat silent again at my side.

I felt my heart beat—just once.

I could sense the disgust in his voice as he looked at me. "I gotta go. I … I'll be back." He paced the room for another moment before hurrying out.

Don't leave me here like this!

I waited, wondering where he had gone and for how long, my mind growing increasingly restless as the minutes passed. I listened carefully for some sign, any sign, that I was not alone. Why would he do this to me?

#

I can't say exactly how long I've been lying here, unable to do anything but ponder my situation, but it has been one of the darkest and most trying experiences I've ever been forced to endure. I've thought about all of the possible scenarios that might have caused him to leave and never return, unsure how long I might continue lying here, immobile and helpless. I wonder if someone will find me and mistake me for dead, and what might become of me then. Will I remain conscious through my autopsy? Will they realize that I am alive before it is too late?

I know I am getting ahead of myself, but I cannot help it. My thoughts are all I have left, even if they too deceive and torment me beyond reason. *I'm still alive*, I remind myself. *But it is unlikely that I will remain so for much longer.* Maybe this is just a *nightmare*, I consider, but I banish that one even quicker than the first; no, I am awake and I damn well know it. Maybe I will survive this, but even if I do, it seems I will be bound to the same fate at Jonathan's. *I will refuse to let that happen to me*, I tell myself. *But it happened to him.*

A good scream. I really could use a good scream.

I try to get up, but I am still too weak. Unable to do anything else, I shift my attention to the television. The news is on.

The anchor, a pleasant young woman wearing a blouse and perfectly styled hair and makeup, is in the middle of her top story: " ... have confirmed that a copy-cat killer has struck the area. Following the same pattern as the Midnight Murderers, the local copycat entered the victim's home in the middle of the night, killing its occupants before setting it ablaze." My mind falls into a whirlwind of revulsion and dismay, terror and bewilderment, and I begin to filter out the anchor's words, too overwhelmed to hear anymore.

I lie here, unable to move, listening intently at the sound of my pounding broken heart. The anchor's words permeate my mind here and there: "crime scene ... killers still at large ... the bloody scenes they have left in their wake ..." *Bloody ... blood.*

I begin to play impatiently against the cut on my tongue with the sharp edge of one fang. I'm hungry. *He'll return. He'll have blood. Yes, he promised he'd return.*

THE END

148

* Leigh M. Lane has been writing for over twenty years. She has ten published novels and twelve published short stories divided among different genre-specific pseudonyms. Her traditional Gothic horror novel, *Finding Poe*, which hit Amazon's paid bestseller list, was named a finalist for the 2013 EPIC Awards in horror. Her other novels include *The Hidden Valley*, inspired by Barker, Bradbury, and King, *World-Mart*, a tribute to Orwell, Serling, and Vonnegut, and the allegorical tale, *Myths of Gods*.

14

Kenda and Kenny navigate the dangers of being little kids in a less than supportive family—getting bullied, missing out on limited resources, being eaten for dinner as punishment.

Eating Our Young
by Casey Wolf

Kenda watched the carnage through the break in the laundry-room wall, sucking on her big toe anxiously. The family was savaging the thin remains of their youngest boy, her twin brother, Ken. Mother nibbled, with her incisors and lips, the tight skin of an ankle, pulling it from its grip on the bone; James sank his teeth into the softer region of Kenny's midriff. A frayed electrical cord hung from the ceiling. The dim, twitching light of a naked bulb gave the meal an eerie look, as if it wasn't normal, didn't happen every day.

The presence of Kenda's toe against her tongue reassured her. She sucked vigorously, closing her eyes. To the sounds of sucking, chewing, snarling over the reluctant cadaver, she sank gradually into sleep.

Morning arrived with the shout of her biggest sister, Enid. "Up! School! Come make your lunch!"

Kenda tripped on tangling sheets as she leapt to the door. All seven kids would stampede to the washroom but she was closest and with luck might not have to wait.

Too late. Enid was mean again and wakened James before the rest. He was the biggest boy and Enid's favourite and slower in the bathroom than anyone. Kenda faltered at the closing door. "Can I come in, Jamie?"

"Wait your turn, Turd-Drop."

She sighed and looked at the bristling line of bigger kids squeezing toward her, and remembered Kenny last night. It was *not* going to happen to her today. She ran back to her room and began to change clothes, then climbed out the window, down the rose trellis, to the dirt. No one guessed her use of the garden. Here behind the rose she yanked her shorts down, piddled, and covered the pee before climbing the trellis again. At the window she listened, peeking cautiously over the sill.

The door had drifted open. Children cried and shouted, doors slammed, water ran. Enid yelled orders. Kenda wanted to climb back in and burrow in the blank oasis of the laundry-room where she and Kenny slept. (Her idea. They'd been sneaking in to sleep together on piles of laundry for so long nobody thought about it anymore.)

No one was in the room.

Kenda slipped inside and went to the kitchen. Dale, their mom, was making coffee. "Morning," she grumbled. Kenda ran over to her. Dale bent down, eyes still on the measuring spoon, to receive her daughter's kiss.

Going to the table, Kenda climbed a padded chair and grabbed a blue-green melma bowl from the pile. Using both arms to lift the box, she shook a mound of flakes into her bowl, then sprinkled on sparkling white sugar. She nearly upset the milk tipping the jug over her bowl. Very carefully, she replaced it on the table.

An assortment of siblings were already shovelling cereal into their mouths, barking at each other, wrestling over the last of the toast or the toy in the empty box. Kenda put her spoon in the bowl and lifted out the first bite.

"SHIT-SMEAR!" James called. Her turn in the bathroom. Get up now and lose her cereal. Don't get up and lose her place in line. She couldn't get dressed till she was clean, and if she wasn't dressed when they were ready to leave…"*Too late!*" rang out her sister Heather's voice, and the bathroom door banged closed.

Crunching softly, Kenda slipped the spoon back into the bowl and lifted out the next bite. At least she'd already peed.

She was the smallest of the kindergarteners and people talked to her like her big owl eyes really were a bird's. They cooed and patted her and talked about her with each other as if she couldn't understand. Some girls got mad when people did things like that, calling them cutie and asking how many babies they would have when they grew up. But Kenda didn't mind. Any friendly attention seemed good. Her answering smile must have been goofy because they'd laugh and say nice things or hug her, and she liked that. So she was happy to go to school.

She looked around and there was Ken, whole and bruised and not meeting her eyes, sitting on his short stool in the kindergarten circle, where they always started their day. She was sad to see him and wanted to look away so she wouldn't have to remember last night. But he was her bestest brother, so she walked over and put her arms around him and said, "Hi, Kenny."

He looked down. There was a raw, lumpy scar behind his ear and his neck was one yellow bruise. She knew from before that the teachers wouldn't see it. She touched him sadly.

"Kenny," she said again.

Ken shrugged her hands off and whispered, "Go away." So she went away and sat on her own stool, hands on her lap.

Miss Streudel (Enid's nickname; she was really Miss Steedle) was as kind and fun as usual, although she was a bit impatient with Ken. He couldn't follow what she was saying and wasn't playing happily or "participating"—Miss Streudel liked kids to participate. Kenda tried to distract her from Ken by being bright and useful, helping her with games and retrieving things from the storage cubes. But this just made Miss Streudel squint at Ken even more. Kenda knew she wanted to say, "Why aren't you like your sister?"

but they weren't allowed to say things like that here. Instead she said, "What's *wrong*, Ken?"

The more she bugged him the blanker he got. Eventually he was sent home with a note, and Miss Streudel had a short, intense talk with Enid, who had to come to pick him up.

That night dinner was a quiet affair. Kenda tried to hide in the laundry-room but they weren't having any of it. They sat like zombies around the table while Enid pointed at the serving platter and Ken obediently crawled up, tears beading in his eyes and dribbling down his cheeks. Even Enid looked stressed.

Dale came in with the carving-knife and everyone stopped breathing. Kenda stared hard at her plate, hands clenched. She couldn't see what was going on, but she *heard*.

She heard the tip of the knife pop the threads that held Ken's buttons, and the shuffle of clothing as it was removed. She heard him settle back on the cold platter (she knew it was a cold platter—she had set it out, and the room was a cold room), and heard his tiny whimper. She imagined him squeezing his eyes shut. She wanted to grab him and run and hide. She stopped her breathing and tried to faint.

That night, for an extra bit of cruelty, they threw the uneaten bits of Ken on the laundry-room floor as a warning to Kenda. She would have to sleep all night with his bloody, pissy-smelling parts only a few feet away. She was lucky they hadn't thrown them on her sleeping pile.

"Come on Kenny," Kenda said the next morning. He had crawled back together in the night and was congealing slowly, regrowing, knitting piece by piece like they always did, the scars and bruises slowly fading as the joins were made complete.

Kenny looked over weakly. She could see he was very tired. It's hard to rest when you have to go through this, and it was his second night in a row. She pitied him.

"Want to run away?" she whispered, knowing what he would say, what he always said.

But this time he didn't say anything. He just looked.

James was in the bathroom. Enid came down the stairs to the laundry-room door and looked in, a pink hairbrush in her hand. Kenda saw the white, threadlike scars along her neck and face, down her arms and even over the bones of her bare toes.

"Is he okay?" Enid asked.

Kenda shook her head and nodded at the same time. Enid sighed hard and pushed up the sleeves of her housecoat.

"Okay," she said. "Turn around, Kenda. Let me brush your hair."

The bathroom door opened and James called out. "Hey, Shit-Stripe! What the hell did you do with my toothbrush?"

He came in holding a toothbrush covered in grimy flesh. His hands shook with fury and his face was red enough to burst.

Kenda was speechless. Ken shrank into the darkness behind the washing machine. Something dark dripped from him. He shouldn't be bleeding; he was all knitted up now.

"Oh, for Christ's sake, James. How the hell do you know it was her? Piss off."

James and Enid faced off for a brittle moment, then he stomped out of the room.

Enid took up the hairbrush again.

"Got to get a new carving-knife," she said. "The old one's getting dull. I think it hurt Kenny too much." She pulled a bunch of bobby pins from her pocket and stuck a few between her teeth.

Kenda held her breath. Too many feelings hit together inside her all at once. She was battered, scared, desperate, tentatively mad. She wanted to bawl.

But.

Enid was right. She would make it better. She would make sure the knife was really sharp.

Kenda turned to her big sister, stared up at her. Enid grabbed her hair and started to pull the brush through it, sending little stars of pain through Kenda's scalp.

It would be better. It would help a lot. Relief washed slowly up. "I love you, Enid," she whispered. Enid's hand jerked, then resumed brushing, maybe a little less roughly.

A small movement by the washing machine caught Kenda's eye. A sick, sad, bloody boy, subsiding hopelessly to the floor.

THE END

* Casey June Wolf lives in Vancouver, Canada. She doesn't normally write horror, but she's no stranger to the grim side of life. In her stories characters must grapple with whatever life brings, and she isn't, damn it, allowed to help. To read (or be read) more of her stories look for: *Finding Creatures & Other Stories*, by C. June Wolf (2008); *The Den Page of C. June Wolf*, to read "Claude and the Henry Moores" ; *Brigit's Sparkling Flame*, to read "The Brídeog", or BEAM ME UP! Podcast, to hear "After Hours at the Black Hole" and "Claude and the Henry Moores".

15
Choose the world you want to believe in and then spend the rest of
your life lying to yourself.

Unbreakable Fetters of Adamantine
Jim Secor

A powder room. A dressing room. A place to change one's appearance. To maintain the mask, the cover-up for the night. Or the day. Day or night, night and day. It doesn't matter for the actor. Actors act on and off the stage. A different kind of love in each case. Adoration. Affirmation. All accolades. All because she can successfully sit before a mirror and change herself over. Put on a sham with an exquisite touch of paint. She is good at it. Very good. Perhaps because she likes it, this character acting. She is an honor roll student at her profession.

"I'm the proud parent of a—"

Only she is no parent. Has no children. She never let herself have any. Never let herself go that much. Never let herself go that far. Never so much as to really be with a man, though she had been with many. Men were part of the territory. She never disappointed an audience.

Making fashion is a forte because it is her guard, holding herself aloof. Maintaining a semblance of the unhad, just enough distance to keep herself clean and alluring. Maintaining virginity. It is the bait which arouses the desire. A carefully decorated hook can also be a disguised piano wire. But there really isn't a man worth his weight, so what's the difference? Not many worth their dicks, either. Maybe there just aren't any worthwhile men! None

157

for her. Men are men. It is all the same to her. It. She takes her pleasure with whomever. Even if he is lousy, she finds something to pleasure her. She has to. Otherwise she can't survive. She can't just lie back and let it happen, hoping it will be over. Using her muscles and hips. There must be something in it to sacrifice herself so.

Once... once she'd had a... pretty good man.

#

Early in history, dressing rooms were called closets. Places where costumes were kept and façades were kept. A place where men were kept, entertained in a teasing sort of way. Then boudoirs came into fashion. More clothes, more fashion, more men crept in. They became the highlight of the evening. Then the boudoir was replaced by the bedroom. Closer and closer to the real thing.

#

"Play hard to get," mom had said. "No man wants an easy piece."

Something she did, though. Sometimes. The easy piece. With ease. A touch of life.

"It's like fly fishing," her father had said. "Keep a loose wrist. The rod's just an extension of your hand. Your body rhythm keeps that line arcing, coming back in better and better ellipses 'till the moment of casting. Then it's just a matter of reeling it in." He was good at playing women.

#

Just a touch of reality was enough. A nose-powdering to take care of the glare. That was good. Just enough to keep him coming.

Then she had the last say. She had to have the last say. She had to come away with something.

The last say. A powdered nose. A touch of reality.

#

But the bedroom changed, too. To the parlor. Here, one could be watched, by everybody. Like an entranceway, comings and goings manipulated with finesse as the affair lost its allure. Its hue. The shadow flying out across the water was the tempting morsel. And so the parlor led to the car seat and sleazy motels and, eventually, anywhere. Anywhere to advantage.

#

She smiled wryly. In she went to get the spirit and out she came to practice the message.

For her, the pre-game show was just color commentary. After that, it was decorum, demeanor and dissembling. Then, back to the closet. A practicing disciple following her long historical precedent. There was no need for her to advertize. No need to shout from the top of the mountain, "I'm a cunt!" No. They knew she was a cunt. Men loved a cunt. Probably because they were just dicks baying at the moon. Big mouth bass coming to the surface to snatch that fly.

Once … once … there had been…

#

She stood at the door to her boudoir. She liked the name: boudoir. It excited the romantic sentiment in her. This was her place. She was the boss here. This was her secret closet. At just the right geometric angle, her large dressing table with its large triptych mirror was placed to good advantage. A man couldn't tell

159

if this woman was watching him watch her. But she was. The widening of his pupils. The slight increase in his breathing. The nonchalance as his pants filled.

She smiled. "Oh, yes," she said, "I like this."

The outer room where her man waited she called her odalisque. There, she had the Romanesque-Art deco divan draped decorously with a woven silk-fringed shawl, which she never wore. But it smelled like her all the same.

The bed was in the next room. Five or six thick, soft hand-made futons piled high so she sank into their plush interior, a vision taking form. And this pile of bedding sat in the middle of the room.

"I am a princess," she murmured.

She liked wide-open spaces, an aesthetic she'd picked up in her travels. And, oh, she had travelled a lot! A lot! Across the room a plush middle-Eastern flying carpet was spread before the ever ready fireplace grating. A few throw pillows and the mirage was complete.

"I do have a pretty face."

The windows to the street were only half-blinded. She liked showing off her well-kept body as much as she enjoyed exhibiting her well-kept face. No one could see below the waist. Seduction. No one could see the lift surgery or the adjustment to her jowls, either. Anything to keep her from looking like her mother, a once-pretty woman who has overused with stretched chipmunk cheeks and turtle-like folds at her neck.

#

"Well," she said to herself, "time's a-wastin'." And into her make-up room, her artist's garret, she went to once again create her magic.

Like every good artist, she had a plethora of masks to choose from. They were ranged about her closet in tasteful fashion. She smiled at them. She smiled at herself. She sat down at her piano bench, back straight as a ramrod, waist so slim an Edwardian lady would have swooned for want of it, gently rounded heart-shaped hips—no Rubensian over-exposure for her, though she did have a finely rounded ass.

Men liked a good ass and she gave it to them every morning with gluteal exercises—and maybe some stomach crunches to flatten her belly and emphasize her mound of Venus. Like everything else about her, she picked and chose her assets. Her exhibition pieces.

Someone had called her a choosy bitch. Once.

#

"I'm so slow today."

She looked at the triple image of herself. Two three-quarter profiles and a magnified frontal. She was much more than a whole person.

"What is it, my love?" She pouted into the mirrors. "What is it, sweeting?" She leaned forward for a better look. "No saggy-waggies under the eyes. Little, feathered-out crow's feet men find so intriguing. And the little chicken pox scar just below the corner of my left eye for the men who like flawed beauty. Like a blue diamond. A little chink in the armor. A hole in the… mask. It always manages to peek through for just enough weakness. A windmill for my men—who are not Sancho Panzas!" She leaned on her elbows. "That's the best of all—no Sancho Panzas. No discerning eyes. God, what would I do with one of them!"

Silence. A stage silence.

"I take what's mine by right. Divine Right. After all, God was a woman first and foremost. Only we give life. And then we give and give and give. And then we have the life taken away from us and made into a damned mystery. A curse. Trivialize it. Isolate it. Give it back so it's ours again. But with something missing.

Instead of life coming into life, we've been burned into a painful repository. A thrusting place to be used, not worshipped. Fucking two-faced bastards! That's why you take what's yours, honey. Your birthright: mother, virgin, whore."

Her body sank in on itself.

"So ... what's wrong with the masquerade tonight, Sadie Lady? High cheek bones with just a hint of youthful blush. Slightly almond-shaped eyes. Long lashes. The full-lipped mouth barely rouged a light coral tint. That wet look. Like I've just done one man and now I'm ready for the next?" A little giggle. "It's so successful, why do I feel I should change it? I must be losing it. I must be! Look at the way I'm sitting. Come on. Straighten up, old girl. It's not long now 'till the need for a veneer won't be so obvious. Cranky old ladies get to say whatever they want. Look however they want."

She leaned forward some more, her forearms stretched along the glass-surfaced table, almost another mirror with the high sheen of the wood beneath. Japanese red cedar to roseate the lifted chin and smooth cheeks. To make her look healthy.

"So, why do I worry? I'm not nearly so old. But I feel like shit tonight? Well, then, let's make a change. Just enough for people to wonder at. What's different about you, honey? They'll be surprised it's me! Just me. The one-eighth Algonquin Indian girl with the... with the... what? Just the right look. Je ne sais quoi. With the white lovers! What a pollution. What's being Indian have to do with anything? A cunt's a cunt. But I'm on the rolls. An authentic Indian fuck. So, I can pay and pay and pay. I'm a pay sausage-making machine!"

She bowed her head. No diluted offspring for her. She was the last of the line.

"Is it any wonder we look for financial stable mates? Love be damned, we need to get something for the time we spend on our backs. Just once ... once..." She looked away from her many selves, then swung back. "Love isn't all, honey. Don't moon. It's what he's got in the seat of his pants that counts. It's the bankroll that sells. Sex is just the way to getting it. If it isn't that good, well, that's the price you have to pay. A lover on the side can liven things up a bit. Who cares? A cock's a cock. It just takes up space. Money, on the other hand... now, there's something you can get a grip on. Do something with. Make something of. Yeah. Something that doesn't use itself up. Money changes a girl. Yessir, it surely do!"

Her voice changed to a sugary drawl.

"It sho do. There ain't nothin' like money t'make a woman's heart go pitta-pat. Atrial fib. A little extra warmth in the chay-est, a tightness in th' throat."

She pressed her hands together and looked up.

"That's why the fashioning is so important. They have to feel I'm worth it." She leaned back and laughed. "Men are so easy! Suckers for a good fly fisher of men. A female Christ. A virgin mother. And I am certainly that! I move with grace and fortitude. Not even number two could fathom my depths. That could be it, though. Stringing them out. I had two lovers with him. Boy did I come out the winner on that one! A house for me and a $48,000 debt for him. What a fool! He still loves me, too. After all I did to him. Raped him. Flayed him. Hung him out to dry and beat him with a switch. All of that love and joining of souls hogwash he believed in. Well... if he wishes to believe that, okay. Let him have his fantasy. If I get too tired, I'll just open the gate again and let him in."

She leaned back, to get a better look, to see her pride.

"His letters are wonderful epistles of love. Maybe I'll publish them one day. A little love-letter package. Proof that men are easy. Ruled by the flesh between their legs. Long or short, what does it matter? It's all the same thing. All the same."

In a frustrated movement, she kicked her piano bench away from the table, slamming it against the opposite wall.

She stared at the assortment of visages, of shrouds that crowded her walls. All around her. Staring back at her with cold, black, blank eyes. Feral animals.

"So many to *choose* from!"

She toned down the lights on her mirrors. She did not want to look at herself any more, not as she was at any rate. Not now. She was dissatisfied now. She couldn't let that get in the way! She had to concentrate on the evening's goal.

She looked down at her red lace crotchless panties. No cunt hair. Her thigh-high silk stockings, shimmering white. No garter belt. No bra. Large teats atop well-fashioned mounds needed no help. Yes. She was ready. But what face would she be tonight?

A new one was in order. She'd been wearing this one successfully for a long time. She called it her Poor Pitiful Pierrette. She'd worn it for so long she'd almost forgotten she had it on. It had become so very comfortable. She had friends because of it. A support group. People who believed in her. And best of all, she was quite successful in business: who could resist such a face?

She thought about the diamond teardrop variation but she was really looking for something different. Which one? There were quite a number to choose from, really. It had taken her a lifetime to build up her collection. Her gallery. Her wallflowers, as she liked to call them. She smiled up at them, spaced so evenly about, a firmament of well-placed stars on a rich azure background. Evenly spaced. Even-handedly spaced. An unmoved mover's geometric logic.

Which one? Which one?

She could sit in her niche for hours looking at these different facets of herself. And she did. She was. Enjoying their brooding lives. Her eyes glittered.

She could make things happen with them. She could put together a world with just one accoutrement.

But she was just a little tired tonight. The deftness and swiftness of choice and characterization was no longer with her.

Her impetuosity had slowed. She'd noticed this happening over time. A slight slowing, like a lingering disease. Or maybe the beginning of one. Early onset intellectual glaucoma. The game just wasn't as easy as before. The thrill was gone.

"No," she whispered. "Not gone. Just… delayed."

There was more of an effort involved now. After these many years. One would think, with her experience and repertoire, she'd have nabbed her fish by now but there was no catch for her. Maybe there would never be. But the times… the times… the old days. The past. The moments of heady success, of stroking her trump card.

Once…

#

The masks around the mirrors were a joy to her. Each new façade the thrill of putting on a show that could never be replaced, would never end. The high of making each new guise work, moving in its world, carrying life through to actualization. The adrenaline rush. Each conceit manipulated to perfection so that life came out of its half-shell. Life, like a disease, took over the wooden body. The mask and the body always bent together. Trout and lure.

She heaved a great sigh. Morbidly vaudevillian romantic. Stilted realistic.

"It's so hard today."

She shut the lights off and then sat in the dark.

She sat an inordinately long time. The masks floating in and out of focus, dancing silhouettes. Now seen, now enshrouded. As her attention took shape, she began to feel funny, displaced and a little dizzy. The cowls were difficult to look at. They framed the three-eyed dressing table and gleamed out of the glassed table top like dark edifices of dead Greek heroes. Ancient armor. Tarnished livery—chivalry.

165

The little dressing room pressed in about her. The air became oppressive.

She put her hand to her throat and drew in a deep breath. She tried to fight the feeling, to let it sweep over her and pass through her so she could better see, better perceive her through-line of action. She began blinking, attempting to wink out the blackness around the edges but she finally flipped the switch and the lights about the triptych burst into flame, casting her regalia with eerie shadow lives. Chins and lower lips. Cheeks. Pieces of rhinestone jewelry.

Knowing exactly what she looked like—would be looking like—was important. It was easy when she knew what was expected. It was the actor's choice: being and knowing of one's being at the same time.

"Self-conscious awareness," she mumbled to herself. "Why am I so jaded tonight?"

In truth, she had been avoiding her closet lately, afraid of the improvisation. The improvidence. Maybe she should simply brush up a bit. But her masquerade beckoned and she could not, after all, resist. So, she'd gotten dressed and entered her little room for the *coup de grace* and couldn't back down. Not now. She knew her prey for the evening. The how and the why and the wherefore. But still she hesitated.

She stood and pulled on a small, thin mantle and folded it about herself. Right over left. She did not use a tie to fasten it but held it in place with her hand. The cloth felt cool and grateful against her body.

She moved into the glaring circle of light and reached out to touch the Columbine. It was smooth and smiled quietly back at her, eyes demurely lowered. But she could be regal, too, not just innocent—and with no more than a slight shift in the tilt of the head. Imperious at a harsher angle upward; submissive down.

This particular shell was her bread and butter. Everyone liked Columbine. So sweet and pure and wanton. A greeting. The absorbing caress of acceptance. This was her ravishment. Taking the beguiled. Number two had particularly found it enthralling. The allurement brought out a duality in him. The gentle, thoughtful dominator. Many's the time they had spent the weekends ensconced in the house—her house—playing Columbine games until exhausted. Fleshed out.

It was times like those that she once had … once … once…

#

This net was good closing material in her business dealings as well. Just a slight hint of sex brought the hardest of men to their knees, contract signed and sealed just as she wanted. No quarter asked, none given. All on the take. And, of course, sometimes the tease would not be contested. That is, sometimes she made a sacrifice. After all, they had to be made to feel in control.

Her hand moved with her eyes and came to rest on Diamantina, the beaten or maybe the beater. In either case, Diamantina could, and would, get what she wanted. Large, heavily lashed, wide-open eyes with deep, deep, pupils. Like a Noh mask, there was no conjunction. She could not only see through tunnel vision eyes, as if she were a split brain, a bicameral mind navigating through time and space with two different maps, but she could be the double persona. And to think they called multiple personalities psychotic!

The slight disorientation, the feeling of loss and confusion, worked because men were so very paternalistic, so cocksure they could take care of her. Diamantina never wanted for a guide. Only, more often than not, it was she who led them down the garden path to the green door where the only handle was on the outside and it was broken.

Was it number three who suffered the consequences of this maiden? Soft and polite, her lilting voice danced jigs and subtle minuets around any man's head. Diamantina, the flashing beauty.

But once they took her to hand, the gig was up. These men were no more than laundry lists. Alimony, a house and a restraining order. That's all it took to defrock the priest. El Capitano brought to his knees.

"Ahh," she intoned as her fingers found another guise. "Fiorinetta. My very, very favorite."

With her, the bait taken was refreshened nightly. Any time, any place, Ms. Rake took hers. Men appreciated being ravished as much as women and with Ms. Fiorinetta, innocence turned into an insatiable little tart. Lascivious Lolita, loyal only to the flesh and capable of far more submissive a seduction than washing a man's feet with her hair.

She sat down and squeezed her thighs together.

"Oh, yes, I remember. I remember. It was with that virile body-builder. Number three. He did my morning exercises with Fiorinetta. Ha-hah! An exercise in futility. Begun in the nude and finished with his masturbating directly into my vagina. Right on target— from how far away? It doesn't matter. In or out, it was masturbation for him. I got off, then, watching his river of come spew over my lips."

She pulled her chemise closer about her.

"It's true what they say about athletes. They peak early. Dammit! A girl has a right, too. Doesn't she?"

Pause.

Or perhaps, as her eyes roved over more of the masters of deception, she'd choose a little less blatant an approach. Possibly pastoral Amarilli would do the trick. Of course, she would do the trick. All of them would! Could. Did. Very well, thank you. That was the whole point: to take one's due. There was nothing personal in her treatment of a man. Why should there be? Two separate bodies. Two separate souls. Ragged, waggish souls. Spirited encounters but definitely not spiritual. There was no way she would let a man rag on her, not since she'd learned to give as she got.

"You give me trash, I give you trash back. Margaret Atwood, hymning a pig."

She sighed and looked way into the darkness around her, the chaos out of which life was born.

In the beginning was the word. And what was the word? It was her. Hers. Hers alone. It never touched another soul except as succubus.

She was tired of the game. That's why tonight was so ... unidentifiable. Perhaps, as she was, untouchable. Unsatisfied. Dissatisfied. But without a mask, without a shield, a castle keep, she was nothing. She needed her enameled skin, her horned dermis, in order to live. Every animal had its skin. Skin was necessary to keep the inside from imposing on the outside. Overwhelming it. The casque. Never once touched. No. Not true. Once...

#

There! That one. That was to be it: Isabelle. The intellectual one. The one who would take a chance on a razed sailor's dream. So... she would take her chance. Tonight. She would reach out and touch what she didn't have herself, intelligence and stupidity. Definition and altruity. A living up to and giving up to. She had nothing but emptiness to give anyway. So, intellectuality was, of course, the correct course.

Isabelle had once gotten her a man. Once. Once upon a time. One day.

#

She faced the mirror front-on, feeling tired and haggard, and began to strip off the mask she had worn for so long. She'd worn it for so long the fiction had entered into the reality and so she tore frantically at her face, she pulled off great patches of fascia. Her fingernails, dermis and DNA encrusted, ripped red valleys into her face. And as she watched the destruction of Aphrodite in Repose, she created the desecration of herself. The face ran with blood and glared out at her from worn, bloodshot eyes.

\#

In the end, she was just feeling. A mass of feeling. A mask of feeling. Her pain became a super-reality, a surreal sketch with nothing to offer but a desert, a desert after its first and only rainfall. She was a Dadaist persona, a destructed personality to be fulfilled only once. In the end.

\#

But she didn't know who she was.

THE END

* Jim Secor is a long time social satirist who grew up during the lively alternative theatre years of the late 1960's and the 1970's. After over-educating himself, he became a disability activist. The local State government blacklisted him and he went to China where he was also blacklisted. Three-time loser.

16
All Norman had to do was deliver some good news. But he
couldn't do that till the evening, and he had no idea what was
waiting for him out there in the darkness…

Across the Tracks
Tony Richards

He'd have preferred to go during the daylight hours but his
was only a small law firm. There were just he and his partner, and
they'd lost their personal assistant a couple of weeks back—she'd
left to have a baby. And there was such a pile of letters to be
written, wills to be altered, claims to be followed, that Norman
Miller was forced to leave the Hudson matter until after work. He'd
already tried phoning ahead, but the line appeared to be cut off.

It wasn't too far, so he made his way on foot. Once he was
away from the town center, the streets of Birchiam grew quiet
around him. Miller lit one of the two cigarettes he allowed himself
each day. He was trying to give them up altogether, but hadn't
managed that as yet.

He had already noticed something curious, simply from
looking at the map. From the town side at least, there were no
roads at all running into the Avontree Estate. The only means of
access seemed to be a footbridge. The housing estate had been
built in the late Eighties. The intent had been to relieve the
pressure on the poorer parts of larger nearby towns. Families from
those locations had been given the chance to move out here, on the
northern edge of this quiet little seaside place, to start a better life.

Except you never saw them or heard anything of them.

Miller thought that over as his footsteps took him closer.

He went past the final row of tidy suburban homes. Beyond them, there was some kind of mini power station. It made a subcutaneous humming on the air, but it appeared to be unoccupied, sitting in the middle of a stretch of open ground with chunks of broken concrete strewn across the patchy grass.

He walked around the building and across that uninviting space until he reached the railway line.

It was a high-speed link that didn't even stop there. And, because of the danger it presented, it had been blocked off with a chain link fence, maybe nine feet tall. Miller could make out several yellow and black warning signs. And then one of the trains went by, there and gone in a few seconds, traveling with such a massive impact that the air around him shuddered.

You wouldn't know that you were anywhere near to the sea, up here. At home, he could smell it in his back garden. But this far north there was only a brick-dust odor and the acrid tang of ozone. This barely counted as a genuine part of Birchiam at all.

Nothing around him was moving now that the train was gone. It would be best, Miller decided, throwing down the remains of his cigarette, to get this over and done with as quickly as possible, and then return to his home, his evening meal, his waiting television set.

He stared at the footbridge that led over the tracks. It was high, and looked rather precarious, the handrail sitting lower than it should. And he had never cared particularly for heights. But Miller steeled himself and started up.

When he reached the top, he paused before heading across. He could see the whole of the estate from here—this was his very first sight of it.

There were six streets crosswise and a dozen more running from top to bottom, precisely the way the map had shown. A grid pattern, which was something you found nowhere else in

Birchiam. It seemed to be made up of terraces of houses, but he knew that wasn't entirely true; The Hudson's address was 27B Callan Street, indicating many of these tight-packed homes were actually maisonettes.

Beyond their rooftops was a high, crumbling bluff, so heavily eroded there was practically no vegetation. But it dipped at its center, so there had to be a road back there. It simply wasn't possible that this bridge was the one way in or out.

His footsteps were cautious and unsteady as he went across. The handrail *was* extremely low. And just before he reached the end, another high-speed train went rushing past below him. The steel and concrete underneath his feet trembled so violently that, for a moment, Miller was afraid the whole thing might collapse.

But he finally reached ground on the far side. Twilight was gathering very quickly. No streetlights had come on in front of him, despite the fact that when he glanced back he could see them in Birchiam. And there were no lights either in the windows of the flat, blank houses. Was everybody still at work?

It seemed rather unlikely in a place like this. Maybe they were saving electricity.

There was no one at all in view. Nobody returning from the local shops or setting out to go there, and no playing children. But a movement to his left made Miller swing in that direction.

A huge black dog, of no definable breed, had emerged from around the corner. It had stopped, and was staring at him. It had no one with it and, peering at the creature, Miller considered going back up the footbridge and forgetting all of this. He stiffened, expecting it to move up closer. Strange dogs had always been a source of worry to him, especially when they were this size.

Except that it did no such thing. It merely stared at him a while, then turned away and ambled off.

He was sweating by this time but figured the encounter had gone better than he'd expected. He recalled where Callan Street had been when he'd been studying the map, satisfied himself that he was facing in the right direction, and then headed off towards the house.

The problem was, he quickly noticed, all the street signs round Avontree Estates were gone. What kind of mindless vandalism was that? Additionally, none of the homes that he was passing appeared to have numbers on their doors.

And because of both those things, he wound up crossing the entire estate without finding the street he was looking for. He stopped at the top end of town, underneath the bluff.

And—good God almighty—he just couldn't quite believe what he was staring at.

He had been partly right. There was a lower gap here. There *had* been a road. But the walls of the eroded bluff had totally collapsed across it, heaven only knew how long ago.

The only street that allowed entry to this place was blocked from one end to the other. So that footbridge that he'd recently crossed really *was* the one way in or out of Avontree Estates. Which was why he'd not seen any cars, parked or otherwise.

This was utterly incredible. Did anybody even know?

How did people *live* like this?

He took a train into London at least once a month. He and his wife went regularly into Brighton for the evening. He drove out of town for visits and excursions. Whereas these people … went nowhere?

Then a new thought struck him. Some people had always lived like this, hadn't they? There were places in the world whose inhabitants never left their own village or valley. And a hundred years or more ago, the same had to be true of England.

It seemed like a bizarre idea in this day and age, but he had no real choice other than to accept it. No one that he knew of ever came in here. And so perhaps the folks who lived here almost never ventured out.

The more he stared around him, the more he began to realize that the whole place looked as if it had been planned that way. He retraced his steps, reached a wide street to his left and then decided to explore it. There was a grocery store, and a newsagent that doubled as a post office. Their plate-glass windows were reflective, and he could not see inside. Beyond them were a clinic, a community center, and even a brick-built, single-storey church. They all looked to be empty and their doors were closed. But maybe they were central to the whole design of this estate. The Avontree had been intended, maybe, to be self-enclosed and self-sufficient.

The streetlights were still refusing to come on and it was getting pretty dark. When he glanced back at the corner he had come around, he caught a glimpse of the black dog again. It was only there an instant before vanishing. Was it following him?

Then, his attention was caught by something else, out on the pavement in front of the community center. Some kind of glass and metal signboard. When he closed in on it, he could see that it contained another map. He squinted and could make out Callan Street, exactly where he'd thought it was.

Turn right at the next junction, left at the one after that, and he'd be there in minutes. Miller shot another glance across his shoulder, making sure the dog had not come back. And then he set off briskly.

It occurred to him that he might actually be engaged on a mission of mercy this particular evening. His visit here might help someone to move out of this hushed and dismal place.

"Mr. Hudson?"

He ran it through his mind while he was walking.

"Mr. Hudson, are you aware you had an aunt, Theresa Shaw, in Bermondsey? That she was fairly solvent and has left you a quite respectable amount?"

But the words in his head trailed off. He was still entirely alone. And not a single light had come on in a window, in spite of the fact that it was now properly night.

This didn't make any sense. Maybe there had been a power cut. But he knew one thing for certain. He was utterly wasting his time here. Finding his way around was going to be practically impossible in this degree of darkness. He could barely see his hands in front of his face. It would be better if he went back home, and returned in the daylight.

And so he turned around and started walking carefully the same way he had come. It would be easier by far if he stuck to the exact same route. But he was halfway down the street when some clouds above him parted and a section of the moon came out. Its glow made his progress a good deal easier.

Except that, when he passed the grocery store again, the moonlight was shining at such an angle that it passed through the front window. Miller could make out that all the shelves were bare. And the same was true of the newsagent—not a single item of merchandise was visible.

He backtracked a little, stood on his tiptoes and peered in through the community center's high and narrow windows. There was what looked like an overturned table, and some balls of paper screwed up on the floor, but not the slightest sign that anyone was making use of the place.

And the truth occurred to him. With only that footbridge in or out, how could big bundles of newspapers and magazines be brought here? How could supplies be delivered?

What exactly did the people who'd been moved here … *live on?* His pace was fast from that point onwards. His chest constricted as he went around the final corner. He caught sight of the massive chain-link fence by the railway track, and he pushed himself towards it.

But before he'd got a dozen yards, the front doors of the houses all around him started coming open. Startled, he faltered to a halt.

#

The people emerged, but they didn't make the slightest sound. There was not a murmur, not even the soft tap of a footfall. Maybe they were wearing trainers with thick rubber soles? Wasn't that the kind of footwear people preferred in dumps like this?

Their movements were extremely measured. Nothing hurried. Nothing sudden. The word for it might be 'languid,' and that included the children. And that last fact didn't strike him as at all plausible and correct.

Miller edged around the crowd. The whole street appeared to be turning out.

Nobody took any notice of him. That struck him as extremely odd. He couldn't see their faces, since the moon had now gone mostly behind the clouds again. But several people passed him by without even acknowledging his presence. They just went to either side of him like slowly running water seeping round a rock, their heads lowered, their attention fixed on the ground.

They all went in the direction he'd just come from, to that wide street with its empty shops. Miller knew he oughtn't linger, understood that he needed to get away, but, nervous though he might be, curiosity overcame him. What exactly did they think they were doing?

When he followed them, he saw that it was not merely this street. Silhouettes were heading in from everywhere. The entire population of the Avontree Estate was gathering.

Those that had already arrived were forming a queue in front of the church, whose doors were now wide open onto gaping blackness. There were still no lights on in the place. The people were simply stopping in a line before it and then becoming very still, waiting for their turn to shuffle forward.

Some of the women had very small children with them—even babies in their arms. For heaven's sake, what *was* this? Not a single gaze lifted up to meet him as he edged in a little closer.

Everyone continued staring at the paving stones in front of them, their heads inclined.

He wanted to go into the church and take a proper look at what was happening inside, only he couldn't see how he was going to manage that. The doorway was choked as solidly as possible with waiting people, and the thought of pushing past them jangled badly at his nerves. None of them had acted dangerously so far. Not a single one of them, in fact, had even acknowledged his presence. Except he couldn't help but wonder how much that would change if he just tried to shove on through.

But then he noticed that there was an alleyway down one wall of the church, so there might well be another way inside.

It turned out he was right. There was a fire door with a metal bar across it down at the far end of the narrow lane. But when he tugged at it, he could feel it had rusted shut. In his frustration, he grasped it with both hands, determined to get through, and yanked and rattled till it finally came loose. The door swung open. He dropped the bar.

Just before he stepped inside, Miller glanced back at the alley's top. The huge black dog was there again, motionless, still watching him.

He flinched and stepped hurriedly into the darkness of the church. There was a smell like old, dried meat. And he believed he could detect some kind of steady tremor on the air. He could hear the people who had come inside shuffling around, and quite close by. But there was no real way to tell what they were up to.

So he reached inside his pocket, found his lighter, flicked it.

There were shrieks. The people in the church were backing away from the brightness of the flame, their hands coming up to shield their faces. The light was actually hurting them.

Soon there was no one standing near him. This gave him the chance he needed to study his surroundings.

The church was barren, all the pews stripped out. Nothing remained but a crucified Jesus etched into the back wall. That, and a big stone altar closer in that had been split open at its top.

Something was oozing upwards from that ragged gap, lifting itself into the air above the broken block. It was large and had no definable shape. Or rather, it *did* have one, but the outline of its edges kept changing.

And the thing was so dark, the yellow glow of his lighter was absorbed the moment that it touched it.

As he continued watching, its outline steadied, then began to pulse like some enormous heart.

It raised itself still higher and then twisted round. The thing had no discernible face, but Miller knew it had turned towards him. It hung for a few more seconds, pulsating. Then it spoke to him.

"I do not know you, do I? Yet. No, you are not from this place, are you? An intruder."

Miller stumbled back, although he couldn't help but answer the voice in his head with his own thoughts.

What are you?

"I am here to help the people in this place."

What are you doing for them? To them? Why?

"Your world forgot about them. Put them here. Turned its back on them. Gave them no more thought. They had nothing with which to make the slightest meaning of their lives, nothing in the world to live for, till I came along."

"What *are* you?" Miller asked out loud.

"I am hollowness made visible. I am emptiness brought into life. You know me by a very simple name. I am Shadow."

A man against the far wall, dressed entirely in black, decided to brave the lighter's glow. With his hands still shading his eyes, he moved in the direction of the rearing creature. And as soon as he had reached it, the thing bent down. Their bodies merged for a few seconds. Then the man swivelled around and moved off again.

The rest of these people were hanging back within the safety of the deeper darkness, but were obviously growing restless, making awkward edgy gestures, like they wanted to step forward too. The lighter was becoming very hot in Miller's grasp, but he still held onto it tightly, feeling that he had no choice.

"I feed them and nurture them," Shadow was explaining, *"in the same way you just saw."*

That simple contact? Was that all?

"And in return, they give me their respect and their obedience."

Where had this thing come from? Miller wondered.

And the creature heard that too.

"There are no such words as 'here' or 'place,' where I was born. I come from outside this thing you call a Universe, and my rules are entirely different from yours."

"But people cannot *live* like this!" Miller shouted.

The creature laughed, a deeply chilling noise.

"No! You are wrong. People can adapt to anything."

Miller glanced towards the crowd again. They were all wearing black. He stepped forwards another pace. Saw he'd got that wrong. There was no clothing anywhere in view. Instead, there was only formless darkness covering these folk.

Everyone was shrinking away from his flame again, but of the glimpses he could catch... A few body parts visible amongst the huddled group. A small cluster of fingers here. The side of a jaw there. A solitary eye and part of the ridged cheek below it. These people had largely become silhouettes, and nothing more.

His gaze went to a baby in a woman's grasp. He raised his lighter rapidly to get some kind of proper look before its mother pulled it back.

The infant was wholly darkened, no features whatsoever, and on top of its head there were two fleshy strands that were waggling gently.

Feelers, so that it could find its way around without there being any light?

"*So you see the truth.*" Shadow said. The creature's voice had taken on a smooth, satisfied tone. "*They continue to adapt, and the transformation is getting faster. They become a part of my world more and more with every passing day. They love me more and more. And me... I love them back.*"

The baby started wailing a high-pitched, inhuman sound. Panic washed through Miller. Reason left him and he fled.

He went down the empty streets at a speed he'd never managed since he'd been very young. While he was lurching crazily across the footbridge, another train went by below him. It didn't even make him pause. He could see the amber streetlights and the lit-up windows of town. He kept his wild gaze fixed on those, and stumbled down the far-side steps before he even slowed.

#

By the time he was most of the way home, cramps forced him to stop. He leant against a streetlamp, gasping hoarsely, his entire body bathed in sweat.

He managed to straighten himself up after another while, his lungs refilling and the tremors in his limbs subsiding.

Don't ever go back there, he told himself, no one ever goes there if they have a choice. There's nothing you can do about it.

And by the time he'd reached his front door, he'd half-managed to convince himself that none of it had genuinely been real. He'd been the victim of some strange delusion, that was all. The darkness and the unfamiliar surroundings… they had somehow mixed up his perceptions.

#

He ate his supper without tasting it, then watched TV silently. The images from where he'd been were slowly fading, his mind attempting to repair itself.

Except he couldn't get to sleep that night. His wife was snoring, so he climbed out of their bed as quietly as he could and fetched his dressing gown.

In the living room, he didn't need to switch any lights on as harsh moonlight was pouring through the window. So he went in that direction.

He stopped.

The same huge dog that he'd seen on the Avontree Estate was sitting on the pavement directly in front of his house like a blackened hole cut in the night, a deeper darkness by far than the normal type. He could make out not a single feature of it, not even a shallow glint around its eyes. But its head came up. Otherwise… it did not move.

THE END

* Tony Richards is the author of seven novels and more than one hundred shorter works, with his fiction appearing in Asimov's, Alfred Hitchcock's, F&SF, Weird Tales, Cemetery Dance, and many top anthologies including Best New Horror. Widely travelled, he often sets his tales in locations he has visited. He has been shortlisted for both the HWA Stoker Award and the British Fantasy Award. His latest novel—Tropic of Darkness—is due out from Simon & Schuster later on this year, and a dark fantasy novella of his is due out from Samhain approaching Christmas of the same.

17

Susan thinks she has finally found the charming cottage she's been looking for all her life; and to add to her joy, it comes with a small shop selling very special merchandise. She imagines it will be the beginning of her grand success story. But is it the fulfilment of her dream or a terrible nightmare?

The Entrepreneur
Mary Firmin

The minute she saw the California bungalow, Susan Hargrave slammed on the brakes of her red Honda Civic. The house boasted a long front porch, freshly painted a sunny yellow. Its double hung windows were flanked by gleaming white shutters. Underneath, sturdy shelves held charming flower boxes fairly bursting with colorful blossoms. It was the kind of home she had dreamed of all her life.

Then she saw the "Business for Sale" sign, and Susan was thrilled... but only for a moment. How could she ever afford such a place?

Wistfully, she gazed at the cottage, and rationalized. She did have the small inheritance from her mother, and what better way to spend it than buying a business? Not that she knew anything about business, but she was bright, and what she didn't know she could learn.

Okay, she'd at least take a look ... but only a look.

She ascended the steps to the porch.

"Emma's Emporium," declared the hand-painted sign posted over a front door sparkling with beveled glass.

A petite, dignified lady answered the bell. She was dressed in a long, black dress with a puff of white lace at the neckline. A round doily of the same intricate lace was perched on her snowy white hair. "May I help you, dear?" she said, peering over tiny Mother Hubbard glasses.

Give me a break! From her fairy tale appearance Susan had half-expected she would speak in poetry. But, since she did not believe in fairy tales, and was not about to spend her meagre bankroll on something stupid, she was cautious. "I saw your 'For Sale' sign and I wondered if I might take a look." She tried to sound nonchalant in case she needed to bargain, but when Miss Emma showed her around she couldn't conceal her excitement.

In fact, the place took her breath away.

The spacious store encompassed both living and dining rooms adjoined by an elegant mahogany archway. Fine taffeta bubbled over brass poles and draped the long elegant windows. Shiny honey-colored floors framed several bright Oriental rugs.

Discreetly, Susan touched the homemade quilts arranged casually on the backs of carved chairs, she ran her palms across the faded silk cushions of a Victorian loveseat. Lovingly, she fingered the crocheted doilies and lifted pouches of potpourri to her nose.

Mmmm, lavender, peach, cinnamon! The blend of odors brought to mind her grandmother's house and tender memories of home-baked cookies and love.

More potpourri, silk flowers, China figurines, porcelain boxes, and many other wonderful treasures were artfully displayed on an assortment of antique tables and bookcases. A dark oak mantelpiece above the green marble fireplace held a selection of old photographs in ornate silver and pewter frames. Susan examined each one before moving on to the dining room where a slightly scratched Chippendale table was set with crystal, silver, and hand-painted china. Around the room, built-in cabinets with leaded glass doors showcased more delicate bowls and serving platters.

Indeed, Emma's Emporium held every type of handiwork imaginable, bringing to mind the chic boutiques in Santa Monica and Beverly Hills. But there was one huge difference. Everything here was phenomenally cheap.

That's when Susan realized what a killing she would make if she could get the place at the right price. Then the downside hit her. She could also lose everything she had. "Do you make all these beautiful things yourself, Miss Emma?" she asked, holding a fragile white doily in her hand.

"Mostly," Emma answered. "But some of 'em comes from the ladies in town … when they got it to sell. Not many of 'em left doing this stuff anymore."

#

Susan had diligently finished her homework. She had checked on the store's sales, the current inventory, and had already acquired the necessary guarantees from the providers of Emma's handmade inventory. In addition, she had hired a lawyer to write the sales agreement.

Within a couple of weeks she was the proud owner of Emma's Emporium. It had cost her a healthy deposit, in fact almost all of the inheritance she had received from her mother when she passed six months ago. But the best part of the contract, as far as Susan was concerned, Emma had promised to continue providing the store with her own needlework. As part of the deal, Susan allowed Emma and her "Baby" to continue living in the small rear house.

Baby? Surely Emma meant her grandchild. She did not linger on this impression since it didn't make any difference to Susan.

Had she been too hard on the old lady? No, Susan had given her practically everything she wanted. Except she had dickered heavily on the price, all the time constantly reminding herself of the old adage, "business is business." Susan already had grand visions of a chain of "Emma's Emporiums" all across the country. In fact, if she could continue to acquire enough merchandise from Emma and her sources, she could sell wholesale to the high-priced boutiques in Los Angeles.

What a coup!

Meandering through the tiny living quarters, Susan felt immediately at home. She hadn't expected much, but they'd turned out to be more than adequate: a cozy bed-sitting room with a fireplace, a small office, and a bright, roomy kitchen.

Later, when Emma retreated to her little cottage, Susan heard strange animal-like noises. *Of course, Emma's baby must be a dog.*

She smiled to herself and felt much safer. They were miles away from town, and quite alone. She was glad to have the added protection of an animal.

#

Susan's first week at Emma's Emporium went by swiftly and successfully. Plenty of street traffic and the customers eagerly spent their money. In fact, she was already showing a small profit. So far, Emma had kept to herself except when she brought items to the store.

On the following Sunday morning, Susan was washing her breakfast dishes when she saw Emma returning from the ice house at the far edge of the property. The old woman carried a large bucket. Probably food for the dog, she thought. It must cost a pretty penny to feed an animal. Curiously though, Susan hadn't actually seen the dog. At night she'd heard thumping sounds and much snorting and snarling, but never heard it really bark, nor had she seen it running or playing in the yard.

The wind chimes announced a customer, interrupting her thoughts.

In the shop, a young sheriff's deputy tipped his hat. "Good

day, ma'am. And are you working for Mr. and Mrs. Harrison?"

"No, I'm not." She smiled and extended her hand. "My name is Susan Hargrave. I'm the new owner."

"Well, the Harrisons didn't last long, did they? Did they leave a forwarding address?"

"I'm afraid I can't help you there. Why don't you speak to Emma? She'll know."

He smiled and shook his head. "I doubt it! You can't get much out of that batty old lady. The name's Mike Nelson." He placed his card on the counter and tipped his hat again. "If you hear from the Harrison's, let me know."

Hmm, Harrison's? Emma didn't mention previous owners. I must speak to her about that.

#

Three weeks later, after a slow afternoon Susan closed the shop and decided to get an early night. For some reason the sounds from the rear house were especially loud and frightening to her, and she could not sleep.

Every hour of so she got up and peered through the kitchen window. Once, she even thought she saw something slinking around Emma's little house. What could it be? A fox? Five minutes later she checked again. Nothing but shadows. She dropped the curtain again and waited. She peeked once more. Nothing but more shadows. Telling herself it was her overactive imagination, Susan went back to bed. She slept only three hours that night.

Next day, while cleaning out some drawers, Susan found a bundle of letters tied with blue ribbon, Emma-style. She flicked through the envelopes and saw that three of them were addressed to Mr. and Mrs. W. M. Harrison. The rest were names she'd never heard of. A flicker of apprehension passed over her. Quickly, she shoved the package back into the drawers and gave herself a chiding. *Why are you such a scaredy–cat all of a sudden?* But she still called Deputy Mike Nelson at the Sheriff's office to tell him about the letters. He was not there.

The next three nights the noises became progressively worse, and several times Susan thought of going back to Emma's little house and strongly requesting she keep her `Baby's' mouth shut. She was fed up. She had to speak to Emma!

The next day, agitated from lack of sleep, Susan confronted Emma when she came into the shop. She questioned her about the strange goings on and the weird noises she was hearing at all hours. "I really must get my sleep, Emma. The shop is so busy and I need to get up early. Why is Baby making so much noise? Surely there is something you can do about it."

Emma was more than apologetic. "I'm real sorry Susan, but there's a storm approachin' an' Baby gits so restless when the weather gits bad." She gave Susan her most affable smile but volunteered no other information.

At this point Susan didn't care if the old lady had a bull elephant back there she just wanted to have a good night's sleep. "You do know that in our agreement I have the right to ask you to move? I really don't want to do that Emma, but if Baby keeps it up, I may have to…" She chose to leave it hanging. Emma would get the message.

Baby was right about the storm! She had to give him that. By four o'clock that afternoon rain was pouring down in torrents and there were no cars on the road.

Susan put up her "Closed" sign and retired to her apartment.

She tried to light the fire in the front room. After an annoying struggle, the logs in the fireplace caught the flame and brought a spark of cheer to the gloomy house. She made a cup of tea, and a chicken sandwich and sat down in the living room to enjoy it.

The night progressed, and the storm worsened. Doors and shutters banged in the wake of the shrieking wind. Bouts of thunder exploded, sending her to the window. Flashes of lightning lit up the darkened sky, like a fireworks display, and exposed all the dark frightening corners in the room.

Susan, not easily frightened, was nervous. (After all, she had lived in the war zone that was Los Angeles.) Emma had no telephone so she couldn't call her for comfort, and she wasn't about to cross the dark muddy yard to the little rear house.

Who could she call? She didn't know any of the locals. Susan hadn't made friends with anyone in the four weeks she had been here. In fact she hadn't even met anyone, except the sheriff's deputy. Haltingly, she picked up the telephone and dialed the sheriff's office, mainly to make contact with another human being. *Damn, the line's dead!*

Unbidden, every negative thought she had ever dreamed up entered her head. The vague uneasiness she had experienced in the past few days expanded to terror, and her knees began to shake. What if a stranger knocked at the door? What if he was a serial killer? What if someone came to rob her? Who would she call? Emma? What about Emma's crazy dog? Maybe he was rabid. He must be pretty big; he made an awful lot of noise. But maybe he would be their protector. Again, she seriously considered going to visit Emma. No, she'd be drenched and muddy the minute she stepped outside the door. Anyway, she might run into Baby and catch him howling at the moon. She shivered at the thought.

The lights went out. Her breath caught. That's when panic hit her like an avalanche and she began to pray. She promised God everything. *Dear God please help me.* Just as quickly, the lights were on and she felt instant relief.

As Susan regained her composure she scurried about the house trying to find candles. She remembered the wall sconces in the living room each had two candles and hurried to fetch the ladder from the kitchen.

The lights flickered again! The storm played havoc with the electricity and the howling wind sent shock waves through her body. She was afraid the huge tree in the back yard would fall on the house. She glanced out the kitchen window. Off to the side the branches of the tree were lashed about by the wind but it appeared stalwart.

The back house was suddenly spotlighted by a bright flash of lightning.

Emma's doggie door burst open!

Susan stood; rooted in fear, staring hypnotically at...?

What was it ... this, this thing ... this entity?

Whatever it was, it was definitely not a dog!

The power flashed off and on. There could be a blackout.

Lights, I need lights! Candles. Candles In the wall sconces by the fireplace.

Forcing herself to move, she grabbed the kitchen ladder and ran for the living room. As she reached the fireplace the fire went out and the house was in total darkness. The store and the merchandise she loved appeared ominous and threatening.

Hurriedly, she erected the ladder in order to reach the fixtures that held candles.

Slam! She almost jumped out of her skin. Was that her kitchen door?

Terror consumed her, but Susan climbed the ladder and reached for the candles. Her hand wavered as she struggled to find the fixtures in the dark. Aided only by brief flashes of lightning, she groped for the sconces, even attempted to light a match.

*There! Another bright splash of lightning! S*he grabbed the two candles.

The storm blew wilder, wilder, drowning out all sound! That's when she sensed, rather than heard, something creeping across the floor.

She fumbled with the match. The candle was lit.

She strained to hear...

The ladder shuddered. Something was shaking it. Oh, God.

She held the candle aloft ... her fear was quickly replaced by such horror and revulsion at what she saw ... she almost blacked out. Teetering precariously, Susan collapsed against the rickety steps of the ladder and tried to control the vomit rising in her throat as the light from the candle confirmed her worst fears.

The naked, dripping creature below could not be called human.

Its oversized head, with its long, matted grey hair, lolled grotesquely to one side. Slowly the thing raised its hideous face to look up at her. A smudge of flesh served as a nose, and under shaggy graying eyebrows bright blue eyes gleamed maniacally. They were Emma's eyes.

For two or three very long seconds, Susan stared in awful fascination.

The thing stared back at her, its mouth dripping with saliva. Suddenly, the mouth opened wider revealing fang-like teeth.

That's when Susan screamed, and she just couldn't stop.

Suddenly it moved. Fast. It rumbled around the ladder and smashed it periodically, trying to shake her loose.

That's when she realized it had no legs! The thing was a mass of un-molded flesh ... a monstrous lump of tissue, tapering into what resembled flippers. Surprisingly, it moved quickly. A fast crawl sustained by stump-like arms. Was it some kind of deformed animal? Surely, it couldn't be human. Could it?

Susan's stomach churned, but she clung to the ladder.

It rocked the ladder again, more ferociously this time.

I can't hang on. Dear God, please help me. Susan clung to the top rung of the ladder as it swayed. The thing was pushing harder now. What did it want? Where was Emma?

She lost her grip on the ladder and tumbled down. Grasping at nothing but air, Susan plummeted to the floor. The candle was out!

In panic, she sprang to her feet. The room was in darkness.

The thing seized her leg. She felt the flesh being ripped from the bone. The pain was excruciating. Wildly, she reached for the butchered leg. Her hand was chewed with shark-like efficiency. That's when Susan screamed, long and loud, into the void.

The back door crashed open and wind shrieked through the house. Emma bustled into the living room, flashlight in hand. "Oh my, Baby," she sighed. "Oh my!"

Emma's torch flashed on Baby's face. Susan saw her own blood mingled with saliva on its chin. The light continued down over its shriveled, deformed body to unidentifiable genitalia. Now she knew why it was called just ... "Baby."

"Emma! Emma!" she cried in relief. "Thank God you're here!"

Emma rushed across the room to the fireplace and grabbed the poker. "I'm sorry, Baby," she cried, as she approached brandishing the weapon.

She flailed the weapon towards them.

The crushing pain in her head jolted her, and Susan felt the briefest moment of surprise. As she faded into unconsciousness, she heard Emma say the strangest thing.

"That's enough for now, Baby. Let's get her to the ice house."

#

The next morning, while Emma pounded the Business for Sale sign into the ground, the Sheriff's Deputy drove up and parked his car. "Good morning, Ma'am."

"Mornin', Sheriff."

"Is Susan about?"

"No, sir. She went on back to L.A. Family problems. Her mother was ill."

"How many times you sold this place, Emma?"

"Four or five times, maybe."

He rocked back on his heels, and smiled condescendingly. "Now that's what I'd call a money-maker. I guess we could call you a re-e-eal entrepreneur."

"Well, I don't know about being no entrepreneur, Sheriff," Emma said, with her most benign smile. "But it sure keeps meat on

≈ೕಣಣಣ≈

the table for Baby and me."

THE END

* English born Mary Firmin was raised in Ontario, Canada, then lived in Santa Monica, California for many years and raised three children. Vice President of a large Real Estate firm she attended writing classes at U.C.L.A. When she moved to the Desert she wrote a society column, many short stories, a screenplay, and a novel, Deadly Pleasures. She now lives in Rancho Mirage, Ca. and is a member of Mystery Writers of America, Sisters in Crime, Romance Writers of America, Women in Film. and Palm Springs Writers Guild.

≈⊱ଓ୫ଆ୫ଓଈ⊰≈

18
How does one outrun darkness?

The Speed of Dark
Clayton Clifford Bye

Richard Bartholomew's little brother sat on the bottom stair and studied the line bisecting the rock walled basement.

"What's the speed of dark?" he asked.

Trying to ignore the sudden knot of pain in his stomach, Richard answered. "Doesn't have a speed, Tim," he said. "Darkness is just the absence of light."

Shadows, lifelike in their furtive movement, crawled a few more inches away from the walls. Richard pretended not to see them.

"Light moves fast?" Tim asked.

"Nothing's faster," Richard said.

Small windows atop the western wall glowed with that special golden light which always seems to be reserved for crisp, autumn evenings. These tiny glass squares of life cast beams of airy gold into the spreading gloom. Billowing ribbons of dust danced along the slender rays, entertaining the watching boys, distracting them until the darkness closed in, until the colour of the light changed and took on the hue of blood.

Suddenly, Richard heard his mother's voice within his head. "Somebody's got to go." She'd stood as a rock in the middle of the hall, blocking the way out to the world. Had taken her purse up before speaking and dug out the keys to the old Motor Cart. Then, casually, as if instructing him to do something as mundane as washing the breakfast dishes, she'd made her wishes clear. "You decide," she'd said. "But I want somebody gone by dark."

Mother had locked them down—as she always did when going out. The rumble of the engine as she eased along their gravelled drive reminded Richard of distant thunder. A cold shiver walked up and down his spine. Bile rose in his throat.

Richard wiped the memory from his mind and joined his brother on the steps. He could feel the younger boy tremble. The cool, dry basement air was sour with the scent of Tim's fear. A centipede scurried across the floor, its serpentine movements and glossy red skin the perfect harbingers of this night.

"How do we get out of this?" Richard asked himself. Action was required. Becky had proved that. Nobody gets to refuse mother. Not even once.

Tim had Becky's eyes. Richard had been able to keep her alive in his mind because Tim had her eyes. Grey. With striations of blue and yellow.

"Wanna try busting a window, Tim?" he asked.

Tim looked up at Richard with their sister's long dead eyes and said, "Can't bust those rocks. So what good is it gonna do?"

"We can't just sit here and wait for it, Tim. She don't take no for an answer. We gotta get out."

"Windows are too small," Tim said. "Ain't no way to change that."

Both boys allowed their gaze to follow the lines of the walls. The basement had nothing in it but the stairs on which they sat, four bare rock walls, a hardened earth floor and a couple of rows of six inch windows. They'd already tried to force the door at the top of the stairs. Hadn't managed it. Not even when there had been three of them.

"Can you make me not afraid, Richard? Can you make it so I don't have to go into the dark?"

Richard started crying.

"Watch the windows, Timmy," he said. "Let the sun fall on your face."

Tim got up and walked over to one of the diminishing beams of light. He turned toward the window from which the beam originated, and then stepped into the path of the reddening light.

"Richard!" he exclaimed. "It's still warm."

The older boy didn't have the heart to tell Tim the warmth would fade, that there was no way to escape the darkness. Their problem wasn't the speed with which darkness travelled, he thought, but one involving the very nature of darkness.

Richard hung his head, tears darkening the soil below. He didn't know how to explain that the dark was already here. It had always been here.

#

Tim fed them for months. Mother was pleased. One day, after finishing a particularly good roast, she even went so far as to say he tasted better than Becky. Richard figured that was because he was younger.

At night, when greasy rain fell on the rotting roof, creating phosphorescent droplets which occasionally fell on his skin and burned him, Richard would conjure up images of what his mother would say when the time came to eat him.

Richard didn't have an ounce of fat on him," she would brag. Or, perhaps, "He made a fine stew."

The boy could hear the smacking of her wet, red lips, could envision her licking juices from claw-like fingers, flat, black eyes studying each morsel as she calculated how to get all the precious meat from his dead bones.

#

On the days Richard wasn't locked in the cellar, when his mother chose not to go foraging for edibles in what was left of the city, he enjoyed walking in the fields. Trees hadn't yet recovered from the firestorm, but clover and hay and the like had come up greener than ever. He also watched dragonflies. They weren't birds, but they were alive. And mother wouldn't eat them.

Richard shuddered, gooseflesh rose upon his arms. Time to head back. Mother was cooking up the last of the Tim steaks. She'd be angry if he was late.

The boy pushed through waist high grasses. Poisoned grasses. Ones he'd contemplated ingesting on many previous occasions, as a way to bring about an end to the headaches and the nausea and the aching in his chest.

But Richard was more afraid of the dark than Tim had been. So, recently, rather than thinking about ways to kill himself, he'd begun to harbour a secret dream. Down in the black place that was now his mind, the boy was cultivating the thought that maybe, just maybe, he could find the nerve to make mother a dessert.

THE END

* Clayton Bye is a writer, editor and publisher. The author of 9 books and a varied collection of short stories, poems, articles and hundreds of reviews, The Speed of Dark is his second foray into the world of traditional publishing. It's an anthology of excellent short stories by some great talents from around the world. And as you will already have discovered, this particular collection is filled with strangely different and disturbing horror stories.

19
A dark figure stalks the cancer center.

9 Vials of Blood

John B. Rosenman

Ramsey found the Lyon Oncology Center to be a calm but chilling place. The atmosphere was meant to be soothing and reassuring as if to say, "You're not really sick, it's just a minor thing easily correctible, and you're going to live a long time." On the surface, the Halloween motif reinforced that message, with grinning pumpkin-head clowns and scarecrows stretching across the walls and counters, perhaps to escort him to a land where his blood count was normal and he didn't get tired so often.

Yes, it wasn't as bad a place as he'd anticipated. Only why did the clowns and scarecrows have to smile so much? There was something creepy about it. And why didn't any of the other patients look troubled by the same word posted everywhere on doors and walls in yellow police tape? Didn't it seem … well, a bit ominous?

BEWARE! BEWARE! BEWARE! BEWARE!

Of course, it was October, and Halloween was nigh. Everybody knew that. Halloween was this country's real holiday, more sacred and beyond scrutiny than even Christmas. Hell, if a gang of bloody axe murderers stomped through here, the patients would probably stand up and cheer.

As if to prove the point, a cloaked hooded figure swept past them in the waiting area. It was a mere shadow, obviously a trick of light, but he rose, filled with foreboding. Who or what was it?

The dark figure turned a corner down the corridor and disappeared.

"Are you all right, sir?" a fat woman across the waiting area asked.

He looked at her, feeling embarrassed. His blood pounded. He swallowed and sat down.

It was nearly one. Most patients had to wait to see their doctors, so volunteers wheeled a lunch cart into the waiting area. Ramsey selected a chicken salad sandwich, a bag of chips, and a Coke. Noticing a Clive Cussler novel on a counter, he picked that too, hoping to bury his nervousness in a thriller.

It didn't work well. He kept reading the same sentence and hearing patients talk and wheeze. A white-haired man with an ample paunch sat down next to the fat woman and stared unblinking into infinity.

Rising, he dropped the book on the chair and walked down the corridor but in the opposite direction from where the dark figure had disappeared. He reminded himself he was seeing a hematologist, not an oncologist. Yes, his father had died of leukemia, but he himself hadn't been diagnosed with any form of cancer yet. This was just a precautionary step. All he was going to do today was answer a few questions, maybe have his chest thumped a little, and last, give a little blood. Well, maybe a lot of blood. Still, this was just precautionary. His primary care physician had referred him to Dr. Needles because his white, red, and platelet counts were a bit low. Nothing more.

Dr. Needles … was that really his name?

He hadn't thought of it before, but didn't the name sound strange? For that matter, was Dr. Needles a man? He'd just assumed he was. He'd been reluctant to visit the Center's site online and do any research. It was as if the mere act would make the seriousness of his problem official.

What if Dr. Needles was the dark figure he'd seen in the hall? What if he had *needles* for fingers?

Ramsey pressed his hand to his face. What was wrong with him? Why was he thinking such crazy thoughts? He was a practical insurance salesman, yet he was letting his imagination run Halloween wild. It all had to do with his fear of doctors and his dread of repeating his father's painful history. His father had died at 53 of leukemia, a disease which had started in his bone marrow and produced a lot of abnormal white blood cells which grew fast and kept on growing, taking him away piece by piece. All too soon his father had been reduced to a screaming shell tormented by agony but terrified of death. Just as he himself might soon be.

Ramsey was only 48 years old now. He might not even live to see 50.

Stop it!

Instead, he stopped walking. He found himself in another part of the Center before another counter.

Turning, he looked back, down the long corridor and the walls which framed it. The chair where he'd been waiting for his appointment seemed immeasurably distant, in another realm altogether. A trick of perspective of course, but he couldn't shake the feeling that he'd come a long way. He didn't even know if he could get back.

Feeling lost, he glanced at the new counter.

Nursing.

There were no nurses present, though. The place was empty. He didn't even see a bell to ring. Instead, a big cat made from plastic pumpkins perched on the counter, looking like it was ready to spring. It had a glossy black shine and consisted of a big pumpkin for the body and a smaller one for the head. A snakelike tail made from a squash swayed in a phantom air current.

To Ramsey, the cat's eyes were scary. Almond-shaped, they glowed a bright yellow and followed him wherever he moved. His damned imagination! As he started to leave, he half-expected the black feline to leap off the counter and come after him.

Just then a sharp hiss split the air behind him.

He knew he shouldn't, but he looked back. The black cat now faced away from him. What really frightened Ramsey though was not the hiss or the cat's changed position but that the sign on the counter no longer said *Nursing.* Instead, bright yellow police tape blared a warning:

Cancer! Cancer! Cancer! Cancer!

It was a hallucination! He staggered on, struggling for calm. *Nerves, that's all it is. I'm scared about meeting this new doctor and imagining all sorts of weird things. Yeah, that's it. I'm worried about my health and what he—or she—will say.*

As well he should be. The low white, red, and platelet cells didn't square well with a diagnosis of leukemia. That was the darn trouble: his regular doctor had no idea what he had. Yes, he experienced some weakness and bone pain consistent with leukemia, but then it might be something else. Torn by doubt and uncertainty, Ramsey felt all alone with his fears and the specter of his miserable, pain-racked father.

A litany of unpleasant terms rattled in his head. Chemotherapy and radiation. Bone marrow transplants and remission. Life-threatening operations he didn't even want to contemplate. Damn it, why did this have to happen to *him*? It was so unfair, especially now when he had rich new clients coming in.

Perhaps worst of all: no one gave a damn about him because he was all alone and had never married. He was an only child, had no family, and all his friends were casual, see-you-Monday ones.

And all his girlfriends were don't-call-me-at-all. Some even accused him of being cold and selfish. Distant and mean-spirited. To him it made absolutely no sense.

When he reached his chair, he found two women had moved into his area, encroaching on his personal space. One was rather pretty and sat talking to the snowy-haired woman of about eighty who sat in a wheelchair before her.

Ramsey picked up his Clive Cussler novel from the floor where it had fallen and sat down. The old lady's shrunken body reminded him of a wasted corpse, but there remained something defiant about her fluffy white hair. He imagined lovers running their fingers through it in days gone by.

"Mother," the younger woman said, "please consider chemo. Keeping your hair just isn't worth it. Besides, it will grow back."

Her mother touched her breasts. "They took these, Miriam. They aren't going to take this, too." She touched her hair with a trembling hand. "It's all I have left."

Lowering her voice, her daughter leaned toward her. "Mother, what's the point of the operation and reconstruction if you don't use chemo to stop the cancer?" She said "cancer" so softly, Ramsey doubted her mother caught the word.

Her mother sat back and shook her head. *No*, she might have said. *Here I draw the line. I only care about me.*

Suddenly the dark figure appeared behind the pair. Ramsey watched in horror as it glided toward them, fuller than before though parts of it were indistinct, and it was still somehow incomplete. His sick blood went cold as the specter stopped by the old woman's chair. He sensed at once he was the only one who knew it was there. The daughter took her mother's hand, looking right through the looming figure.

The sight of the visitor, however, made Ramsey want to scream. Somehow he knew that beneath its hood, its long, lean, predator's body had been spawned from five million years of human misery. A smiling slash of a mouth mocked every human dream. And its twisted hands fed human lives like candy down its gullet.

As the mother and daughter prattled on, Ramsey saw the cloaked, hooded figure raise its hand and lay it on the old woman's shoulder as if appraising her. Only Ramsey recognized who or what it was: Death.

Remembering his father's whining, hate-filled, final days in a hospital, Ramsey reflected that such a vile presence belonged in a place like this where human misery, meanness, pettiness, and selfishness ruled. Where people not only struggled to live but so often cared only about themselves and acted their very worst.

To Ramsey, this self-pitying old woman richly deserved her dark suitor. She had spent so much time and pain reconstructing her breasts to save her life, and then what did the selfish bitch do? She refused to take chemo and didn't care one bit about all her daughter had done for her. The probable result? She would die anyway. And why? Because she was so vain about her stupid white hair! The old crab acted like she had a whole stable of hot young studs panting to get into her bed. And the worst part was she had a daughter who tried to talk sense and wanted only the best for her. A daughter who would be crushed by her death and obviously loved her deeply.

While he had no one who loved him at all.

Ramsey saw the dark figure's hand tighten on the old woman's shoulder.

At that moment, the mother's white hair started to twitch and stir. A black beetle appeared within its frothy, nest-like folds. The beetle glittered and extended tiny antennae, feeling its way around.

Another beetle appeared.

Another.

More beetles materialized as if from nowhere. Now there were dozens, swarming throughout the woman's white hair. In horror, Ramsey glanced at the daughter. Surely, she should see something by now. The daughter, however, wasn't looking, had changed the subject and was talking cheerfully about some recipe she'd discovered.

Swallowing down nausea, Ramsey looked away at the walls. *BEWARE! BEWARE! BEWARE! BEWARE!*

He looked back. The old woman's entire face and body was a solid black mass of death beetles now. They crawled over her and dropped heavily to the floor. *Plop! Plop!* Frantically, Ramsey raised his foot and brought it down repeatedly on top of them. *Crunch! Crunch! Crunch!*

The shadow figure—Mr. Death—danced and whirled in delight, his cloak spinning.

For the first time, the old woman's voice faltered. She sagged forward in her wheelchair and started to fall.

"Mother!" Her daughter leaned forward and caught her.

The result of her touch was miraculous. The mother straightened with a jolt as if she'd been reborn. "Sorry, Miriam, I don't know what happened. I must have nodded off."

"Are you sure? Do you feel all right now?"

"Don't be silly. I feel fine."

The dark, cloaked figure faded, as did all the beetles. A moment later, they were gone.

Ramsey shuddered and felt faint. Dimly he heard a voice call his name.

As if in a nightmare, he rose, wanting to run. Instead, he tottered toward the nurse. She recorded his weight, handed him his paperwork, and led him to a small room where she took his temperature and blood pressure.

Why had he seen death's shadow? Was he losing his mind? No, no, he was just getting worked up again. It was the deep fear that he was repeating his father's history and would waste away to a bleeding shell riddled by painful infections. He would calm down once he got this matter settled and knew something, one way or the other.

The nurse smiled. She had a pleasant, ordinary face which inspired sanity. As a matter of fact, this room seemed so ordinary and normal, so different from the waiting area where he'd imagined a laughing shadow of death and a swarm of black beetles. It was hard to believe the two places could exist in the same building.

"Mr. Ramsey," the nurse said, "please make yourself comfortable. Dr. Needles will be in soon."

She left, and he tried to relax and not think of meeting this new doctor and what he would say. As Ramsey did so often, he thought of his profession: selling insurance. How ironic there was no insurance against losing his mind. The idea actually made him chuckle.

The door opened, and Dr. Needles walked in.

Like the nurse, Dr. Needles was pleasant looking. He immediately inspired confidence with his impeccable white coat and neatly parted brown hair. Ramsey's eyes went to the man's fingers, finding no needles. He raised his hand barely in time to receive the proffered handshake.

"Mr. Ramsey? I'm Dr. Needles."

"Hello, Doctor," he responded. "I'm glad to meet you."

Dr. Needles consulted his chart. He looked up and smiled.

At first the examination went well, with Dr. Needles asking routine questions about how Ramsey felt and if he was in any pain. Then, mostly because he was nervous with doctors, he ran into his usual fate. Ramsey found the man's technical terms slipped rapidly from his memory as new ones he couldn't even pronounce shoved them aside. He tried desperately to hold on and understand, only to lose them as more medicalese rushed by.

Finally, he raised his hand. "Doctor, could I have cancer?"

He waited, unable to breathe.

"Mr. Ramsey," Dr. Needles said, "we can't be sure until we've conducted tests, but it's unlikely."

Tension escaped him in a whoosh. "It's unlikely." Just two words, but what relief! They didn't guarantee perfect health, but no doctor could. Only, why did he feel so tired now and then? Why did his bones ache?

Dr. Needles coaxed him onto the examination table. "Your fatigue is keyed to your low red blood count and may be caused by one or more of your medications. As for your bone pain, you do have arthritis and need to see a rheumatologist." He felt Ramsey's midsection. "Your spleen feels fine."

"What about my low white blood and platelet count?" Ramsey asked.

Needles started to reply, but then Ramsey glimpsed something move from the corner of his eye. He turned his head only to have it elude him. Where was it? *The ceiling.* Looking up, he saw a faint shadow steal across the tiles to the far wall over the door. The shadow shifted there from side to side and seemed to hesitate. Then it slipped to the right and came toward him across the wall closest to the examination table.

There it darkened and assumed a deadly shape. It pounced at Ramsey with long sharp claws. He leaped off the table with a muffled scream.

"Mr. Ramsey! Are you all right?"

"Y-Yes."

"Good. You startled me." Dr. Needles frowned. "Before you leave, I'd like our staff to draw some blood."

Trembling, Ramsey searched around for the shadow, even peering behind the examination table. Thank God, it was just a bright, safe room.

He tried to joke. "Uh, blood. My doctor said about three or four gallons."

Dr. Needles smiled. "I promise we'll leave enough for you to get home."

#

Outside the examination room, Ramsey leaned against the wall. *Please tell me the shadow was just my imagination again,* he thought. *As long as I know the difference between fantasy and reality, I'm still okay.* The shadow had resembled a panther, but he'd known it was really the evil creature who had touched the old woman's shoulder.

It struck him for the first time that the specialized language of doctors he found so opaque and intimidating resembled the terminology he sometimes used to sell clients and customers insurance policies they couldn't afford and didn't need. He smiled.

He was very good at manipulating these people. He had always been a talented person. Only why was he so alone, feeling at times like an empty wasteland?

Clutching his medical paperwork, he forced himself to walk. In the waiting area, the daughter had swung her chair around to sit beside her mother. Ramsey passed them and stopped nearby.

"Mom, you'll feel so much better once you've had your chemo," the daughter said as her mother sobbed into a handkerchief. "And after the treatments, your hair will grow right back, maybe thicker than ever."

"Will it, honey?" A hitch in her breath. Stick-thin shoulders shuddered.

"Yes, sweetie. You'll be good as new." Her daughter leaned close and kissed her shrunken cheek. Ramsey saw the daughter's gaze rise and meet his, then return to the mother as if she were the most precious jewel in her life.

And I guess if her hair doesn't grow back, you'll have enough love for the both of you to make her accept it, just as you had enough love to save your mother's life with a touch when Death placed his venomous hand on her shoulder.

Ramsey himself had never known such love. His mother had died when he was young, and the closest person in his life had been his cold father, dead for thirty years now in a grave he'd visited once. Yet, for the first time in his life, he felt a yearning stir inside him as he watched the mother and daughter embrace. Tears moistened his eyes, and his lips opened, trying to express what he dimly felt.

"I wish," he whispered. "I wish I could start all over again and be different…"

His nurse appeared. "Are you lost, Mr. Ramsey?"

He shook his head at the interruption. "But how can I change?" Despite his uncertainty, he felt the beginning of hope.

"Mr. Ramsey?"

The promise faded, leaving an old emptiness. "Yes," he finally said. "I'm lost."

She touched his arm. "The blood lab is this way."

He followed her to a room where two rows of people sat facing each other ten feet apart while having their blood drawn. Ramsey thought, *Offerings to the Great God of Blood, who is always thirsty.*

He sat through the ritual as a woman checked his name and date of birth, set out the tubes, asked him which arm he preferred, applied a tourniquet tight enough to make the vein bulge, gently patted the vein and examined its size, swabbed him down, and slid the needle into the vein as smoothly as if it were melted butter.

Ramsey counted the tubes as she removed them and inserted new ones. Nine vials of blood, all of them to be vilely filled. He suppressed his disgust, knowing he should be pleased. He'd actually received good news today, for it looked as if he didn't have leukemia like his father.

A spider crawled out from under one of the tubes. Ramsey recognized it at once. It was a black widow, for it had a shiny, jet black, globular abdomen with a red hourglass marking. It looked exactly like the one which had bitten and made Dicky Martin so sick in the seventh grade. He remembered how he'd laughed at his classmate's pain and vomiting.

The technician didn't notice the spider. She wrote his name on the label of another tube with a magic marker.

Another spider appeared. This one was big, red, and fluffy. He didn't know what species it was, if any.

More spiders crawled onto the scene, a growing horde of them. The woman wrote his name on more tubes. Her mouth opened, and a large tarantula emerged and dropped down inside the front of her uniform. She licked her lips, suspecting nothing.

Ramsey wanted to scream. Couldn't.

He saw the people in the room were now covered with scuttling spiders of all colors and sizes. They emerged from mouths and noses and scurried across the floor. They coated his body as well, squirming eagerly beneath his clothes.

Across the room, one of the technicians turned to him with a broad smile.

He was the dark specter who'd placed his hand on the old woman's shoulder. Only now, as he threw back his hood and dropped his cloak to the floor, Ramsey could see the creature perfectly, every dreadful feature of his naked face and body.

The thing's hands were as savage as claws and his bone-white body starved like a sinner's from hell. Ramsey knew he was very hungry, hungry for something besides food. The worst thing, though, the very worst...

The face he wore was *Ramsey's* own.

The specter laughed, not silently this time, but with a hellish screech of joy. "Oh my dear boy," he crowed, "you are so much more worthy than that vain and selfish old hag you sat next to. Essences like yours, when I'm blessed enough to find them, are very rare and a gourmet's absolute delight. They are the most precious and exquisite additions to my collection."

Ramsey struggled to rise and almost fell. "Please," he cried to a room filled with people who looked up in alarm, seeing only a frantic, upset patient, "I want to learn to love, to change my selfish, empty life. Won't one of you touch or kiss me before it's too late?"

The dark man swept forward, pressing his claim and his lips to Ramsey's as he wrapped him in a tight embrace. Ramsey felt the vile lips taste him, deeply and forever.

At last the specter pulled back. "It doesn't really matter," he said, his loathsome hands caressing him like a lover's. "Dr. Needles was quite wrong. Your cancer is not only subtle but deep. You will die within a year anyway."

The End

214

* Two of John's science-fiction adventure novels recently became audiobooks and are available at www.audible.com. They are *Beyond Those Distant Stars*, winner of AllBooks Review Editor's Choice Award for 2010 and his African deep-space epic *A Senseless Act of Beauty*. At Norfolk State University, John designed and taught a course in writing and publishing Science Fiction, Fantasy, and Horror, and he is a former Chairman of the board of HWA (Horror Writers Association). John and his wife Jane have been married 45 years, and they have two children. John likes to hear from his readers. You can email him at jroseman@cox.net and also visit his blog at http://johnrosenman.blogspot.com and website at http://www.johnrosenman.com. He invites readers to check out one of his interviews at http://www.milscifi.com/files/inter-JBR-BS.htm.

20

A grieving widow faces hellish terrors attacking her home and mind, and is forced to face an unknown evil.

Out of Nothing
Micki Peluso

I sit and stare through the small French window overlooking a seedy, neglected yard. It is my only pastime, this gaze into nothing, awaiting the day when I will join the emptiness that whispers my name, which teases my deadened senses. My soul is winter yearning for the spring that will never come.

Fierce, unearthly screams interrupt my stupor. Sounds of horror which started recently—days, perhaps weeks. I do not recall the passage of time, except the change from daylight's brightness to the dark of night. First the scratching hits the house like branches from my tall oak trees, slowly at the onslaught, and then furiously; matched by tornado-like howling that rises to a crescendo matching the elevation of my terror. I am alone, surrounded by a soul-wrenching discord that accelerates a slow and aching heart to a pounding and thumping that seems to echo throughout my home.

The assault continues, I know not how long, spewing evil vileness, yet the sound is seductive and somehow familiar. I must not yield to it. It will be the death of me, an unpleasant death, unlike the repose of the beckoning abyss. Let me die in my own bed, not tortured by this spawn of Hell. The old house continues to creak and shift as if dancing to the sounds of imminent dread. We shudder together, the house and I, in apprehension of an unknown peril.

The wind-like wailing ceases abruptly, as always, yet each new episode seems amplified and of greater length. The afghan pulled up around my shoulders soothes the chill brought on by the frigid house and the fear that has no name. And as that fear recedes from my shaken body, a sweet languor causes me to doze, perhaps to finally sleep free of hideous nightmares that cause me to scream aloud. What monstrous thing delights in such torture?

The doorbell rings, jarring me awake. Cranking the window open a crack, I call down, "Who is it?"

"It's only me, Mrs. Romano—Meals on Wheels. Can I come in?"

"Come right on up."

"This door should be kept locked," says the delivery man, as he reaches the top of the stairs.

I ignore this, for I know the thing from which I cringe will not be deterred by a locked door. The man sets my dinner on a tray in front of my chair. The same old fare—watery instant mashed potatoes, a gray slab of meat, some bread, and an apple to challenge my dentures.

"Why, thank you, John," I say, managing a slight smile.

"I'm not John, Mrs. Romano."

"I know, I know," I answer, mechanically biting into the cardboard passing as white bread.

"It's cold in here," he mutters in exasperation, checking the old gun-metal radiator for some sign of heat. "Did you forget to pay your gas bill?"

"My husband pays the bills," I answer, pulling the afghan up to my chin.

"Mrs. Romano, your husband's been dead a month now."Don't look at me like that. I know you remember."

His words thrust stabbing pain into the pit of my stomach. John and I were married nearly fifty years, decades of oneness and intertwined love. He was my stability in an unstable world. We raised one son, our finest achievement, only to lose him from a tainted blood transfusion. How ironic of God to spare his life after being struck by a car, only to take it in a twist of fate.

John followed him a year later, never recovering from his sorrow. Only our grandson, Jonathan, carries on the legacy of those I loved.

I need to be with John, to replenish the part of me that is missing. I cannot exist in an empty world lighted only by the trusting smile of a four-year-old boy. A boy whose face reflects my loss, a face I can no longer bear to look upon. *John*, my heart cries out, *Come to me and take me with you.* My heart is a century cactus, its outside barbed and safe, its inside soft, vulnerable to the mockery of death. Somewhere beneath the layers of grief, anger lies ready to lash out. John had no right to leave me alone, denying the focus of my existence. It isn't fair. My anger flares, then flickers out in desolation.

"You'll have heat in a few minutes," the man said. "The thermostat was set too low. Will you be all right now?"

"Of course, dear, I'm always all right when you're near me."

He shakes his head somberly and walks down the stairway to the front door, locking it behind him. My husband is such a thoughtful man.

My mind tries again to embrace the limbo that holds insanity at bay—that shuts down the mind. If only the raucous noise would stay away I might empty my soul of the anguish of consciousness. I wish to die but not by the brutal grasp of a wicked entity pounding on my doors.

The telephone rings until I can no longer ignore it, another intrusion keeping me from the dream of eternal slumber. Jonathan's mother asks me how I am doing. She means my mental health, but cannot say it. I leave her to her speculations. I know too well that I am sane, and whatever is reaching out to devour my sanity desires to eat away at the fragments of my mind. It is the sanity that is unbearable.

We have little to say to one another. The common threads of our life lie buried in parallel graves in a cemetery not three blocks from my home. It is not a place I choose to visit, for my loves are not there, only the shells that housed their splendor. She wants to bring Jonathan to visit.

"Not yet," I say. I do not tell her the pain still pulses like an open wound. Jonathan will survive. He will learn to call another man father, and the memory of the lean, white-haired grandfather that he called "Pa" will slip from his young mind *like the tenuous threads of dreams.*

"He cries for you," she tells me. I harden my heart and block the picture of the cherubic reminder of better days.

#

The racket seems more intense today. The intervals of numbing silence grow less frequent. The hellish sounds, demanding in tone, reverberate throughout the house, vibrating within my body, lodging in my soul. Clamorous noise from something ungodly now hurls itself against my door. Again and Again. I can bear no more.

The sun has slipped below the horizon and day grows dim in anticipation of nightfall. I rise slowly to confront this relentless intrusion, this formidable being that prevents me from embracing the timelessness of grief. Another screech sends me reeling back to my chair. This thing will not let me go. Desperation lifts me to my feet. I must greet my fate, for I can tolerate no more of its torture.

I take one step down the narrow staircase and nearly fall. The railing braces my frail weight. My legs tremble, my heart rapidly beats what must be its final serenade. Hands, gnarled from arthritis and shaky from a touch of palsy, dance like mimes along the banister. The dizziness in my head settles into a persistent fog as I try another step. And another. Some time later, I find myself on the landing facing the front door.

Once unlocked, the door groans and opens a crack, then a little more. Something fierce and quick slinks through the door and leans against my tremulous legs. The sounds and wails from Hell subside at last. Gray fur, standing upright in indignation, relaxes as its warm body entwines about my feet, emitting soft contented mews. I don't remember owning a cat.

I follow the animal's insistent trail up the stairs toward the kitchen. It seems to know the layout of the house. *My gait is slow, but there is levity to my step, and a spark*, just a spark, illuminating my heart. *Tomorrow, I must call Jonathan.*

THE END

* Micki Peluso began writing as a catharsis for grief, which culminated in 30 years as a short story writer, staff journalist for the award-winning newspaper, The Staten Register, freelance journalist for other newspapers and author of *And the Whippoorwill Sang*; a funny, poignant true family saga of love, loss and survival. Her next book—a collection of short stories called, *Heartbeats... Slices of Life* will be released in 2013.

21

With the death of her husband, and her children busy making their own lives, Lillian has little to do but feel sorry for herself. One day she takes a walk on Pacific Palisades and her life is changed forever. She finds a new quest in life and it is an altruistic one. Or so she thinks.

Taking Care of Mother
Mary Firmin

On a sparkling June morning, Lillian Hartley, feeling much younger than her seventy-two years, walked briskly along the bluffs at Palisades Park. She yearned for something to happen, anything, to bring meaning to her placid widow's life. Lately, she'd caught herself observing the world like a spectator and decided to come here to immerse herself in nature and experience the vitality of young people.

How she loved the park before the crowds arrived, loved to feel the energy of designer-clad runners sprinting single file along the path. She slowed her pace to admire the movements of a young couple practicing Yoga, and then turned her attention to four graceful Tai Chi dancers easing slowly into ancient postures.

She purposely avoided the eyes of the `homeless' people meandering on the grass, and turned away from the sad-eyed, derelict men as they emerged from burrows in the cliffs to face another day of roaming the streets and scavenging for food.

Lillian couldn't bear to look at them so she hastened on.

The warm sun had already burned off the marine layer and the sky was clear, allowing a spectacular view of Santa Monica

Bay and Catalina Island. A brisk wind whipped and crested the waves, icing the sea with fluffy white curls. Leaning on the cement railing, she focused on a curve of lacy foam embroidering the waterline, and was fascinated by the intricate patterns it created on the sand.

Moving on, she tuned in on the whir of a lawn mower and inhaled the sweet scent of newly-cut grass, mingled with the heady odor of jasmine. It permeated the air like a cloud of French perfume. How lovely, she thought.

The fragrance was interrupted by a sour stench as Lillian neared the white gazebo where many of the vagrants slept. Her first inclination was to hold her breath and hurry away so she wouldn't inhale the millions of germs she knew must emanate from such a place ... but something drew her to a tattered pile of clothes. She leaned forward. Suddenly, the whole raggedy bundle heaved and writhed!

Lillian jumped back, startled.

Cautiously, she watched it undulate again, as if inhabited by some strange reptilian creature. Eventually, an unkempt woman about her own age emerged from the pile and wriggled into sitting position. She looked surprised, as if she'd expected to wake up somewhere else. Then she caught Lillian's gaze, and for one long moment stared back, a terrible rage burning in her pewter eyes.

Lillian turned away, feeling not only horror at the venom in those eyes, but strangely enough, embarrassment, as if she'd caught the poor woman naked. When she glanced back, the animosity was gone, replaced by submission.

Lillian walked quickly away, determined to take a different route home.

Forty-five minutes later, as she fumbled with her key and finally unlocked her front door, Lillian heard the telephone ring inside the front hall.

She rushed into the house and grabbed the receiver. "Hello-o?"

"Hi, Mom."

Lillian warmed to the sound of her daughter's voice. "Hi, Priscilla."

"How are you, Mom?"

"I'm fine, dear. How are my darling grandchildren?"

"They're just great, keeping me busy as always."

She tried not to whine. "When am I going to see them?"

"Have you heard from Robin?"

This was Priscilla's way of transferring the heat. "No, I haven't talked to your brother since he left for Australia."

"That was three months ago."

"Yes, dear, I know. Priscilla?" She spoke hesitantly. "Could you and David bring the children to dinner next week?"

"I can't, Mom. Next week is little league play-offs. Nancy has a recital coming up. Every day is filled with something."

"How about the following week?"

What she got was another apology from Priscilla, and a whole lot of concern.

"No, I'm not angry with you dear," she repeated twice.

"The week after, I promise. And, Mom, I love you."

"Yes, I love you, too, dear."

The clang of the receiver echoed in the cavernous marble foyer, reminding Lillian of the emptiness of the stately old house. She walked slowly through the grand dining room containing her lifetime collection of antique furniture and dishes. It had been such a joyful place when her husband, Edward, was alive and Priscilla and Robin were still home. A small tear formed in the corner of her eye.

The terrible truth about getting old, Lillian thought, is few of your friends make it, and you're left to do it all alone. She could count on one hand those who were still alive, and most of them were unable to leave their house. Gazing around the empty kitchen, she asked herself, "Now, what will I do all day?"

At four o'clock that afternoon, unable to concentrate, Lillian put down her book. Try as she might, she couldn't get the old woman out of her mind. Maybe she was still in the park. She had to find out.

She found her at the gazebo sitting between a sleazy young man with dirty dreadlocks and a full-bellied blonde woman who was holding a sign which read, "HUNGRY, HOMELESS, and PREGNANT."

The man wore a soldier hat, and his sign stated, "HUNGRY, HOMELESS, VIETNAM VET".

She dropped a five-dollar-bill in each can, and handed ten to the old lady. Her conscience appeased, Lillian went home.

Next morning she was back at the latticed bower.

The old woman had just awakened. Lillian donated another ten dollars. The indigent nodded as if she'd expected it.

Every day Lillian found herself more and more obsessed with the homeless woman's welfare. Every morning she gave her money, and every night she worried about her sleeping in the cold, at the mercy of the elements and any and all madmen wandering the streets.

On Saturday, she was shocked to read in the newspaper that the police had chased all the transients out of the area. Unsure which was worse, getting thrown in jail or being left on the street, she rushed to the park. The woman was nowhere to be seen.

For a moment Lillian panicked. Then, to be truthful, she felt almost relieved and headed home. Rounding the corner of her street she saw her—a dark, formidable crow in an oversized brown dress and dirty black shawl, sifting through the trash.

Approaching her, Lillian asked. "Where will you go?"

The old woman raised her frenzied, pewter eyes and shrugged. "Dunno. Around, I guess." Pursing a crinkly mouth, slashed with orange lipstick, she adjusted the dark green turban to better cover her matted hair.

"I'm sure you'd like some food," Lillian said, impulsively.

"Mebbe." Although her eyes had lit up at the mention of food, the woman was cautious.

"Come with me," Lillian ordered. "I live down the block."

She helped to push the grocery cart full of the woman's trash-bagged belongings. For a moment she wondered what her yuppie neighbors must think, and then realized she didn't give a damn. For the first time in years Lillian felt useful.

One week later while sitting by the pool in the back yard, she asked her new friend. "Would you like cream or lemon?"

Rosie, bathed, powdered and dressed in a peach velvet robe, tittered. "Nothin' for me ma'am. I likes my tea black 'n strong." She fingered the pearl comb, holding back her straggly grey hair.

Lillian watched her with pleasure, and yes, gratitude. The last few days, since Rosie had been staying with her, she hadn't been lonely for a moment. It felt so good to have someone to look after. And now Donna was also living here, she even helped with the housework. The poor girl was six months pregnant and no one else would give her a job. And since Donna carried his baby, Mickey, the veteran, had moved in too and replaced the gardener.

Who knows, Lillian mused, if everything works out I might keep them on permanently? Now all she had to do was find a way to explain all this to her daughter.

By the time Priscilla called, two days later, she was ready.

"How are you, dear?" Not waiting for an answer, Lillian forged on. "I want you to know that I've taken your suggestion and hired a companion."

"Did I say that?"

"Yes, you did, dear. Don't you remember?"

"Who recommended her?"

"Oh, she has excellent references." Anticipating the next question, she continued. "And of course, I verified them."

"That sounds great, Mother. Can I come by tomorrow and meet her?"

Knowing when her daughter called her Mother, something serious was going on, she replied. "That sounds urgent, Priscilla."

"Yes, Mother, it is. How about four o'clock?"

"Yes dear, four o'clock will be just fine. I'll see you tomorrow, dear."

The next day when Priscilla arrived, the antique tea table was covered with a starched Battenberg tablecloth, tea was steeping in Lillian's best sterling service, and fine *Limoges* plates overflowed with tiny sandwiches and thick English scones.

Lillian introduced a very reserved "Rosalind" to her daughter.

Rosie wore a black skirt, and a creamy silk blouse pinned with Lillian's lavender jade brooch. She prepared to pour the tea. "I'm pleased to meet you Ma'am. Would ya like cream or lemon, Ma'am?"

While Lillian chatted with Priscilla about the children and Robin's trip to Australia, the old woman kept a discreet silence.

As Lillian knew she would, Priscilla soon got down to business.

After explaining how she must hurry home, since she and David had a dinner engagement, she began, "I'm so pleased you've found someone as dear as Rosalind." Priscilla beamed at Rosie.

"Now I won't feel guilty about going to Europe with David and the children. We'll be leaving in two days."

Completely taken aback by the announcement, Lillian asked. "But how long will you be gone?"

"At least three months. I know this is sudden, Mother, but the opportunity came, and it will be so educational for the children, we had to take it. We'll be moving from country to country. You know I'll call you often."

"Of course you will, dear. I'll miss you and the kids." *As if she ever saw them anyway.*

"You know I wouldn't dream of going, Mother, unless I was sure you were going to be all right."

Lillian nodded.

Priscilla rose and hugged her mother, kissing the air behind her left ear. Then, grasping Rosie's hand, she asked. "You will take care of Mother, won't you, Rosalind?"

Rosie nodded, and smiled.

Outside, Mickey was mowing the lawn and Lillian silently thanked God she'd convinced him to cut his hair.

Ignoring him, as if he didn't exist, Priscilla climbed into her black Jaguar. "I'll send you postcards from everywhere," she called, and sped away.

Two days later, Priscilla, David and the children left on their trip, leaving only a vague itinerary and no forwarding address. Lillian still hadn't heard from her son, Robin, but had little concern as she settled into a pleasant routine with her three house guests.

#

One afternoon, busy at her needlepoint in the sunlit living room, Lillian heard Rosie screaming orders to the others. "Donna, Mickey! Get the hell in here, we're gonna have us a little conference."

Within minutes they had all gathered in front of the couch.

Smiling, Lillian looked up, but the smile quickly froze on her face.

Rosie was staring at her with more rage in those pewter eyes than even that first day in the park. In fact, all three of them displayed such hatred, Lillian found it hard to believe they were the same nice people she'd taken into her home.

Rosie snarled. "Mickey, throw the bitch in the basement!"

Nobody moved.

Lillian looked around, bewildered. What was she talking about? Surely Rosie wasn't calling her a bitch. And this business about the basement, well … ?

Rosie screamed again. "I said throw her in the basement!"

Mickey grabbed Lillian and shoved her towards the cellar door in the hallway. At first she didn't react. But feeling Mickey's strong fingers bruising her arm, and his dirty nails digging into her flesh, she began to struggle. Donna moved in, grabbed her by the hair and yanked her across the room.

My God, she's going to scalp me. "Hey, stop it, you're hurting me," she cried. But her head burned so fiercely she found herself shuffling along in an effort to keep up with the woman.

When they reached the hallway Rosie called a halt. "Hold on a sec, Mickey!"

They all stopped, but Mickey kept a strong grip on her arms.

Lillian almost fainted so great was her fear of what was coming next. She turned to Rosie, expecting the worst.

Rosie waved Lillian's checkbook in the air. "First, get her to sign these here checks," then, as an afterthought. "Oh, and Donna, get those goddamn rings off of her fingers."

Donna twisted and pulled at the rings. Lillian fought back, clenching her fists in a desperate effort to hold on to her wedding ring. But it was her arthritis-swollen joints that helped in the end, or Donna would have gotten them all.

Rosie handed Mickey the checkbook and a pen.

Determined not to co-operate, Lillian pressed her lips together and refused to sign the blank checks — no matter how hard Mickey pinched her arms.

Rosie laughed. "She'll sign 'em in the morning. Then we're gonna have one helluva party 'round here."

To the sound of Rosie's cackling Mickey and Donna hauled Lillian down the stairs into the dank, dark basement.

Lillian couldn't fight at all. Her knees had turned to jelly, and she felt so weak she could barely stand up.

Scream, she told herself. Scream, you must scream.

But who would hear her? Edward was dead and the children?

Even when Mickey chained her to the gravity furnace in the cramped basement Lillian couldn't cry out, she couldn't even move. She simply curled up on the earthen floor and whimpered to the only One who could hear her. *Dear God, please help me.*

And then … something was on her legs. Something crawly.

Almost insane, she imagined all manner of vermin scurrying across her skin. She quickly came to life. Twisting and turning her body, she shook her head every which way. And spit. Again, she told herself. Spit. Keep them away from your mouth.

But the spiders and ants worked their way under her clothes and nested in every warm, moist spot they could find. Weakly, she tried to squirm them away, but nothing helped. Soon, her body was covered with itchy welts she couldn't even scratch.

Eventually, her arms bruised and sore from Mickey's abuse, her head throbbing from Donna's hair-pulling, and her whole body weary beyond belief, Lillian gave up. What was the use? She was surely going to die here all alone, with no one to help her. And then, a horrible thought. Her terror turned almost to madness.

Rats. Black, hairy rats. They were here, in this cellar. She knew it.

She'd seen them, set traps for them. "Dear God," she pleaded out loud. "Don't let me fall asleep."

Lillian tried to lie still and listen, but her heart was pounding too hard. Quiet, she told herself, try to be quiet. With a great deal of effort, she calmed down, and listened. Through the awesome silence came the dreaded sound.

Tiny razor-sharp claws were scratching the dirt. She could hear them.

Somewhere in the darkness of the cellar, they waited.

Vicious, hungry rats, lingering patiently in the shadows, ready to feast on her flesh the moment she lost consciousness.

"Why is this happening?" she wailed. "Why? Why?"

What was Rosie going to do? Kill her?

Whatever it was, Lillian prayed it would happen soon.

Hours later, she had no idea how many, every scrap of resistance was gone.

There was no hope. She was about to die, and it was only a matter of time.

Her eyelids drooped, and she drifted off. Suddenly, she was startled awake.

Something was on her face? She tried to knock it away. Couldn't move ... her hands were tied. Oh, God. What?

Pointy nails. Pain pierced her gums. Her mouth was filled with blood.

Something furry, grasping, clawing, trying to climb her face. A rat? No-o-o! But it had to be a ra-a-t! Spitting as hard as she could, Lillian tossed her head from side to side ... her mouth opened, and she heaved.

The rat loosened its grip, and fell to the floor.

That's when Lillian screamed, and she just wouldn't stop.

In an effort to shut her up they took her upstairs.

Anything was better than the basement so Lillian drank the cold tea, even though she guessed it was laced with drugs.

#

Time went by faster when she slept. She didn't know or care who gave her what anymore.

Their faces faded and oozed into the rose chintz wallpaper in her bedroom. Most of the time they left her alone, except when they put her on display in the yard, presumably for the neighbors' benefit. Both times Priscilla telephoned, Rosie held a knife to her throat. The rest of the time she slept.

Knowing little of her captors before her imprisonment, Lillian soon learned that Mickey had never been to Vietnam, and

Rosie couldn't get Social Security, because, in Mickey's words, "they don't give free money to old ho's from Ohio."

They fed her barely enough to keep her alive, and sometimes forgot to feed her at all, but every day they brought her something else to sign. It didn't make much difference to Lillian what she signed, or what she ate for that matter, as long as they didn't put her back in the basement.

Time went by, and she lived in a fog.

She tried, but couldn't remember where she was or what was happening.

Nothing mattered, except when she would get her next fix, and go back to sleep.

Late one night Lillian awoke with a start, sweating. A fiery pain seared her chest; her heart was pounding so hard her body shook. A crushing weight pressed hard on her ribs. That's when she saw him. Her husband was there … in the distance.

"Edward," she cried. "It's me, Lillian."

He called her name. She heard him. He moved toward her.

Closer, closer, Edward was there, at the foot of the bed.

Beckoning, he whispered. "Come, Lillian."

"Edward, it's really you."

He reached out his hand … Lillian took it.

#

One month later, Priscilla was screeching at the top of her voice. Donna stood at the door listening to her. *No wonder the old woman was whacky, this bitchy daughter of hers would send anyone 'round the bend.*

" … you haven't heard the end of this! I'll take you to the Supreme Court if I have to. You people had no right to bury my mother without my knowledge. You could have found me if you wanted to. And I want her jewelry back right now. And all the antiques that were here in this house. I don't care if you sold them. I want them back!"

"Come along Priscilla, this won't do any of us any good," David, said quietly, trying to guide his wife outside.

That's right, get her the hell outta here, thought Donna.

Robin, the brother, had already stormed out of the house, which was now Rosie's house, according to the new will Lillian had signed.

Donna moved aside as the enraged couple swept past her and slammed the front door. For a moment no one said a word.

Finally, Donna spoke. "Is that it?" she asked. "Everything's ours?"

"It sure is, honey chil'. Ha! Ha! Ha!" Mickey roared, and hopped gleefully around the room.

"Waddya mean, ours?" Rosie sneered, a fierce gleam in her eyes. "Everything's mine, all mine. I'm the one as found her!"

Mickey's dance came to an abrupt halt as he stared at the old woman. "But Rosie, Donna's your own daughter."

Breathing heavily, Donna rolled her pregnant body off the couch and lumbered to her feet. Her eyes seething with contempt, she glared at her mother in stony silence. Then, with a cruel smile, she turned to Mickey and growled. "Throw the bitch in the basement! Oh, and make sure she signs them there checks on the table. And be sure you take them goddamn rings off her fingers and give 'em to me."

Just as he had done with Lillian weeks before, Mickey dragged old Rosie, kicking and screaming, to the basement door and dumped her, unceremoniously, down the concrete stairs.

He smiled, wickedly, at the sudden silence, and walked back to the living room, rubbing his hands. "She'll do as she's told by tomorrow."

Donna smiled and leaned back into the plush velvet couch.

She placed both hands on her corpulent belly and felt the child she was almost ready to deliver. Thump, thump, thump. The baby kicked, wildly.

And just for a moment ... one brief uncertain moment ... Donna wondered.

THE END

* Mary Firmin was Vice President of a large Real Estate firm in Santa Monica, Ca. and previously worked for many years at Arthur Murray Dance Studios in Hamilton and Toronto, Ontario. In later years she studied Writing at UCLA, belonged to a private workshop given by her mentor, and attended many writing conferences and seminars. She has written two books, one as yet unpublished, Voodoo Fire, a screenplay, Rhumba, and lots of short stories. Her novel, DEADLY PLEASURES, was the winner of Reader's Favorite Internatioal Book Contest in the mystery/thriller category. It received rave reviews from Kirkus, Clarion and many readers. Blueink Review called it "Sex and the City meets James Patterson." She presently lives in Rancho Mirage, Ca, and is hard at work on DEADLY SECRETS.

22

She was a child, lost and pathetic. What had sent her out into the night alone and too afraid to speak?

Sowing on the Mountain
Lyn McConchie

I always liked being on the police force in Wellington. In many ways being on one beat for a long time is like working in a small town. I know a lot of people around here, they talk to me and sometimes they tell me important things. It helps that I'm distantly related to Granny Ngaire and Patti Paiwai too. Everyone knows them around here, maybe that's why the police force has kept me on this beat. I don't get promoted but that's okay. I like it where I am and my bosses like me there too, so no one has any problems.

And what I do reminds me of the saying that the more things change, the more they stay the same. I started walking a beat in the city when I was twenty-one and just out of police training school, then they put us into cars for years, and now in 1997 we're back walking a beat again, because that's how the public likes it.

So my partner and I were walking up by the old Bolton Street cemetery around two a.m. on a weeknight when everything was dark and quiet. I was thinking about the latest rash of vandalism in my area—probably ring-led by the Thompson boys who lived up Tinakori Road way and were real little nuisances—when I caught sight of the small figure trudging down the road towards me. Ten futile minutes later I was on my radio to dispatch.

"Constable 147 Olsen reporting. My partner and I have found a child in the street, female, about eleven. She's in nightclothes with bare feet and she's freezing."

"Dispatch to Constable Olsen. Can she tell you who she is?"

"I've tried, dispatch. She could be in shock. She's shivering very badly and seems unable to talk."

"I'll have a car with you in a couple of minutes. Take her to the hospital. I'll have them drop you back once she's hospitalised, and you and your partner can look around the area. Do you think she's come far?"

"We're not sure. She looks healthy enough although she's very thin and she seems to have a lot of bruising on her arms. I guess she could have walked quite a way."

"Ask the doctor if he can get an address from her."

"Will do."

#

"She was just walking down the street towards the cenotaph, Doctor. I spoke to her, she turned to look at us and then passed out on the pavement. It was just briefly, though, as she was already trying to sit up when I kneeled down beside her."

"But she hasn't spoken?"

"Not a word. Dispatch said we should bring her here and have her checked out. She's so cold I thought she could be in shock for some reason, what with her not talking either."

"She is cold, but it's freezing outside, it could just be that— however shock is always possible. I am able to tell you one thing right now though, Bob. I think it probable someone's been beating her over a period of time. These bruises of hers tell a fairly clear tale; some are very recent, others are a few days old, and there are others that are nearly gone—they'd be about a week to a week and a half old. I'll get her into a cubicle with a nurse and take a proper look once you've gone."

#

The Doctor

Bob went out to see what he could discover, and I got the girl into a cubicle. I knew it would take time to examine her properly, and it did. In the end we had no choice but to sedate her so I could make a proper physical examination. I was disgusted at what I found—although I have to say I wasn't greatly surprised.

What had been done to her isn't unusual in a major city. Although even in small towns this sort of thing goes on. I've worked in small towns and in cities and the fact is it's more likely to go on in small towns without anyone laying a complaint, because that's where people know each other and are reluctant to tell tales.

#

"Constable 147 Olsen to dispatch, we've spotted a house nearly a kilometer from where we found the girl, but I'm fairly sure this is where she's come from."

I was quite sure this was where she'd come from, I remembered her now.

"The front door's been left wide open and all the lights are on. I know the occupants, and they'll make a legal fuss if I go in without a warrant, so should we enter?"

"Constable 147, in view of the circumstances you are cleared to enter the house to check status."

I guessed what I'd find as soon as I approached the front door. The smell told me. I sent my partner to check around the outside of the house to see if there were any signs of a break-in. I entered the hall, looked in the rooms that opened off the passage all the way from the front of the house to the kitchen at the back. I swore, returned through the place, and stepped outside into the clean air on the front porch to phone back.

"Dispatch, there's four bodies in the house. I knew them as the occupants, one adult male in his forties, one adult female around the same age, and two young boys. I'd say they all died in their beds, but there's vomit in the hall by the front door. This has to be where the girl came from. I remember her now and she lived here."

"I have detectives on the way as of right now, Bob. Hand the scene over to them once they arrive, file your reports and go off shift."

"Thanks, dispatch. Constable 147 Olsen out."

One thing about our discovery in the house ... I could stop worrying about the current vandalism in this part of the city. I wasn't happy about how it had been stopped, but I was pleased that it had. I didn't appreciate seeing the cenotaph lions wearing black felt-tip mustaches all the time—and I suspected they didn't like it much either.

#

"I'm Detective Ainsley, Madam. What can you tell me about the Thompsons, the family two doors down on your right?"

"Nothing much, Detective. They're religious although you'd never know it from the way their boys behave. I think they adopted his dead sister's daughter about three years ago."

#

"I'm Detective Haddan, sir, what can you tell me about the Thompsons, the family next door to you on the left?"

"Why?"

"There's been an incident, sir. They're dead, everyone but the little girl. What can you tell me about them?"

"Malcolm, who is it?"

"The police, dear. They say the Thompsons have had an accident and they're all dead but the girl."

"It's no more than God's judgment on them."

"Why do you say that, madam?"

"I don't like to speak ill of the dead, but they ill-treated that poor child. She was always working, some jobs were far too heavy for a girl of that age, and he used to hit her far too often. I saw him do it several times."

"Did you ever report this abuse?"

"I couldn't do that, Detective, but I let him see that I knew. I stared him right in the eye last time I saw him by his front gate, and I know he got the message."

"How was that, madam?"

"He looked guilty and went hurrying indoors again, that's how."

#

"I'm Detective Ainsley, Madam. Is your husband in?"

"John's in Auckland for several days on business, Detective. Can I help?"

"What can you tell me about the Thompsons, the family next door to you on the right?"

"What's happened?"

"There's been an unfortunate incident, madam. They're all dead but the little girl."

"Poor child. I'm sure that's a blessing in disguise for her."

"Why is that, madam?"

"Well, the Thompsons used to punish her a lot—and when I say "punish," I mean that they beat her and that may not have been all. I mentioned it to him once and he said "spare the rod and spoil the child" and gave me a very nasty look. I asked her to help me move a couple of pieces of my furniture a while back and when we'd finished I gave her afternoon tea. She was polite, but, Detective—she ate as if she hadn't had a decent meal in days. I'm sure she was starving and that isn't right.

"I didn't say anything to the Thompsons at the time, but I saw her adopted mother at the shops a week after that and I just said that Pam seemed to be very thin. Mrs. Thompson gave me a nasty look, said something about fasting and repentance being good for the soul and walked away. I'm afraid the Thompsons really may not have treated the child very kindly."

"Did you tell anyone?"

"Like who?"

"Well … Social Welfare or us, madam?"

"Oh, I couldn't do that. It wasn't really any of my business and neighbors have to get on, don't they."

\#

The Police Commander

"Olsen, check with Doctor Ross at the hospital. He says they have an interim medical report on the child's physical condition."

"Yes, sir."

I love my city, but there are times when the "don't see and don't want to see" attitude of people angers me. I'd heard about the interviews and what had been said in them from the detectives. That poor kid. Half the people in her street knew she was being beaten and maybe starved on a regular basis and no one did anything about it. No, of course not. They might have to testify in court—still worse, if they talked someone might talk about the testifier's own sins and that would never do.

\#

The Cop

"What can you tell us about the kid, Colin? What about the bruising on her arms and legs that I noticed?"

Colin Ross is a good doctor, he likes kids and they mostly trust him on sight. He looked angry as he glanced at a report and started talking.

"She's suffered long-term abuse. She's been regularly beaten. She's also been raped repeatedly and she is definitely malnourished. In my professional opinion she's been underfed, overworked, and badly abused for two or three years. She is also suffering quite mildly from some form of poisoning."

I looked up at him sharply at that. "What sort of poisoning? Could she have taken something herself?"

"It wouldn't be surprising if she had." Colin told me bitterly. "Life must have been hell on earth for her. Why didn't anyone notice? What do the neighbors say?"

"That the girl seemed to be overworked and hit a lot but they didn't want to get involved. I can see why, I knew Thompson, and in my opinion he was a nasty piece of work. All piety and biblical quotes, but using them to justify whatever he wanted."

"Wonderful. It reminds me of the saying that "the more I see of people the more I love my dog.""

"I know," I told him. "Is she talking yet"

"A little. I've been told her family were found dead. Under the circumstances the shock of her finding them when some poison had already weakened her could well have produced traumatic amnesia. She might never remember, she certainly doesn't appear to recall anything from the time she went to bed until the time she found herself standing on the street looking at two policemen."

"Could a hypnotherapist help?"

"Possibly, but it's unlikely Social Welfare would agree—to the experiment or to the expense. They have a foster home arranged for her to go to as soon as she can be discharged. At least there may be money for her once she's twenty-one. I presume that as the only surviving member, she'll inherit whatever the family owned?"

"I hear she was adopted, but yeah, I guess so. Under adoption laws it counts as if she's a natural daughter and so far as I know the Thompsons didn't have any relatives who'd be closer than this girl."

"Well, let me know if there's anything more I can do," Colin offered. "I imagine the postmortems on her family will be interesting."

#

The Police Commander

"Ainsley, you'll have to interview everyone in the Thompson case again."

"Why, sir?" I was annoyed about that. I'd done a comprehensive job the first time, talked to almost everyone in several blocks and now he wanted me to go over the interviews again?

"The postmortem reports have just come in and they say that they'd all ingested weed-killer. One of the nicotine-based poisons with a very high concentration. The pathologist has identified it as Pestaway, That's a powder concentrate intended to be diluted at a teaspoonful per forty liters of water. It gets sprayed on fruit trees I'm told."

"I see, sir. Yes, I'll talk to all the neighbors again."

I would, although I didn't think they've have much more to tell me.

#

The Detective

"Is your husband home now, Madam? He was out when I called three days ago"

"Yes, he got back from Auckland last night, I'll just call him.

"John? There's a policeman wants to speak to you about the Thompsons."

"Detective Ainsley, sir. You'll have heard about your neighbors?"

"Yes, I heard. It's a terrible thing. I'm told they were poisoned?"

"That's unfortunately true, sir. They seem to have eaten or drunk weed-killer in some way."

The Thompsons neighbor looked at me and his mouth fell open in shock. "Oh, my God, I told him. I warned the fool!"

Ah ha, it looked as if I might have been wrong about further interviews being a waste of time. There had been a bit more to find out after all.

"Sir? What did you warn him about?"

"He was chatting to me over the fence last week while he made up the spray for his fruit trees. He turned around without looking and knelt on the plastic bag. It split so he went and got an empty container from the kitchen and he put the remaining spray powder in that."

"What sort of container, sir?" Could this be the explanation?

"He had a sweet tooth, you know, old Thompson did. His wife used to keep icing sugar in the kitchen in one of those shaker containers with holes in the lid. She sprinkled it on half the desserts they ate. I know because my wife had tea there a couple of times in weekends when Thompson was home. She and Mrs. Thompson were on a school committee together for a term last year."

It looked as if it was the explanation. That'd be good. It would mean we could stop interviewing and tell the coroner to hold the inquest.

"I saw what he was doing and I said to him that it wasn't a good idea putting weed-killer in a food container. He said he'd label it and then he gave me a very nasty sort of 'mind your own business look' so I did. You know, Detective, he wasn't the sort of man who appreciated advice from anyone—but I really should have said more about it."

"I don't see what more you could have done, sir. You could hardly insist. It was his decision."

"Yes, but I still feel I should have done something. If I had maybe they wouldn't all be dead."

#

The neighbor
I did feel guilty, that was true, but only a little bit. As a neighbor, Thompson had been a complete pain in the neck, and I'd loathed the way they'd treated their niece. She always seemed to be a nice, polite little girl, if terrified of Thompson and his wife. My wife hadn't liked them any better than I did, and she said she was delighted when Mrs Thompson wasn't nominated for the PTA the next term.

Thompson hadn't exactly been chatting to me either. It had been one of his endless diatribes about how I should trim my trees better, cut my lawn more often, and paint the dividing fence on my side to improve the value of his property. And I hadn't been nearly as definite about the dangers of weed-poison in a food container as I'd suggested to the detective. In fact, I'd carefully said just enough to put Thompson's back up. He was a man who liked everything his own way, and he absolutely hated to be told anything.

When I saw him use the icing-sugar container to put the Pestaway powder in, I must admit that it just crossed my mind how very convenient it would be if his wife made a mistake with it and we got new neighbors. None of the family—apart from the girl, and my wife said she was positive the child never got anything decent to eat and certainly not sweet desserts—would be missed by anyone in the area.

Mrs Thompson was a spiteful piece of work who loved making trouble on any committee to which she belonged, and the boys were complete hooligans in the making. If the police didn't know who was responsible for the latest outbreak of graffiti around the cenotaph and the cemetery, I did. I also knew better than to say anything to the police—even Bob Olsen—about that.

Friends of mine who lived in the next street had once complained about the Thompson boys' depredations to their father, and when that hadn't worked, they'd mentioned it to the police as an official complaint. That week their garden shed burned down and nearly took their house and the garage with it. We could all guess who had been responsible for that, but this time the silence was deafening.

It would, I thought with some satisfaction, be a much more friendly area with the Thompsons gone. And the girl had survived too, which eased any guilt I might have felt about the other four.

#

"All right, Ainsley, where are we with the Thompson case?"

I'd been working on it for ten days after we found that the cause of the deaths had been poison—along with everything else I had to do. I'd talked to Bob Olsen who knew the family and knew just about everyone else in the area as well. He'd not been able to suggest any possibilities other than what I was about to tell my boss.

"I think the coroner is going to bring it in as death by misadventure, sir. We've been all over the crime scene several times, talked to all the neighbours, and it seems to have happened like this. Thompson made up the Pestaway powder as spray for his fruit trees a number of times. The last time he used the powder he knelt on the bag and it split. There was only a small amount of the Pestaway left so he put it in one of those icing-sugar containers that have holes in the lid so you can sprinkle the contents on desserts. His next door neighbor has told us he saw the whole thing and admits he warned Thompson about it. He's made an official statement on that."

247

"How exactly did they ingest the powder?"

"They had sponge cake with fruit salad for dessert. The neighbor's wife has given us a statement saying that she ate with them on a number of occasions last year when she and the wife were on the same committee. She says that Thompson indulged heavily in sweet foods and they all liked to sprinkle icing sugar on any suitable dessert.

"Thompson told his neighbor that for safety he would label the icing-sugar container that he used for the Pestaway and at first we thought he hadn't done that as he said he would. Then we found the label under the stove and the container shows signs that it did have an additional label originally. They keep their sugar, icing-sugar, and salt in canisters on a shelf above and to one side of the stove.

"It looks as if steam from the kettle may have steamed off the label Thompson used, and it landed under the stove, probably from a draft when the back door was opened. We checked that and it's all possible, the glue on the label he'd used was from an old box of them and the gum was perished. The draught when the door is opened can blow a label—if it's on the floor below the shelf—under the stove.

"I can't believe that the man was so stupid, but there's only his fingerprints and his wife's on that container. And we have the neighbor's evidence that gives us a clear and believable story of why the poison was in the container where it was found.

"The child has talked a little. She still doesn't remember anything at all from that night, but it appears that the Thompsons were in the habit of starving her in punishment for things they saw as sins. Sometimes she was deprived of three or four meals in a row. As a result she often unobtrusively ate any minor amounts of leftovers from their plates before she washed them, so she would have ingested a tiny amount of the Pestaway too. Enough to make her vomit and become faint and disoriented, but that was all."

"And you're happy with the coroner's decision."

"Yes, sir." I certainly was. I couldn't find any evidence the deaths had been other than accidental, caused by Thompson's own stupidity. And I'd seen the doctor's report on the way the Thompsons had behaved toward their niece. I thought that there was a special place in hell for people who treated a child that way. I hoped the Thompsons had had a taste of where they were going before they died and from what I'd heard from Doctor Ross of Pestaway's symptoms, they probably would have.

"Close the case then. I hope the foster parents they found for that kid treat her well. I saw the doctor's report and she deserves it."

"Yes, sir!" I agreed.

#

Years Later—the woman who adopted the child
"There's enough money for you to do what you want to, darling. Now you're eighteen all of it is yours."

"I know, Mum, don't worry. I plan to use some of it to get my law degree and the rest can stay in the bank. I'll use it for the deposit to start a practice of my own eventually."

"That's my sensible girl."

I smiled at my foster daughter. She was most of my world these days. My husband had died of a sudden heart attack last year and it was Pam who had seen to everything for me, Pam who'd been my support. I remembered the skinny, bruised, silent child we'd taken in and how, very slowly over the years, she had become the kind-hearted, friendly, and socially conscious young woman that she was now.

She'd known for some years that she'd inherit money from her dead family, but she'd never been foolish about that. She'd worked very hard, gained her High School qualifications, then left to work at the local lawyer's office for a year and save her salary before going on to university. Mr. Bycroft specialised in Family

Court problems and Pam turned out to have a talent for dealing with frightened or traumatized people. Now the money from her uncle was released to her she planned to get her degree and work for Mr. Bycroft for a few years before striking out on her own.

Mr. Bycroft was becoming overworked. Once Pam had her degree she could work with him in Thorndon and consider setting up on her own or buying into a partnership with him once she had more experience. She was a good and loving child to me, so kind and gentle. It was a miracle she'd turned out that way after the years she'd suffered at the Thompsons' hands. It was God's mercy that she could remember little from the time they'd had her and nothing at all of the night they died.

"Mum? I have to go out for the evening. I promised Di I'd try on my bridesmaid's dress. You'll be okay on your own? What are you looking so serious about?"

"I was just remembering how you came to us, darling. Yes, go and try on the frock, I'll be fine. Have you had a reply from your application to the University? It's fortunate you have the money, I couldn't have managed to send you otherwise, not with it being so expensive these days."

"I know, Mum. Isn't it lucky you don't have to try? Yes, I had the letter of acceptance this afternoon. I meant to tell you. And I've decided I'm going to use a bit of my inheritance when I get it next month to trade in my old car and buy a better one before I start at the university."

#

Years later—The adopted child

I sat on the bed remembering how I'd inherited the money that would give me the life I wanted where I could speak for the powerless ones, the children who might suffer as I had. I recalled the Thompsons' increasing brutality once I was safely in their hands. Even the boys had enjoyed tormenting me and had been permitted to do so without restraint. I remembered my pain and

250

terror, the deliberate blindness of the neighbors and, very slowly, my lips peeled back from my teeth in the sort of smile my adoptive mother would never see.

Silence was safest, and from the beginning I'd made everyone believe I remembered nothing at all of that night. Some of what I remembered I knew to have been impossible, but I did remember it and I relished everything that I recalled.

I'd prayed with all my heart and strength to God to help me and he'd done nothing. So I'd prayed to anything I thought might hear me, even to the cenotaph lions towards the end. I knew my brothers made fun of them, painting moustaches on them with felt-tip, and I'd heard some odd stories about the lions from one of the Paiwai kids at school in my three years living in the area. So I prayed and someone or something may have answered.

I had come out of my bedroom around midnight that night, feeling wretchedly sick myself—as I'd expected—but too intent on other things to really notice. I watched those who'd brutalized me for the past three years writhe and die, in too much agony to even scream for help. They could only gasp hoarsely and whimper, eyes bulging, hands outstretched imploringly to me for the aid I was happily refusing.

It had taken almost two hours for them to die and for all that time I'd watched what happened and let them see me standing there, enjoying their pain as they had enjoyed mine. After that I'd walked off into the night leaving the door open and all the lights blazing. Something inside my head whispered that a child wouldn't remember to turn off lights or shut doors. I walked until someone found me … and my life was changed.

It wasn't even as if I'd done anything to cause their agony, not really. He'd been the one stupid enough to put his poison in a food container; I'd only overheard the man next door warning him about it. He'd been the one to use an old label and she always boiled the kettle too long. I'd just changed the containers over, or at least I think I did. The label fell off when I did that and went fluttering under the stove in the draught from the half-open kitchen door. He dumped the usual heavy sprinkling of icing-sugar on his jam-sponge , as did the other greedy pigs on their own plates of the dessert.

I was never allowed anything nice to eat, and often enough I wasn't fed at all. This time I licked his plate carefully, but only a couple of times before I washed up. I was too young to know just how much of a risk I was taking but it had worked. Their deaths were brought in as death by misadventure as the coroner directed.

It was true; it was just their misadventure that he'd done most of it to himself and his family. It had been an act of God as their minister had claimed at their funerals. And maybe it truly was a god of some sort because something had looked out for me on that night when I decided I'd rather risk death than stay alive with them.

Fingerprints? There weren't any of those, I think because it was freezing at 3 a.m. so I must have been wearing woolly gloves as I sneaked into the kitchen and changed the position of the tins on the shelf. Yes, I'm almost sure that has to be why there were no fingerprints.

I do have a sort of odd memory of that night where I never touched the containers, where they changed over as I watched them move by themselves. The label fluttering to the ground and under the stove in the draught as the bolted kitchen door swung half open and shut silently again.

That has to be wrong of course. I'm remembering some dream I once had. Things like that don't really happen. I was only eleven, and I never knew about fingerprints at the time, and it was cold so I wore gloves. I'm sure that's the reason there were no fingerprints.

I do remember that at the funeral we sang the hymn that goes, "Sowing on the mountain, reaping in the valley, you're going to reap just what you sow." I guess in the end, whoever or whatever was responsible for their deaths, me or something else, they reaped everything they'd sown—with generous interest!

❧❦❧❦❧

THE END

* Lyn McConchie shares her 19th century farmhouse with her Ocicat Thunder and 7,527 books. She'd been professionally writing and selling for 23 years and has 29 books published and over 250 stories. her latest book was *Rustic (And Rusted) Daze*, seventh in her humorous non-fiction series from Avalook Publications in Australia. Lyn's blog and site are at www.lynmcconchie.com

23
Love's Second Law of Thermodynamics: it takes two
to deteriorate.

Tangled in the Net of Ruin
Minna van der Pfaltz

One day, two people fell in love. It was not a sudden, romantic falling in love, for they had known each other for some time. They lived in the same village. But one day they realized they were in love. Once they discovered this, they went to her parents.

Her parents tried to dissuade her from making this match. "It will be a mistake," they said. But their daughter persisted. The boy bowed low and said all the appropriate things in order to win their good graces. There were problems, however, that made her parents shy away from sanctioning the marriage.

Finally, the girl convinced her parents. She was, after all, not a child any more. So, they acquiesced, saying, "There's no help for it." But they had conditions. He must leave the village and make his way in the world. Even though this meant the lovers would have to be parted, they agreed. After all, they were in love and love would outlast any separation.

On the day of his departure, the lovers walked to the bridge at the edge of town. He carried two bags with him. At the top of the arc of the bridge, they stopped. This was as far as she could go with him, according to her parents. They turned to face each other. They held hands for awhile and then they kissed. They stood apart and were silent a moment.

He handed her one of his bags.

"What is this?" she asked.

"This is my flower. The grammar of my craft. It is a Book of Masks and a Book of Dance. You must keep them for me."

"I will hold these against your return."

"Without them I am a man with no direction."

"You know they will be safe with me. Here is my gift to you."

She took from her pocket a large case.

"You cannot give this to me."

She stepped back so he could not return her present.

"This is too precious." He held it out to her. "This is the family heirloom. You are the last in line."

She put her hands behind her back.

He sighed and took the case to his heart.

There was nothing for it.

They vowed to meet again in one year to assess their fortunes.

Each year, for many years, they met on the bridge. She showed him his books. He did not have good news for her but she gave him a new gift each time.

But then came their fateful meeting.

"My parents have forbidden us to meet again. This must be our last assignation."

"And my craft?"

She handed him the bag.

"There's only one Book in here! Where is my learning? Where is my book of Dance?"

She was silent a moment. "You must be mistaken. There was ever only this one volume."

"No! There were two."

"Perhaps your memory is bad." She looked down at the wooden planks of the bridge and stepped away from him. "It is not so. There was only this one teaching."

"You're wrong."

"I have no gift to give you. My parents have forbidden it."

"But—"

"I cannot stay. They are waiting at the door for me."

"Next year, then."

"I cannot. It is forbidden."

He watched her run down the bridge and into the village. Her betrayal left his shoulders heavy and his feet stupid.

At her house, her parents were waiting for her. They questioned her before they let her into the house. They took the bag with its single Book from her. They smiled secretly.

"We will throw this one on the fire, too, for retribution. He has stolen for the last time from us. You know we are right. You will not be so headstrong now."

She went to her rooms and sat down on her veranda looking out over the garden with its dried-up pond and untrimmed bushes. There were no blooming flowers and no scents.

Then, one day, her lover returned. It seems he had made his fortune. Her parents were very shocked and sent him to her. She still sat as she had so many years before. The garden was overgrown with weeds. The pond was nowhere to be seen in the tangled mess.

"I am surprised to see you," she said.

"I told you I'd come back."

"Then you have come to kill me."

"I have not."

"You have, for I have betrayed you."

"You have waited for me."

"Yes. And I have waited for my death."

"You won't die. I'm here now. I've fulfilled my bargain. We can marry now."

"It is not to be. My parents imposed on me. They took your Books and burned them."

He did not say anything.

"I did not stop them. They said you were a thief and a vagabond. This is how they have paid you back for your promises and the gifts I gave you. What could I do? I had given you all I had but you had not become successful. They were angry and I am only their daughter."

He took a large case from his pocket and placed it before her. Then he went to see her parents. Standing before them in the main room of the house, he opened his pants and urinated on the floor.

#

At the centre point of the arcing bridge, he jumped into the river and drowned himself.

From that day forth, the bridge was called Love's Ending Bridge. There was a sign marking the spot of his jump. A little inscription explained that this was the only place in the land where a lovers' suicide had included only one person. Often, young lovers would come to this bridge and touch the balustrade in hopes of gaining luck in their endeavor.

It is not known what happened to the girl. But it is rumored that she turned into a plum tree to bloom in deepest winter and bear no fruit.

THE END

* Minna van der Pfaltz was born into a Walloon-speaking Belgian family and now makes her home in French Glen, OR, because she has to have an address, that is, belong (to) some place. Her favorite haunt is Whorehouse Meadows at the foot of the Steen Mountains.

24

Most people, especially cops, know that the past loves to sneak up
and bite you...

A Fair Cop
Megan Johns

Barbara gazed at the blanket of rust-coloured ivy draping the
mellow Cotswold stone.

"It looks nice," she concluded with a tight smile.

"Nice?" Her husband threw a look over the old building and
grimaced. "Not the word I would use. More like dilapidated. And
it's hardly a prime location for a restaurant. We're in the middle of
nowhere."

His voice sounded odd, almost disturbed. She shot him a
sidelong look, but he evaded her gaze. Fingering back a stray hair,
she straightened her shoulders.

"People will travel miles for a top class restaurant once word
gets around."

Grenville cast an eye over the deserted road and grunted,
"These twisty lanes are lethal at the best of times. And they're even
worse after dark. A drink and a momentary lapse of concentration
is all it takes..."

"Bundle of fun tonight, aren't you? You're always picking
fault; the location will be a great selling point, you'll see. People
will flock here in droves once Justin's built up a reputation."

Ignoring her husband's, "And that can take years," she
pressed the buzzer with a sudden determination.

It was a characteristic Grenville still found daunting, despite their many years of marriage, and he fell into silence. He watched his wife push her nose against a frosted window pane.

"I can see someone moving around inside."

"Why the hell don't they open the door? It's freezing out here," he complained.

At that moment, the door swung open. A waiter stood in its frame. He twitched a grin, though his eyes, Barbara noted, were sombre.

"We're here for the launch. Actually, we're the proprietor's parents," she asserted.

"He's very busy. Follow me. *I'll* look after you." The man didn't sound welcoming, but his tone was commanding and they followed without argument. The pace was so brisk they struggled to keep up. As they scuttled past the dining room, Barbara craned her neck to catch a glimpse of the tables draped in vivid pink cloths.

"Are we the first to arrive?" she addressed the waiter's back.

"Yes." He responded without turning.

Rather curt, she thought. Still they forged on down a long corridor lined with faded damask wallpaper stained by acrid swathes of mould. Snatching a handkerchief to cover her mouth, Barbara gagged at the stench.

At the far end, a lone door of varnished wood that had blackened with age confronted them. The waiter flung it open with a flourish of the wrist. "The snug."

Barbara regarded the sparse room that looked anything but snug with growing scepticism.

"I'll fetch you a drink while you wait."

She threw the waiter an up-and-down look. Despite the standard black and white attire, his spiky bleached hair and yellow bow tie didn't gel. Surely Justin would demand higher standards of his staff.

Grenville, however, seemed to have rallied and was rubbing his hands at the mention of a drink.

"How long do we have to wait in here?" Determined not to let the waiter off the hook lightly, Barbara made a show of dusting the seat of the old, worn sofa before perching on the edge.

"Until we're ready for you."

"Do we know you?" Grenville was studying the waiter closely. "Never forget a face."

"I'm Mark," he said with a sniff. "We met once, but you were drunk."

Clenching his fists at the waiter's impudence, Grenville inhaled a ragged breath and tried to remember. From a corner of his eye, he saw Barbara screw her face into a knot, looking more disdainful by the minute.

"It's so shabby in here. Look, there isn't even a light shade. And it's cold." As if to prove it, she shivered.

"A little snifter will soon warm you up." The waiter threw the remark over his shoulder as he withdrew.

"Who the hell *is* he?" Grenville hissed.

"How should I know?" Barbara snapped. "He must be a friend of Justin's."

"But what's he *doing* here?"

"I'm acting as maître d'hôtel." The speed with which the young man re-appeared brandishing a cocktail shaker took them both by surprise.

"Oh." Barbara's tone was tart as she recalled how her offers to help her son had been declined. She forced a measured response, "That's nice. I'm sure you need all the help you can get for the opening night."

"How the hell…" Grenville's gaze flitted from the waiter to the door.

Shaking the mixer like a sole maraca, the waiter gyrated his hips in tune to the rhythm.

"Why are you so early?" he asked.

"Early?" Barbara repeated. "We're bang on time."

"Six o'clock," her husband concurred with a grunt. "Ridiculous time for dinner, if you ask me."

"But the invitation was for eight."

Was that a grin the boy was stifling? Grenville battled with an urge to wipe it off his face. Frowning deeply, he glared at his wife. "I specifically checked the calendar and it said six."

"Don't look at me like that! It was your handwriting." Yanking her handbag on to her lap, she delved inside and produced her diary. "There! Eight o'clock. It says so clearly in here." She pushed it under his nose. "Six was supposed to be your dental appointment."

Rubbing a hand over his cheek, he suddenly remembered his aching molar.

She watched the waiter place two cocktail glasses on the small table in front of them and stared at the green liquid with its chunks of tropical fruit skewered by paper umbrellas. Her gaze lifted to scrutinise him. His visible amusement irritated her. Was that diamond earring in his right lobe appropriate for a maître d'hôtel of a high class establishment?

"One of my special cocktails," he informed her. "I call them bull's eyes. Hit the spot every time." With a little snicker, he left.

They both eyed the drinks.

"It's green!" Grenville hissed.

"I can see that."

"What the hell is it?"

"Oh, just be quiet and drink it."

"S'pose it might dull the pain…" Snatching the glass, he downed the contents in one.

"*Really*! You're supposed to savour a cocktail." Raising her glass, Barbara took a delicate sip as if demonstrating to a child correct social manners. The liquid hit the back of her throat, making her splutter uncontrollably.

"Serves you right."

Ignoring his derisive snort, she put her glass down and turned her attention to inspecting the room.

Unsightly strips of paper peeled off the walls. Even the rug that had been thrown over the uneven floorboards was threadbare. She tried to imagine a fire burning in the Franklin stove, but she doubted anything could counter the inhospitable feel. The crazed mirror above the hearth caught her attention. She studied the itinerant pattern, mesmerised. Her eyes drifted out of focus until illusory shapes began to form as if from the squiggles of a magic eye picture. Rows and rows of faces appeared. She shook herself. It *was* just an illusion, wasn't it? She felt uneasy.

"Why do we have to sit in this horrible room? It looked much better in the dining area."

"Maybe this is Justin's living room. Nothing would surprise me."

She twitched her nose. "And what's that smell?"

"Damp I'd say."

"No… It's slightly scented."

"Probably his perfume."

"Don't you dare start one of your tirades," she glowered.

"Why not? Nobody would hear me from here. We're half way to Siberia."

"Not quite." They both jerked round to see the waiter was standing by the door.

Barbara glared at her husband.

"Drink up," the waiter tacked another mirthless smile on his lips, "or Justin will think I'm not doing my job."

"Where the hell is Justin?"

"I told you he's busy."

"Wouldn't take a minute to say hello," Grenville grumbled.

Appraising the remains of her cocktail with an air of trepidation, Barbara snatched up her glass. Screwing her eyes, she gulped down the liquid and stuffed the chunks of fruit into her mouth. She banged her empty glass on to the table with the force of a hammer.

"Drunk already," her husband mocked.

"No, I'm not." Barbara shifted in the seat and sat upright. She saw Mark had gone again and blinked deeply.

"He's like Houdini, that boy," Grenville reflected her thoughts.

With a little gasp, she clasped her cheeks. They were suddenly on fire.

Grenville observed her with a cynical snort, then a scuffling noise diverted his attention and he cocked an ear to one side. "Mice, I expect. That would be a fine start for Justin's venture, wouldn't it? A mouse infestation."

Barbara jolted upright. "So long as it's not rats."

Impervious to her alarm, Grenville continued his attack. "This place is a dump. Justin had such a brilliant future ahead of him with his Law degree. Could easily have been a barrister. To think he's ended up in a dead-end backwater like this."

"At least he's happy." Barbara skewered him with a glare. "And you had such a wonderful career in the police force, didn't you? Remind me, how many times were you overlooked for promotion?"

Before he could answer, a low buzzing noise diverted their attention. They stopped squabbling and stared at the light flickering in rapid bursts.

"Don't tell me the electricity is on the blink. Wonderful!"

The motion became suddenly violent as if someone were repeatedly flicking a switch. In his peripheral vision, Grenville detected the shadow of something obscure. The flickering ceased as abruptly as it had started and he found Mark beside him with more drinks. Suspicious, he stared at the waiter, only vaguely aware of Barbara picking up a replenished glass.

"I didn't hear you come in," Grenville looked him up and down.

"Didn't you?" The waiter tilted his head thoughtfully. His eyes looked dark and reproachful. "Perhaps you should be more careful what you say."

"Now hang on!"

"Grenville!"

She took a sip of her drink and Grenville regarded the crimson glow of her cheeks. He caught the colour of the cocktail and blustered, "Jeez, it's pink!"

"Quite nice though. Sweet. Yes, very nice."

He glanced at his watch and rolled his eyes. "How much longer do we have to wait in this room? This place feels like a prison cell. And it's bloody rude of you to push us so far out of the way."

"Nearly over. Everything's running to plan," Mark informed him blithely.

Turning away from the waiter with a low growl, Grenville jabbed a finger at his wife, "You tell him, will you?"

Clearing her voice with a little cough, Barbara went to protest, but the look in the waiter's eyes silenced her.

"What's stopping you? You'd normally make mincemeat of a minion like him."

"Just be quiet, will you? You're getting on my nerves." Taking an indelicate slug of her drink, Barbara glared at her husband.

He saw how her eyes were crazed by a labyrinth of broken blood vessels. Surely she wasn't really drunk? Inhaling a long, deep breath, he slid a hand to his chest as a familiar ache crept over it. He swallowed a large mouthful of the pink potion to relieve the tension pain. At least, he hoped it was just tension. It was happening more frequently, but with the amount of bickering there had been recently with Barbara it wasn't surprising.

He took a second draught of the cocktail, treating it as if it were a pint of beer on a hot afternoon. But the alcohol content was considerably higher than he expected from a pink drink for women or so-called men like Mark.

"Where's he gone now? I didn't see him leave."

"I expect he's busy helping them prepare. He must be rushed off his feet. We've obviously caused problems by turning up so early."

He picked up the glass again. Pink wasn't a manly colour, so he quickly downed the rest of the drink to get rid of it.

He looked at Barbara. She had a silly grin on her face.

"It's nice, isn't it? Sweet and strong."

"Like him. Or *her*, should I say? Well, sweet, anyway."

"You're such a bigot!" Barbara glowered. "I've had enough of this. I'm going to find Justin." Struggling to her feet, she took a step toward the door and then paused to check her reflection in the mirror. Immediately, a violent scream ripped through the room, making Grenville jump in his skin. His gaze shot to her and he watched her crumple like a concertina. Her hands were clasped tightly over her eyes in terror.

"What the hell's the matter now?"

Something crawled up behind and leant on her shoulder, making Barbara freeze. When she realised it was Grenville, she let out an hysterical shriek, "Can't you see? It's horrible!"

Slowly peeling away her hands, he forced her to look at the mirror again. "Come off it, old girl, you don't look that bad." Despite attempting levity, the intensity of his frown betrayed him.

Her eyes stung with tears. The face staring back now had drained of colour, but at least it was hers.

Grenville guided her back on to the sofa and sat close beside her.

"What's going on, Grenville?"

"I don't know, but I intend to find out."

Storming toward the door, he yanked the handle and pulled on the solid wooden structure. "Bloody thing's jammed." He yanked with the weight of his body—an almighty pull. Still no movement.

"Maybe it's locked," Barbara sniffed in a small voice.

"Don't be ridiculous, Barbara." Kicking the door, he winced against a stab of pain, and then limped back to the sofa. "Anyway, the other guests will be arriving shortly. We'll be able to join them in the dining room."

"If we ever get out of here..."

"Now you're being silly."

"This room gives me the creeps."

He watched her wring her hands, then grip so tightly her knuckles turned white. Before he could gather breath, Mark materialised with another drink. Blue this time.

"Green, pink and now blue. Like the flag of some banana republic," Grenville spewed hostility from every pore.

"You're nearly right. But not pink. Red, blue and green, and that's the Gambian flag. But peanuts are what they export. I don't know about bananas."

"Real little smart arse, aren't you? How do you know that?"

"We're *all* educated here, present company excepted."

"How dare you!" Clenching his fists, Grenville made to lunge at the boy, but Barbara summoned the strength to catch the tail of his jacket and pull him back.

"That's right. Hit first, think later. Not a very good advertisement for the police force, are you?"

"That's the final straw. I'm going to find Justin. Tell him what a rude little apology of a man you really are."

Grenville struggled to free himself from his wife's clutches. Whether she was restraining him or clinging on for dear life, he could not tell. Her air of desperation confused him; this was not the Barbara he knew. When he finally extricated himself, the waiter was nowhere to be seen. He pushed against the door once more. "Bloody thing's stuck again. Justin does know we're coming?"

267

"Yes, though I'm beginning to doubt he knows we're here right now…"

A low moan sounded and her eyes jerked to Grenville. "Was that you?"

He shook his head. "Must be the wind."

Another moan, more like a howl, resonated around the room and she turned a panic-stricken stare on Grenville.

"Just an old house creaking and groaning in the way they do," Grenville tried to reassure her.

She stared at the hairs on her arms standing on end. "I want to get out of here."

"Calm down."

Even Grenville was unconvinced by his contrived bravado. And when the lights flickered again, he visibly shuddered. This time it was more violent, like a rapid Paparazzi bombardment. On, off, on, off, they reached a crescendo of blinding white before exploding into darkness. Suddenly the air was so still you could hear a pin drop.

"Grenville, I don't like this…"

Unable to placate her, he knew his battle with fear was lost. Banging his fists against the door, he bellowed, "Let us out of here!"

"It's no use," Barbara snuffled. "There's no-one about.

Returning to the sofa, he clutched Barbara's hand.

"Not frightened of the dark, are you?" The waiter's voice sounded out of nowhere.

"What the…" Grenville searched the gloom "How the hell did you…"

"Get in? Maybe I'm even cleverer than you think. Anyway, I've got you some candles."

"The door was jammed only a moment ago. Anybody would think you'd locked us in here."

"As if..." Affecting a tone of mock innocence, the waiter positioned two dimly glowing candles on the mantelshelf. "I've brought your last drink too. Not long to wait now."

"Are the other guests here yet?" Barbara's heart was racing. In the flickering candlelight, shadows danced across the wall, fuelling her paranoia. She just wanted to get the hell out of this room.

"They'll be here soon."

"*If* they can find a backwater like this," Grenville checked his watch and grimaced.

"*You* found it. But then you've been this way before, haven't you? And don't forget a backwater's a pool still connected with a main river and lots of important, big fish often go there for a rest. That's what'll be happening here. But, of course, what can a little queen like me know about running a business? A *cottage* industry, maybe. You'd believe that."

"When did you come here before?" Barbara stared at her husband in both surprise and fear.

Grenville's gaze shifted to one side, evading her. "We used it as a cut through in the panda car occasionally."

"Yes, used to use it like a race track, didn't you?"

Even in the dull light, Barbara could see the blood drain from Grenville's face.

"What's going on, Grenville?"

"It's him," he jabbed a thumb at Mark. "There's something weird about him."

"You *have* been rude to him with all your prejudice," Barbara heard her voice slur and inwardly cringed.

"*My* prejudice? You were as surprised as I was to find him here." The sound of ice being dropped into a glass distracted him. "You still here?" he glowered at the waiter. "Makes a change."

"Yellow this time. You may not think me manly, but my drinks are strong. I don't know what flag this is, but enjoy it."

Taking a gulp of the yellow drink, Grenville belched loudly. Unapologetic, he waited for his wife's reproach, but the waiter's voice piped up instead.

"Manners!"

"I daresay the guests will do far worse. Knowing Justin, they'll all be queers or low-lifes."

"Perhaps..." The waiter had a wry smile on his face.

The man's smugness was a red rag to a bull and Grenville struggled to refrain from lashing out. He turned to Barbara and saw her slump back on the sofa with a little sigh. She looked chalk grey. "Christ, she's passed out. This is your fault. What the hell was in those drinks?"

He stared at the waiter angrily. Where had he seen this boy before? That spiky yellow hair, the diamond earring reminded him of something. "Who exactly are you?"

"Starting to remember are you?"

Grenville swallowed a nervous gulp.

"All this talk of a backwater..." the waiter circled round him and whispered from behind, "but I know your dirty little secret."

With a sudden whoosh, he was only inches from Grenville's face.

Overwhelming tension turned Grenville rigid. He opened his mouth, but no words would form.

Still his taunter persisted, "And you've kept it quiet all these years. Let's see, how many years exactly?"

"I don't..." Grenville's voice was weak. A bead of sweat ran down his brow.

"I'll tell you, shall I? It's three years since you mowed down an innocent young man in your patrol car and left him lying in the road outside."

"But I thought he was..."

"Dead?"

The light from the candles stuttered, and Grenville stared in horror as the flesh receded from the face before him, leaving vast,

夏

dark holes for eyes. Shock vied with the fear tying him to the spot as he witnessed the twisted body begin to evaporate. Fine tendrils of smoke spiralled away, dispersing into mist.

"It was in all the newspapers." A disembodied voice hissed. "A tragic hit and run incident. A young man killed by a speeding car and left in the road to die. Of course, nobody came forward to own up."

The room seemed to be getting darker as the flames of the candles guttered wildly.

"I've waited a long time for you to come back, Grenville."

Grenville made a frantic search of the void before his eyes. Everything seemed blurred and he could see nothing clearly beyond the darkening haze of the mist. A gust of wind passed through him and he descended into panic. Seizing his wife, he shook her violently. "Barbara? Barbara?"

"Too late. She's gone already."

With a sob, he shook the lifeless body again. His cry ricocheted off the fading walls and echoed back to him as if from far away. "Why? Why Barbara?" he wailed.

"Guilty by association."

"But she did nothing wrong," he howled. A desolate emptiness filled him. His gaze fell unsteadily to the glass lying abandoned and shattered beside his wife's body. Suddenly all the candles snuffed out.

And as she and the remnants of the room swirled away into the dark, a voice whispered, "Your turn now, Grenville. Drink up. There's still a drop left in your glass."

#

It was midnight before the last guest left. Although exhausted, Justin was proud of his achievements. The evening had fulfilled his every expectation. Everything augered well for the

271

future. Thank God his parents kept away. They seemed to court trouble wherever they went.

Settling on a bar stool, he allowed himself a moment to bask in glory, then his gaze fell on the cocktail shaker sitting on the polished wooden surface. With a grin, he inspected the yellow concoction inside. Just what he needed to help him unwind. He certainly felt he had earned it tonight. And, reaching for a glass, he began to pour himself a generous measure...

THE END

* Having 'escaped' from London several years ago, I now live in a pretty village in the UK countryside complete with a duck pond and stocks on the village green!

I always loved writing, although juggling a lecturing career and a family left little time. Now life has slowed down I enjoy the freedom to write in earnest.

My reading tastes are eclectic, but I tend to focus on writing contemporary romance novels 'with teeth'. When I was invited to write a horror story, it was a complete departure from the norm for me. In the event, I had a ball playing with the story and characters in 'A Fair Cop'.

&CBBEOCR&

25
'Twas the night before Christmas. A creature's a-stirring.

The Little Door
Gerald Rice

Rick sneaked down the creaky stairs. Last chance for milk and cookies. He also wanted to search for his wedding band again. He'd taken it off before wrapping gifts and had since come to the conclusion he'd wrapped it with either a Furby, a Dora playhouse, or a music box. But it could have just as easily been in with any one of the twenty presents he'd put under the tree. He had to find that ring tonight if he wanted to avoid a razzing from his wife.

By some miracle, Cindy hadn't noticed already, and maybe it wasn't that big a deal, but it was all he needed to come down here. He really wanted those cookies. His wife had steadily been chopping things off the list of foods he was allowed to eat over the last few years and sweets had been the latest casualty now that it looked as if he was about to become a type 2 diabetic.

With his diet under constant surveillance, the holidays had become almost unbearable with his better half. She was omnipresent around the house, appearing anywhere he was; his workroom in the garage, the exercise room in the basement, the bathroom, the deck—it was all he could do to get a moment's peace.

It wasn't that he didn't want to spend time with her. Rick adored his wife, but… well, it was a family joke that the 'C' in Christmas stood for 'Cindy'. For someone so concerned about his health, she had no problem having him climb on the roof to string

273

lights, drag the tree out of the attic, put out electronic reindeer, and run any number of holiday-related errands that had to do with lifting something heavy.

Now Rick supposed it had been silly, but at the time, taking his ring off had seemed a kind of pressure release. It had been the first time he'd taken it off in years and he'd only meant to keep it off for a few minutes, but he'd gotten so involved in wrapping the gifts, especially when she'd cracked the whip for him to pick up the pace, that he'd simply forgotten to put it back on.

His wife had just begun snoring and she would get much louder before eventually waking briefly in an hour or so. But even that was a risk as she was always a little extra restless on Christmas Eve and might snap awake from even the slightest noise. Rick had to be as quiet as a mouse. It had been freezing in the bedroom, and he knew it would be even colder once he was downstairs. He cinched the belt of his robe even tighter.

The grandkids would be here by six-thirty at the latest and their grandmother would no doubt be wide awake with breakfast. Their son, Kevin, shared his mother's zeal of the holiday season and it was more than enough that he would be making comparisons to Rick's Santa Claus-like girth. Rick would have to be sure to pluck the cookie crumbs out of his long black beard before going back upstairs. He made a mental note to turn on the powder room light which would remind him to check his face after he was done.

Rick made it to the landing, letting go of a lungful of air. He gripped the rail as he took the two final stairs to the living room.

There. He'd done it. All the way down those old wooden stairs without so much as a—

Creeeeeeee—

Rick shifted his weight and listened. Cindy gave a quick snort and resumed her regularly scheduled program of nonstop z's. As frustrating as his wife was with this whole diet thing, he loved her even more because of it. She'd been going to bed promptly at nine for the last fifteen years and even though he was more than

274

ready by the time the hour struck, sometimes he just wanted to stay downstairs longer. Or at least conscious longer. It was like a spousally imposed curfew and he'd wanted to protest on the principal he was a grown man, but had always relented. She was still the cutest woman in the world, so far as he was concerned. Maybe that was just corny nonsense, but it was rare and infrequent when he refused her anything. So the sleepy baby had to go to sleep—wasn't she really just doing him a favor? Of the few times when she'd stayed over her sister's or when she'd helped out Kevin and his wife after the first grandbaby came, Rick had stayed downstairs in his reclining chair and it had never turned out the way he would have planned.

Once, he'd made sure he ate a thick, juicy steak and drank four beers and attempted to stay up until eleven watching Skinemax. But the side-effect of his boy's night in had been a hangover, a twenty-four hour angry stomach, and an even angrier wife when she'd wakened him at six the next morning, glaring down at the broken plate on the floor and grease stains on the armrests. He hadn't even made it to the climax in the plot of *Alien Housewives from Uranus.*

No, he had no desire to get caught in the Wrath of Cindy. That's why his cover story was so perfect. It was romantic and it covered his butt. 'Honey, I just couldn't sleep. I just know my ring is wrapped up with one of the grandkids' presents—won't you help me look?'. Who knew—maybe Cindy and he might fool around right next to the Christmas tree. He wasn't averse.

Rick carefully plodded, avoiding the areas of the floor he knew would make noise. He cringed and froze at every tiny squeak until he got to the powder room and flicked the light on. Something caught his eye on the wall by the floor. Before it could register, his stomach clenched and the skin of his cleanly shaven bald head wrinkled as his eyebrows went up. He looked directly at it and panic settled in even deeper because what he was looking at made no sense.

It was a door. A little door.

No more than maybe ten inches tall, complete with a doorknob, the little white rectangle was a tiny version of all the interior doors in the house.

And it was ajar.

Without thinking, Rick got on his hands and knees and crawled toward it. He half expected the door to be shut before reaching it, half expected it to evaporate and he would come to the realization it hadn't been there to begin with. But the closer he got, the more concrete the realness of it became. He stopped when he was just inside arm's reach. Rick held out a hand, heart racing. He pinched the little doorknob between thumb and forefinger, turning it slightly left and right.

It was *real.*

He noticed there was something on the other side. The mudroom was *supposed* to be on the other side of this wall, but this room, whereever it was, wasn't in a part of his house. In fact, it wasn't a room at all. This was outside. Not outside *his* house, but some kind of lush forest. Green covered everything and all manner of vegetation was everywhere he could see. Rick's neck ached as he tried to look up to see the sky. It was daytime in this place even though he knew it was black as pitch outside. Even Santa was sleepy at this hour.

"Where in the world?" he said.

Something to his left came to a scuttling stop and Rick turned to look. It was a little man-thing, about seven inches tall, covered in some kind of loin cloth and hood, carrying a spear longer than it was tall. It had beady blue eyes and a leathery, wrinkly face.

Rick coughed a laugh, not sure if he could believe his own eyes. The thing stared at him, its pseudo-human facial features registering shock.

"Fee! Fee!" came a small voice somewhere above him. Rick didn't have time enough to move before something that felt like two warm quarters landed on his neck. But then came a sharp pain next to them and he knew he'd been cut. He instinctively drew back and slapped his neck, pinning the thing beneath his palm. Its tiny body felt extra soft and he immediately withdrew his hand in revulsion. It fell and hit the floor and Rick looked at the creature inches away from his fingers, either dead or unconscious.

The one that had spotted him and froze must have shaken off the shock of seeing a human because it had taken the spear into both hands and was charging right for Rick's eye. He sat up, moving his head out of range. The thing stopped beneath him, looked up and sweeped skyward with the spear. Rick jumped, knowing the thing couldn't reach him. Couldn't reach his head, at least.

After catching nothing but air, the little guy turned and stuck his spear in Rick's thigh. Rick clapped a hand over his mouth to keep his scream from boiling out, swatting at the creature stabbing him as an afterthought. It was quick, withdrawing its weapon and rolling out of the way. It dashed for the door and Rick snatched its feet from underneath it, flicking it into the bathroom to get that spongy, greasy body out of his grip. It somersaulted end over end until it smacked off the wall and lay still.

Rick examined the half inch wound in his thigh. It wasn't that bad, in fact, it had only bled a little and had already stopped. With herculean effort, he got off his knees, almost every bone in his body below his belly button crackling. This was going to take five—no, six cookies to process. At least.

What the hell were these things? They looked human, but *rattish.* Rick's heart fluttered. If it weren't the only organ he'd never had any trouble with, he might have thought he was on the verge of a heart attack. The one that had chopped his neck began to stir. It sat up and shook its head. Rick spotted the tiny, cleaver-like tool lying next to it and slid it away with his index finger. He wiped his hand down the front of his robe, not wanting to touch the creature again, but not seeing any way around it. He didn't want this thing here, but he didn't want it running away, either. These creatures were in his house and he wanted to get rid of them. Permanently.

But put them where? They probably could get out of the ninety-five gallon garbage can in the garage, although that would take some effort. And that door. If they could make one of those that went off into another place, Rick was still refusing to fully accept it as another dimension, they could probably just as easily make their own door to get back inside if he just threw them out. No. Had to kill them.

They'd had a mouse problem in their first apartment and Rick had taken care of it himself when the super had been unwilling. The man had denied there was a vermin problem even as a mouse ran between them while Rick was discussing it with him. So Rick had moved all the furniture away from the walls, found several holes the size of Cindy's fist and patched them all up. Then for good measure he'd poured cat food through the super's office rent slot in the door (which also led to his apartment) and tossed fistfuls all over the floor outside. The exterminator had arrived the next day.

But as he took hold of the little guy's leg, Rick knew he was appointing himself as exterminator. He walked quickly to the kitchen sink, trying to imagine it was something more pleasant— like a snake or loop of intestine. He cleared the dishes out left-handed, hurriedly stacking them on the counter and was about to stuff the creature down the garbage disposal. But Rick saw it was doing something out of the corner of his eye.

He forced himself to look at the ugly little thing and saw in the nest of its wrinkly face that the creature's eyes were closed. Its hands were clasped together in a universal gesture of pleading.

He froze.

The little guy was begging for its life.

That meant it had thoughts. And—and feelings, maybe even a soul. Worst of all, it *knew* what he was about to do. Or had been.

No way he could kill it now. It knew he was about to kill it and had begged for mercy.

"Oh my God," Rick whispered. "You're real. I mean, you're really real. You're not just some … some…" He didn't know how to finish the thought, but it had ceased being a thing and was a step closer to being human. Well, not human, but maybe somewhere around the neighborhood of a dog—an ugly, one-legged mutt, probably, but still.

The odd, squishy-feeling he'd had, holding it in his hand suddenly felt soft and a little damp. He righted the creature, letting it stand in the palm of his hand. It cringed as if waiting for a killing blow, but eventually relaxed and stared timidly back at him, the two transfixed by each other as if seeing and being seen for the very first time.

"What … are you?" Rick asked. The little guy shrugged as if to say it didn't know or maybe didn't know what he'd said.

"Wuh … aiyoo?" it said. It sounded like any number of the cartoon characters his grandkids watched on the TV. Rick jumped back in surprise. He laughed.

"You can talk!" He clapped his hand over his mouth then pointed in the general direction of the bedroom. "Gotta be quiet. Cindy's sleeping upstairs." It looked at him, not understanding and Rick set it on the counter, then put both hands together and laid his head on them like a pillow and mock-snored.

"Ah! Moag-dammo," it said, its voice sounding reverential.

"M-mowg—"

"Moag," it said, correcting him. "Moag-dammo."

"Good?" he said, smiling and pointing upstairs.

The creature puffed its body up, hunching over and growling. It made a mean face and its teeny voice dropped low. "Moag-dammo rak-lek ah pet-*ol*." It threw its arms up in a placating gesture and its voice went high. "Moag-dammo, *ip*-wee-mit fud iz."

Rick smirked. If he had the little guy's body language and intonation right his people were afraid of Cindy or *Moag-dammo.*

He pointed at himself.

"Rick."

"Rick," it repeated. He pointed to the creature and it looked down and then behind it, not understanding he was asking its name.

"Rick." He pointed to himself again, then the creature.

"Rick," it said then looked around, trying to figure what he was pointing at. Maybe they didn't have names. Maybe the little guy didn't have a name. It didn't seem to have one for him.

The creature stepped to the side and looked around him.

"Fee-fee!" it shouted and he turned. That was the same thing it had said just before attacking him. But it seemed more a warning or maybe a warning off. Rick turned to see what it was looking at and was shocked to see something like fifty-plus more standing behind him, watching.

One of them spoke rapidly and they all growled low, staring at Rick. He didn't know whether to be afraid or cuddle them, honestly. It appeared to be the same one he'd tossed after it had stabbed him in the thigh. In fact, it was. The little creature was pantomiming their encounter, explaining to the group with actions and whatever their language was how he'd charged and attacked Rick before being brutally savaged and thrown aside.

It was pointless to run. They were between him and any path out of the kitchen; he'd be overwhelmed in seconds. His best bet would be to fight. Rick eyed the drawer with the silverware, hoping he could get his hands on a couple knives before they were on him.

"No!" the little guy behind him shouted. Now there was a word he knew. "No! No!" Rick turned to see it waving its hands wildly in the air to get the tiny mob's attention. Most of them looked, but a few only had eyes for Rick. So far, none of them moved. So attacking him wasn't a lock yet. The little guy said something in their language rapidly; this time Rick didn't recognize any of it. The creature leapt off the counter and onto the floor, walking into the group and talking nonstop. He bumped into several of them that weren't looking at him, seizing some by the face to force them to look at him.

The talking went on for several minutes and Rick got the impression he must have held some position of esteem within the group. Rick began to pick up bits and pieces from his intonation and gesticulation.

There was some kind of war between this clan and another. Maybe several others. But they all lived in fear from the deity Moag-dammo. Figures. Cindy had always teased that he thought he was God's gift to women, but she was the one feared by an entire race of creatures as a demigod.

After about five minutes, the mob seemed less agitated, less on the verge of lynching him.

Actually, they seemed downright happy to see him.

It was in their blue eyes, Rick noticed, that they seemed to look at him almost with reverence. Four of them quickly stacked atop each other and one squished his body between the doors of the fridge and popped it open. Several scuttled inside, sliding out the orange juice and dropping it onto the ones waiting on the floor. Two were carrying a cup Rick hadn't seen them take and after a particularly smallish one got the top off they poured him juice without spilling a drop.

Rick took the cup gratefully and slipped his hand into the white cookie jar, vaguely designed to look like a cat. Something nipped his finger. He yanked it out and one of the creatures popped its head out of the jar. They stared at each other until he looked away. His mind kept defaulting to none of this being real, to it all being a dream. His eyes kept reaffirming he was wrong.

The lead one, the one he'd befriended, tugged on his robe. Rick looked down, his head still filled with a dreamy sensation. He took another swig of OJ and bent to let the little guy crawl up his arm. It wriggled up to his shoulder and stood by his ear.

"Moag-dammo, vik-vik," it said. It punctuated the last two words with a stabbing motion into its chest. Rick thought a moment. Did they want him to kill her?

"Moag-dammo bad-bad?" he asked. He didn't know why he'd doubled the word 'bad', it just seemed the right thing to do. It folded its little arms and seemed to consider this a moment.

"Ai-o!" it said, nodding. "Ai-o, bad-bad golo."

He leaned back on the kitchen counter, his head swooning. He had no doubt these creatures were telling the truth, but there had to be some mistake. This Moag-dammo couldn't be Cindy. It had to be some sort of mistaken identity.

Rick had to show them.

He grabbed a fistful of paper towel and mopped his brow. He looked at the cookie jar again and three were standing in front of it. Like bouncers outside a nightclub.

"I want a cookie," Rick said. They didn't move. "If you want me to 'vik-vik' the Moag-dammo, then gimme a cookie. Matter of fact, two." The three looked at each other and then to the leader. He nodded and they scrambling, two lifting the lid while the third crawled inside to grab a cookie.

"One more," Rick said, gobbling with one hand and waving for another with his free one. It crawled back in and retrieved it.

"Everyone follow me," he whispered after he'd finished and blindly combed through his long beard. They all looked as he slowly stepped through the group, careful not to squish anybody. In his own kitchen in a bathrobe at three in the morning he felt like he was in the lowest budgeted Godzilla movie ever. He made his way toward the stairs and en route spotted the Christmas tree.

His ring!

In all… *this* he'd completely forgotten.

He turned to them, holding his ring finger with the thumb and index of his other hand. "My ring," he said to them. "I need my ring." He had to think of a way to make them understand. He felt like it would be important. If he could show them that the Moag-dammo wasn't this evil god or that Cindy wasn't the Moag-dammo at all then maybe there was a way to bring peace to the whole situation. Maybe he could even help them to end their own conflict.

Rick noticed a few of the creatures wore rings. He knelt and gently grabbed one by its four-fingered hand. It looked confused, but didn't struggle as he pointed and said, "Ring." He pointed back to his own hand and repeated, then pointed to the presents under the tree. "Lost."

They slowly looked around and began mumbling amongst themselves. Rick remembered the gesture of the leader and did the same, putting his hands together and getting on his knees.

They descended on the presents, finding seams in the wrapping paper and squeezing their squishy little bodies inside without tearing the paper or popping the tape. All but a few had submerged themselves within the gifts and it was creepy to see presents he and his wife had wrapped for their children and grandchildren writhing on the floor as if they were alive.

But a moment later one of them emerged holding Rick's wedding band high (relatively) in its hand.

"Fee-fee!" it said. The others came out as it handed the ring back to Rick. He slid it on his finger and held it up.

"One miracle down," he said.

They were looking at him again with those expectant eyes. Rick was nervous, not sure how he was going to pull this off. He thought just by showing his beautiful sleeping wife to them they would understand, that they would realize he couldn't be married to the monster they were so afraid of.

He slowly trudged in the direction of the stairs, passing by the little door, complete with two (relatively) bulky sentries standing to either side. What could have been two females were peeking out (or was that in?) and withdrew hurriedly when they saw him. Rick heard scuttling feet ahead of him, but couldn't make out more of them in the shadows. He stopped at the first step, turning to the group one final time. They may not have had names individually, but perhaps they were called something as a group. If Rick knew what their people were called, he might be able to use that to reach out to them. He hoped.

"Rick," he said, patting the flat of his palm against his chest. He held his hands out to them, palms up, in a gesture he hoped asked, "And you?"

There was a grumble from the group again. The uniform sound of his name being chanted filtered through them until Rick had to shush them. Despite the strangeness of the situation, he didn't want his wife awakened. He repeated his name and pointed to them. They looked confused.

"A-Tooru," one from the back said. Rick repeated it, was corrected, and got it right the second time. Little creatures called A-Tooru had magically entered his home and now wanted him to murder his wife.

Rick rolled his wedding band on his finger with his thumb.

"All right, let's get this over with." He turned back to the stairs, being careful to avoid the squeaky spots, but still managing to trample over a few on his way up. About a hundred or so little feet scuttled up the stairs behind him. His heart was thudding so hard in his ears he couldn't hear the gentle susurrus of her snoring until he was halfway down the hall. If he knew his wife, she was maybe ten minutes away from coming half awake. She'd roll over on her side and snuggle up to him, lacing an arm across his chest and gripping his bad shoulder. But what would she do when he wasn't there?

Rick refused the temptation to look behind him, hoping they had disappeared. That they were either a figment of his imagination or maybe being this close to the Moag-dammo that they'd evaporated.

Finally, they stood at the door. He turned the knob, feeling the weight of each breath on the door like it was jacked into his nervous system. The door squealed as he opened it and Rick let go of a lungful of air like a lead weight.

How was he going to do this?

Rick didn't ask. He turned and grabbed the first A-Tooru he could. What looked like a thousand tiny blue lights stared at him. Rick stifled a scream, realizing they had little glow-in-the-dark eyes. He walked over to the bed and held it over his wife's sleeping body.

"Look," he said a little too loudly. He shook it slightly and the creature squirmed in his hand. He dropped it on the bed next to her. Cindy was on her side with her back to him, sleep mask on, hand cradled next to her face, her little mouth slightly ajar. "No Moag-dammo." He couldn't begin to think how to explain to the creature—to all of the A-Tooru—what he already knew. He patted his chest then hovered it over Cindy, pleading with his eyes as hard as he could. "Rick."

The rest of them were still at the door. The one on the bed looked at Rick, then to Cindy, then it sat on its haunches like a dog. It cocked its head to the side as if considering what he'd said.

"Moag-dammo?" It looked at him, its hand out by Cindy. The little A-Tooru made a sound in its throat. It rattled off something in its language, stood and continued speaking to the others. They mumbled amongst themselves, blue lights dancing as the majority of them shook their heads.

"No Moag-dammo." It ran up to her head, shaking its own. "Cin-dee." The A-Tooru placed open hands to its chest, presumably where its heart would have been.

Had Rick misunderstood?

"Moag-dammo." It pointed down at the bed. Rick scrunched his face in confusion. "Under."

A tentacle wrapped around Rick's ankle. It pulled him off his feet and he landed on his butt, his tailbone singing as several sharp somethings dug into his calf as the thing beneath the bed began dragging him under. There was a high-pitched scream at the door as one of the A-Tooru was grabbed by the same thing that had Rick and the creature yanked beneath the bed.

Rick spotted the rest of the A-Tooru waiting outside the room, holding each other and pulling away. He wanted to cry out, but found he didn't have the wind to speak. Instead, he slapped the siderail of the bed, trying to rouse Cindy. But she snored on. The little guy on the bed looked down at him. Its face set in grim determination, it leapt off the bed and onto Rick's paunch. It took out a tiny, triangular-shaped weapon and charged toward the Moag-dammo. There was a deep, unearthly groan and the toothed tentacle loosened enough for Rick to pull free.

He turned, wanting to snatch the A-Tooru back to safety, but saw it stuffed into a large, blue eye-and-tooth-filled maw in a hole the width of their king-sized bed. The eyes glowed the same as the A-Tooru. Deep, rattling sounds emanated from it and Rick realized the sound was in time with Cindy's snoring. Tentacles wriggled and flailed all around it and Rick got the distinct impression that even though it was currently enjoying eating the A-Tooru there had been a price to pay for it.

Rick scuttled on his butt, back-pedaling toward the door. Somehow, he knew the top of the bed was safe, but his legs wouldn't work, they wouldn't get under him so he could stand. Rick flopped over onto his stomach and tried belly-crawling to the door. The remaining A-Tooru waited at the door, beckoning him to come, afraid to come in the room. Two tentacles wrapped around his legs and snatched him back.

Rick slid across the floor, his hands uselessly attempting to find purchase. He grabbed one of Cindy's errant shoes and tossed it behind him. He felt his feet fall into the hole beneath the bed and his socks were sucked right off his feet as something wet and fleshy touched them. The tentacles gripped tighter and he looked back to see several others had lifted the bed slightly to make room for his big body. Rick finally thought to scream.

"What was that?" Cindy said. The bed clapped to the floor as she turned her light on.

Rick was about to let go with another scream when he realized the tentacles were gone. He opened his eyes and saw the A-Tooru were gone too. He didn't think they'd just left, though. The air felt different. Like a layer had been removed from everything around him. Rick turned onto his back, raising up on his elbows and spreading his legs to see nothing but hardwood floor beneath the bed. He pushed away from the bed a few feet before standing.

"Rick?" Cindy pushed up her sleep mask and stared at him with puffy eyes.

"Yeah." His voice cracked and he cleared his throat. "Yeah."

"What are you doing? Come back to bed, I had a nightmare."

"You?" he said, near hysterical, bending over to touch the spot where the tentacles had bitten in. There were three thin cuts just above his ankle and not even bleeding anymore. What had just happened?

He went to the toilet for a pee, grateful for an extra minute-and-a-half to slow his racing heart. By the time he was done washing his hands, Cindy had turned off the light and was just about sleep again. Rick draped his robe over the footboard, peaking under the bed before crawling under the covers. Cindy curled up to him, clenching his bad shoulder extra tight.

"Honey?" he asked.

"Hm?"

"What were you dreaming about? Just now, I mean."

"I don't know," she said after a long yawn. "Can't remember."

But Rick knew all too well. He'd barely survived it.

THE END

* Gerald Rice is the author of several short stories and novels, including "Mona" in Graveside Tales *Harvest Hill* anthology and *Fleshbags*, available from Razorline Press. He is currently at work on his first vampire story, *Heartbreak Hotel*, due out Valentine's Day, 2013. You can follow him on Twitter @GeraldRice and visit his website, www.razorlinepress.com. You can read his free short story, "30 Minute Plan," for free on Amazon.

26

Be careful of what you create.

Characters
Cynthia B. Ainsworthe

Kelly Elliott was nearly finished with her manuscript. Only a couple of chapters needed to be written; then she would be able to email her newest creation off to her agent in Los Angeles. Never having had difficulty in finding the right ending for her previous novels, this time was different. *Why can't I resolve this thing? It should be so simple, and I'm coming up empty.* The blank page stared back at her with mocking arrogance, forbidding her to even try writing. She typed *Chapter 30* a third of the way down the page. Getting up from her laptop, for yet another cup of coffee, she ambled to the kitchen. Her mind searched for a captivating hook that would grab a reader's attention. *I must have a catchy line; a surprise of some sort. My readers have come to expect that.* She glanced at the calendar posted on a cabinet door. A red circle was scribed around the thirtieth with the words "manuscript due!" She glared at the reminder, as if it represented a principal chiding a small child for a minor infraction. Kelly spoke out loud to her two attentive toy poodles, Gigi and Jacques. They sat at her feet. "Why do I allow myself to work under such pressure? I should've started the last few chapters a week ago. Now, I only have four days left." They rewarded her attention with wagging tales and smiling eyes.

Kelly's cell phone rang. She furrowed her brow, dreading the call. She hoped it wasn't her agent calling again to check up on her progress. The caller identification gave no clue. She shrugged thinking it was a wrong number.

"Yes," she answered.

An unknown male voice replied, "Don't do it."

"Who is this?" she inquired.

No reply came. A dial tone hummed in her ears. *Must be a wrong number or some prankster. I don't need to be interrupted with such foolishness.* She dutifully walked back to her laptop.

Kelly always wrote in the cozy study with her computer balanced on a small table. She found a formal environment stifled her creativity.

As she looked intently at the blank page, a faint image came to view in her mind's eye. *Dare I do this? Paul is such an endearing character, so very kind and loving. I wonder if my readers would hate me for it.* Kelly's fingers tapped aimlessly on her knee as she pondered a new plot twist. Gigi and Jacques curled on each side of her and gave gentle kisses, begging for attention. Her voice was kind, "Not now, kids. Mom has to get this work done. I can't waste valuable time petting you. How about a nice long walk after I finish this chapter?" Their wagging tails affirmed their understanding. Then the two poodles settled down to enjoy a nap.

Kelly took a deep breath, as one would before plunging into a swimming pool from a high diving board. She began.

Paul sat in the driver's seat of his SUV. He was lifeless. A dried trail of blood from his left temple marked the entry of the bullet.

A chill ran through her. She had killed off one of her main characters. This was painful. *I created Paul, gave him depth, a voice and life. Through endless pages he evolved into a breathing person in my mind with all the failings that people are born with. Paul loved too much. Understanding was his fault; a fault that is convenient to contrive his demise. This is one of the qualities my readers love. They've told me so many times that my novels came to life before their eyes, making them laugh or cry. This will be the perfect solution to the love triangle. If Paul dies, then Taylor and Larry will have a happy ending. A divorce is too predictable, can't use that ending. Romance must have a happy ending or at least a happy for now finish. Who will be the criminal? Hmmm, that is a problem.*

Her stomach growled. She looked at the antique clock on the mantle. The sound of the pendulum promoted a feeling of peace. It was a sound she had grown up with from childhood. She remembered her mother would regularly wind the mainspring. Since her parents' death, Kelly clung to mementoes of her past. And with her husband on regular business trips, her writing filled in the loneliness she might otherwise feel. *It's almost noon, I might as well fix something to eat. Maybe I can think of who should be the murderer on a full stomach.*

Kelly stood in front of the open refrigerator, perusing its contents. Nothing seemed to spark her appetite. Gigi and Jacques reached up to her from the kitchen floor, pawing at her legs for a treat. "Yes, my little darlings, Mom hasn't forgotten you," she responded to their pleadings. Grabbing a package of ham and a jar of mayonnaise, she closed the door with of shove of her hip. *A ham sandwich is better than nothing. I'll have to make a mental note to spice up my grocery list.* She absentmindedly gave the two poodles a small piece of ham. They rewarded her with wagging tails. Their large brown eyes asked for more. "No more for now," she answered their silent questions. "You'll spoil your dinner."

While finding a plate, a thought came to her in a flash. It would be the perfect answer and one that her readers would love. Kelly spoke to the poodles, "Linda will kill Paul. She's perfect. I created her character as an unstable sort, and then shoved her into the background ten chapters ago. What a fantastic surprise! No one will see it coming." Gigi and Jacques cocked their heads as she looked at them. "You understand every word I say. Don't you, my babies.' Charged with new energy, she rushed back to her laptop.

Reaching for her sandwich, and eager to end the novel, she looked at the computer screen. Her eyes grew wide with astonishment. *This can't be. Was I merely thinking I had typed those sentences?* All that was on the page was *"Chapter 30"*. She rubbed her eyes and looked again. Leaning closer to the computer, Kelly hoped this gesture would magically cause the previously typed sentences to appear. Still, the chapter title was all she saw. She looked at the poodles who had resumed their place beside her. Kelly petted them, to reassure herself that she wasn't in a dream. She could feel the easy rise and fall of their breaths. *I can't be dreaming this! It must be the stress and lack of sleep from trying to make this deadline. Never again will I procrastinate!*

The phone rang again. Its sound jarred her senses. She immediately got up to answer it.

"Yes," came her greeting with irritation.

The same male voice calmly stated, "Don't do it. We warn you."

Before she could reply, a dial tone ended the call. *I don't need this kind of foolishness. Jerks making stupid prank calls.* She could feel her pulse quicken.

Taking a seat at the laptop, Kelly typed again; *Paul sat in the driver's seat of his SUV. He was lifeless. A dried trail of blood from his left temple marked the entry of the bullet.* Before her eyes, she watched the letters disappear one by one, as if the computer had a mind of its own. *This is absolutely ridiculous. What a time for my keyboard to act up.* She looked under the backspace and delete keys for some foreign matter that might have been lodged there. None was found. She typed a simple sentence as a test. No problem. Then she pressed the backspace and delete function. All were in working order.

Computers! Can't live with them and can't write without them! Maybe it's my software? Exasperated, Kelly went back to the kitchen for another cup of coffee. *On second thought, maybe I've had too much caffeine. Water would be better.*

292

She returned and for the third time, she typed, *Paul sat in the driver's seat of his SUV. He was lifeless. A dried trail of blood from his left temple marked the entry of the bullet.* The words remained. She looked up at the clock. *I guess three times is the charm.* The familiar tic-toc had stopped. *That's very odd. That clock has never stopped before. Well if this is the trade-off, I'd rather have a malfunctioning clock than computer problems.* She was ready to type the next sentence when she heard a sound. Someone cleared their throat. She immediately looked up. She was unable to speak. Fear filled her. She wondered why Gigi and Jacques didn't notice anything wrong. Four figures stood in front of her. Kelly recognized them. She had given birth to these beings.

Paul started first with his hands sunk deep into his pockets, "Why do you have to kill me? Is that my reward for being loyal and kind? You created me, but that doesn't give you the right to murder me."

"But, but…" was all she could utter. *This is not real. What is happening? Is my stress causing hallucinations?*

"This is very real," came Taylor's reply, as if she could read the author's thoughts. "You never asked me if I wanted to be a cheating wife. You put me into situations that I would never have agreed to, all for your own creative ego."

Am I going insane? Is this the reward for the creative process? Her heart pounded with terror as an orange-size lump formed in her throat. Droplets of perspiration trickled from her forehead. She felt cold and clammy. Tightness gripped her chest. Her breaths grew short and rapid.

Larry took a step closer. He began with a warm gesture of open arms, "You're not having hallucinations. I am real." He continued in a kind and pleading voice, "All I wanted was my music. I was happy with my career. Why did I have to be the other man to Taylor? She was happy with Paul. You never considered my feelings."

Linda moved toward Kelly. "You made me a murderer and an unstable nut-case for your own purpose. How would you like to lose your mind like that?"

Kelly thought, *I think I am; I'm going insane.*

"No, you're not. We are very real. You created us without any concern for our feelings. Forever, I'll be known as 'Linda, the unstable fool who killed Paul.' Well, I won't have any of it. Paul, Taylor and Larry are too kind to make things right—but I am not!"

#

The newspaper article read:

Well-known author, Kelly Elliott, was found dead Monday morning by her husband, James Elliott, after his return from a business trip. The perpetrator committed the crime in their home sometime Sunday afternoon. Police officials stated the fatal wound appeared to be a bullet which entered her left temple. Police stated no weapon and no forced entry were found. Her two toy poodles were discovered curled up to the body, licking at the wound. Investigation remains on-going. Police authorities request those with any information to contact them.

END

* Cynthia B. Ainsworthe was inspired by Barry Manilow's words, "Do what you love, and the rest will follow." Her novel, Front Row Center received a five star review from Midwest Book Review as "original and riveting..."

27
Be wary of superficial people. Their shallow nature is infectious.

Plastic People
Lisa Lane

It all started on a warm summer evening. I was sitting on my porch, watching the stars emerge one by one in the dimming sky. There was a full moon that night, so big that it looked like it hovered right over town, looming overhead like a spaceship from Hell, just waiting to swoop down over the unaware and the unwitting. On a night like this one, I think it very well could have done just that.

I was trying to spot constellations in the sky. The Dippers are the only ones I really knew, although I'm pretty sure I had found the Zodiac belt. Anyway, I was stargazing as Alison Franco came up the sidewalk with her stupid cocker spaniel. I hated the bitch with a deep passion, but I smiled politely. She smiled back, taking my gesture as an invitation to chat. She walked up the path to the house, keeping to the stepping-stones as if my lawn were molten lava. Her dog was not so courteous.

Her smile grew the closer she came to me. It was that nosey, I'm-still-better-than-you smile. I'm telling you, I cannot even put into words how much I hated her. She had been a ruthless shit to me all through grade school. She had reveled in the embarrassment and grief of all the "unpopular" kids, but she had always been the worst with me. Once, she had spread a rumor around the whole school that I heard voices and talked to imaginary people. "Psycho" became my nickname for a couple of months, until the novelty of my humiliation wore off, I suppose.

There was another time when Alison had convinced all of her friends in class to go, one by one, to my desk and slip in belongings of theirs when no one was looking. They had then taken turns going to the teacher and telling him that they had seen me stealing out of their desks. They all had giggled as the teacher went through my desk and took inventory of the "stolen" items, glancing at me with a scornful frown. Once again, Emily Johnson had been brought to tears. Another game point for Alison, and at a record-breaking ten a.m. I assume that the display had been quite entertaining, as Alison and her friends had insisted upon finding different creative ways of pushing me into similar breakdowns on a regular basis.

High school had been ten times worse, if you can even fathom that. I really did hate that bitch. Why she thought that we were suddenly old high school buddies simply because I had become a prestigious artist and a pillar of the community is beyond me.

"You've been crying," she said with dramatic concern.

I wiped away my tears, my jaw going tight. It was one thing to pry, but it took real nerve for her to feign such regard. For a fleeting moment, I considered planting my clenched fist into her face.

"How's that little one of yours? I bet he's getting big."

I nearly lost it right then and there, but I forced myself to hold back. She would have enjoyed the show way too much. She didn't know anything, and yet she knew far too much. She always seemed to ask just the right stupid questions precisely at the most inconvenient of times, and I hated her all the more for it. She was a master of feigned sympathy, playing the bleeding heart just well enough to feed her personal supply of town gossip. Bitch.

I smiled again, trying to remain pleasant as I watched that dog of hers sniff my lawn for an appropriate place to relieve itself.

I spoke with much difficulty, a knot lumping up in my throat. "David's in the hospital."

She tried to look surprised, but she was never a good actor. By now, the whole town had to know what had happened. "I'm sorry. Is he okay?"

The knot tightened.

Her dog was now working on my lawn, having found just the right patch to burn. I hated that dog, too. Fucking cocker spaniels … can you think of any stupider breed? Definitely "kick me" dogs, if you ask me, but I'm sure I'm offending a small group of you with that admission. Anyway, the stupid thing crapped and peed on my lawn, and I'll be damned if Alison didn't pretend not to notice.

"Well, you know," she began with a sparkle in her eyes, "if you ever need to talk, you just give me a call."

Yeah, right. So you can be the first to blab all of the juicy details across town…

I cleared my throat. "I'll be sure to do that."

She smiled, looking satisfied.

I stood, pretending I was cold. "I'm sorry. You'll have to excuse me." Without waiting for her response, I turned and entered the house, leaning up against the door with all my weight as soon as I could get it locked behind me.

And then I began to cry. I cried because I knew that talking— to anyone—was futile. Nothing could help me now. I knew my son, my beautiful David, was going to die.

And I could have prevented it.

I received the call around nine that night. I was not surprised at all by the news, but all the same, I was still quite overwhelmed by it. All of a sudden, I was completely alone. No one was coming home. All that was left was an empty house filled with depressing memories.

I had stopped going to the hospital on Wednesday, when my husband, John, had died. It had come as a shock to me because he had already survived two days. He was such a strong man. Given the severity of both of their injuries, I had fully prepared myself for the possibility that David could die. But John? I couldn't believe it.

It felt as if reality was crumbling, slowly but ever so steadily.

I had to get out of the house. I could no longer stay there ... there was no one to stay there for. I wanted to burn it down, watch every last memory held within its walls crumble to ash, but instead my legs took me directly to the front door. I walked for quite some time, my mind racing with so many thoughts that I couldn't even keep up with them all. I noticed at one time that I was thinking about three different subjects simultaneously, as if my mind were running on a number of different tracks. I found it fascinating and made a game of it, concentrating on how many "tracks" I could use at once without confusing myself.

I labored my brain, finding my limit at—try to comprehend this—counting from one to five, while counting from six to ten, while counting from eleven to fifteen, while counting from sixteen to twenty, all simultaneously. It consumed my thoughts for quite awhile, leaving no room to grieve. But it could only distract me for so long, and the painful reality of losing both my husband and my son struck me again soon enough.

I found myself at a nearby park, and I sat down at a bench for a while and allowed myself to cry once again. I buried my face in my hands, my pain creating a brief pool of tears that I watched slip away between my fingers.

"Why are you crying, lady?" I heard a little boy ask.

I looked up, startled by the company. I had thought I was alone, and it surprised me to see a boy so young out so late.

I ignored his question, instead asking one of my own: "Where's your mommy? Does she know you're out here at this time of night?"

He shrugged. "Why are you so sad?"

I thought for a moment. "Because I'm lonely."

"Not anymore," he said with a smile.

"Are you lost?" I tried again, concerned.

He shook his head. "I know where I am. Do you know where *you* are?"

298

I heard several dogs barking in the distance, and I looked around to see if the source was as close as it sounded. Again, I thought about the little boy. "Are you supposed to be out—"

I was surprised to see that the boy was no longer there. I looked around, but I saw no one. "Little boy?"

No answer.

I was alone again. I searched behind trees and bushes, down the walk and into the center of the park. The boy had disappeared. Deciding that his whereabouts really was none of my business in the first place, I decided to continue walking. It was beginning to get cold, and I remember wishing I had thought to bring a jacket.

The barking got louder and, again, I looked to see if I could spot anything. Still nothing, but the dogs sounded close enough to be passing through the street right in front of me. I thought about the boy again, and I hoped that he wasn't in any danger. I wondered if the dogs might be wild, but at the same time, I realized how absurd the idea of a pack of wild dogs running the suburban streets truly was. Dogs ran wild in parts of the city, especially throughout the ghetto, but this was *downtown suburbia*. The thought of running into them scared me nonetheless, being I had never been much of an animal person. They can smell that, you know, just as well as they can smell fear. That really gets them going, so I've been told. They'll hunt for sport sometimes, too, chase down anything that will run from them. I decided it best to continue walking. I hoped a quicker pace might not only keep me from running into the dogs, but also warm me up a little.

Clouds slowly rolled over the town, but they weren't like any I had seen before. They had a strange darkness to them, an ominous feeling that chilled me straight to the bone. They didn't look quite like clouds, but rather the culmination of hundreds of thousands of tiny particles of dark energy, pure evil, scurrying about in the sky like a massive swarm of gnats. I could see, every now and then if I looked really hard, particles of light trying to take over in the darkness, and lightning would suddenly dart through the clouds and strike it down, crackling with apocalyptic fury.

My fear grew even more intense as it began to drizzle. Those abominable clouds were now beginning to shed malignant rain down upon me, and I wondered what might become of it. A new plague? Mutagen from the heavens? The beginning of the end? I wasn't about to find out—I'm telling you, I could feel the evil—so I quickly took shelter under a large oak tree.

The drizzle soon turned into rain, and the wind began to howl through the trees. More light tried to infiltrate the swarming of darkness, and lightning shot wildly through the black void, the evil gnats chasing it down and striking it out of existence.

They fed on the light ... and whatever they were they were multiplying.

I heard the dogs again through the howling wind. I no longer had any idea where they were coming from, so I thought it best to look for some temporary indoor shelter. I looked around, my vision hampered by the downpour. The tree no longer held back the showers, but rather collected each drop and patiently waited for enough with which to create a deluge of heavy drops to fall down onto me. Apparently, the darkness was slowly infecting the rain, as now even the trees were against me. I dodged a number of water bombs, but they just kept coming.

I spotted a small shopping center across the street, just as the trees began to show irrefutable evidence of assimilation. The wind still howled, but the trees took on a life of their own, writhing hideously like creatures struggling to climb straight out of Hell. I tried to scream, but my throat was so tight that the only sound I produced was a faint, strained wheeze.

The trees reached for me, trying to hold me where I was. I broke free and darted across the street. The rain hit hard against my face, then soaked my clothes. It was a freezing, biting rain. I could feel the evil trying to enter me, trying to soak through skin and bone and move clear into my soul. Shaking off as much as I could, I took shelter under the eaves of an unfamiliar clothing store. I shivered violently.

The store looked closed. Lights were on in the far back, but most on the sales floor were off. However, the "open" sign still rested in one of the display windows and the front door was unlocked.

When I opened the door, a gust of warm air blew over my body. This place was safe—for now. I pulled myself in, the evil coldness struggling to suck me back out. I pushed the door closed, a sudden feeling of security and warmth engulfing me.

"Hello?" I called out. "Anybody here?"

No one responded, but the cold, wet clothes sticking to my trembling body moved me further into the establishment. Although the sales floor was dim, I was drawn to a rack of comfortable-looking sweat suits with bright multi-colored designs. I looked through them, and I picked out a pair of purple pants and a matching sweatshirt decorated with swatches of pink and blue. It was my size, so I took it to the dressing room to change immediately. I really did think it would be okay. I was horribly wrong, but at the time I had no idea what I—what the world—suddenly was up against.

Warm and dry, with two clothes tags in hand, I set out to find a cashier. She would just have to understand the circumstances, and hopefully, she would not freak out and accuse me of being a thief when she spotted me wearing the store's merchandise. I knew I'd be met with little hostility if she'd had a chance to see the clouds outside. I searched several minutes, but I found no one.

I decided to check in the back. Perhaps someone was there doing closing paperwork, I thought. I found no one. I jumped as I heard a slam and lock of the front door, and darted to the front of the store. I tried the door. It was locked and the "open" sign was facing me. The closing manager must have been in the back when I had initially entered, I reasoned, and then she had gone up front while I was searching for her in the back, leaving without ever knowing of my presence. Yet I still felt the company of someone—

or something—locked in with me.

Had *it* come in when the manager had opened the door to leave?

I looked out the foggy window and spotted a young woman in a long skirt. She had an umbrella, but the rain still pummeled her. I called out to the woman, banging on the window, but she didn't notice me. As I saw her cross the street, I could swear that something about her changed. Perhaps it was a shift in her posture, I don't know, but it was enough to send a chill down my spine. She stopped and looked up at the trees, and then she screamed as the branches found her and wrapped themselves tightly around her thin body. And then she disappeared, pushed down into the muddy earth with one final, terrified cry.

I backed away from the window, suddenly realizing that the cold was seeping in through the cracks between the front door and its frame. It was coming to finish me, to take me wherever it had taken that poor young woman.

I wondered how long it would be until the store filled with the cold, misty air. My body broke into a cold sweat, and I began to shake. Was I already infected? I could feel the evil spreading through the air around me. I ran toward the back and locked myself in one of the dressing stalls. And then I prayed ... on three simultaneous tracks.

I'd never been a religious person, but I became one that night. I believe God touched me, my soul. I know people who call me crazy for this, but I also know people who understand. I have talked to others who have faced the cold, dark evil, and we hide together in a safe place.

I'll get into that at a later time, however. For now, I must tell you how I came to be where I ended up, and how the demons almost stopped me ... because you, the Readers, are my only connection to the outside, and I know you're out there. I can *feel* it.

I summoned the courage to begin searching the store, the hollows of the clothing racks, searching for the eyes that followed me. It was quite cold now, the evil closing in from all directions. It was watching me.

The rain beat harder against the roof, demons dancing some wicked stalking ritual over my head. Thunder trailing the flashes of lightning rattled the windows like sonic booms. I quickly whipped around as I heard someone approach from behind me. I saw no one, and so I worked to convince myself that my nerves were beginning to make me a little paranoid. I should have listened to my intuition. I should have run while I had the chance.

A mannequin stood before me, poised gracefully with one foot inclined at a right angle to the other. She smiled, her glassy eyes staring directly into mine. I moved a step backward, gasping at how life-like those eyes suddenly seemed. I could have sworn I saw them blink. Fear raced through me. There was something evil about her.

The evil chill bleeding in through the door?

I moved back a few more steps, and then turned to run, stumbling into and falling over another mannequin. I heard laughing, but when I looked around for a source, the laughing ceased. I moved away from the fallen mannequin, and then I glanced back at the one with the staring eyes. They were still locked onto me, despite my movement. I looked back for the fallen one, but to my horror, she was gone.

The walls suddenly seemed to be closing in on me. I felt dizzy. I looked around, bewildered, because everything kept changing. It was almost as if the mannequins were moving systematically as I had my back turned to them.

"Who's fucking with me?"

Silence.

The sudden crackle of thunder startled me, and I jumped. Laughter once again emanated from the shadows. Despite the cold, my face dripped with sweat. I could hear my heart over the beating of the rain.

"I'm paying for the sweats, so you can stop with these games!"

I continued. I knew, however, that this was no game. The cold, dark evil was slowly transforming the interior of the store, just as it had transformed the trees outside.

My eyes focused on a female silhouette moving through the shadows on the other side of the floor. I could barely see her.

"Who's there?" I called, clinging to one last bit of hope that another human being might be locked in there with me.

The silhouette froze, camouflaging into the gradation of shadows cast by the dim fluorescent overheads in the back.

"What's the deal?" I asked, slowly moving toward her. "Is this your idea of a joke?" I prayed that the figure would burst out laughing, give me a good pat on the back, and then send me on my way, although deep down I knew I was only deluding myself. I desperately wanted it to be a joke. I wanted to prove my fears wrong, that the evil outside would pass without taking me with it, but a nauseating feeling deep in my gut told me otherwise.

She had her back to me, her head angled so she could peer at me through the corner of one eye.

"I'm locked in." I tried again, my voice cracking.

She remained motionless.

I heard another quick bout of laughter coming from all around me, which died again as soon as I turned to spot my hecklers. I turned again to the woman, keeping my distance.

"What's the deal?" I demanded, trying to suppress the fear that now threatened to consume me.

She turned to me with mechanical grace. Her glassy eyes stared me down as she scowled, her smooth plastic face stretching unnaturally. She looked like a puppet as she spoke: "Are you trying to start trouble?"

I gasped, unable to believe my eyes. I tried to back away, only to bump into more mannequins. I swung at them, knocking them over, and then ran back to the front door. I frantically searched for a latch, some way to unlock the door that didn't require a key, but I had no such luck.

The evil danced around in the rain outside, laughing at me through the wind. I wasn't sure what was worse, being locked in here with very clearly demon-possessed entities, or going back outside and directly exposing myself to the source. Fear overwhelmed me, and I found myself crying once again. I thought about John and David, all of the things that should have been ... the life and security I had grown to take for granted, all shattered in the dire crash of a speeding car. One night of needless drinking and arguing—all my fault—and never even a chance to apologize. It didn't have to happen, or perhaps it did, because now I was here for reasons only God knew ... perhaps only the Devil. I truly do not know.

I turned around to find a circle of plastic people around me. The fear was maddening, and it took every bit of strength to keep from blacking out. They moved slowly and precisely, closing in on me. I staggered, retreating backward to the door, shuddering at the feel of cold glass against my shoulders.

"What do you want?" I cried.

The closest one stepped even closer. She spoke with much conviction, seemingly their leader. "You chose to trespass at a most unfortunate time."

My throat went tight and dry, and I struggled to utter a few words in my defense. "I was just passing through."

"Now you have two choices: join us or die."

They closed in on me, backing me into one of the display windows. "Join or die! Join or die! Join or die!" they chanted.

The window was empty, save a thin metal post used to prop up a mannequin and a panoramic backdrop of a mountain range.

"All I want is to get the hell out of here!" I cried.

"That wasn't one of your options," she replied. "I guess we'll have to decide for you. You'll be our new lookout." She shoved me toward the metal post.

I quickly pushed away from it, the closing circle of mannequins giving me little room to move. I swung my arms wildly, frantically trying to get away from them. I hit two of them, but that only made them more determined. The group advanced on me, and I struggled to break free.

"It won't hurt," the leader said, her eyes suddenly glowing demonically. "We're just going to shove a post up your leg."

I kicked and punched, throwing them off me. I hit the leader squarely in the face, and she dived at me, knocking me to the floor.

"Is this your way of saying you'd rather die?"

I tried to kick her away. "Go to Hell!"

The group laughed ... and then a strange thing happened. Their faces ... I recognized every one of them. Alison Franco was amongst them, so was Jenny Hansen, the cheerleader bitch with that annoying curly handwriting (with circles for dots!) and enough freckles on her hideous face to create a three-dimensional dot-to-dot. Everyone I hated, they were all there, all the plastic Barbie-doll bitches who had trampled my childhood self-esteem and destroyed my spirit with endless jokes and ruthless tricks. I had entertained the thought more than once that they were all demons of some sort. Now I knew. They were working with the cold, dark evil. They always had been.

The leader, a woman whose demeanor was so absolutely nauseating that I had actually blocked her name from memory, moved forward yet again and struck me down.

I felt like a beast cornered for the kill. The leader moved to strike me again and I flinched, terrified.

She cocked her head, amused, lowering her hand. "Death would be too easy!" she laughed with a sudden enthusiasm.

She beckoned to the others, and they immediately advanced in on me as a group, dragging me back to the post. There was nothing I could do. They lifted me into the air, one tearing off my right shoe and sock, and I screamed as they pierced the metal post through my foot as if it were cellophane, working to force it beyond my ankle and up into my leg.

I cried out, feeling my bloody foot slowly transform into

plastic, the pain of the post tearing through my flesh and shattering my anklebone. I kicked my free leg with all my might, my arms flailing madly. I thrust my weight against the mannequin closest to the window, setting the entire circle off balance, sending her crashing through the window in a rainfall of broken glass. I fell out with her, screaming with the snap of my foot as the flesh and bone tore away from the transformed plastic. Three other mannequins crashed down on top of me.

I rolled over, moaning in pain, splinters and chunks of glass adding to my agony. Blood gushed from the stump where my foot had once been ... and four damaged mannequins lay motionless beside me in the bitter cold. I lay there in too much pain to move. It took only minutes before I grew light-headed and passed out.

When I woke, the first thing I noticed was the intense throbbing of my foot. The pain shot all the way up my leg. I looked at it, crying at the reminder that it was no longer there, and in its place lay a bandaged stump where phantom pain replaced what had once been. My foot was gone, even though the staff here did their best to assure me otherwise. I knew better, though; I knew my foot remained a plastic artifact of the attack I had survived back at the store.

I tried to explain myself countless times, but who could believe such a crazy story? I sure as hell wouldn't have had I not seen it with my own eyes. The evil had retreated, for one reason or another, but I knew it would be back even stronger than before. I could feel it.

And that is why I must tell you to prepare. I'm safe where I am, under the most ingenious cover, and I am planning ... planning for the next cold, evil rain, because it will be back.

Excuse me for a moment, please...

Sorry about the interruption. That was Nurse Bradley. She's a royal bitch, always pretends she can't hear me when it's quite clear that she can. She's had me tied up in a jacket for hours now, and my right arm is getting a little numb. That always makes me feel very much like screaming, I must say. She gets mad at me for talking to you, but we'll see how long she lasts when the shit hits the fan. If only she knew, then she wouldn't be forcing those terrible pills down my throat.

But where was I? Oh, yes … you, my friends, must find the other Readers and give them my story … because you all must prepare. I've seen the cold evil and the destruction it can do.

It all started on a warm summer evening…

THE END

* Leigh M. Lane currently resides in the beautiful mountains of Montana with her husband, editor Thomas B. Lane, Jr., their two very spoiled cats, a leopard gecko, and a grumpy, geriatric turtle. Having grown up on reruns of *The Twilight Zone* and *The Outer Limits*, combined with her mother's extensive Stephen King collection, Leigh writes a broad spectrum of science fiction and horror, all of which contain strong psychological or speculative twists.

≈⊰⊱⊰⊱⊰⊱≈

Visit us at:
http:shop.claytonbye.com
and every other large book provider on the internet.

Get in touch at:
ccbye@shaw.ca

STRANGELY DIFFERENT HORROR STORIES BY TALENTED AUTHORS WORLDWIDE

THE SPEED OF DARK

CLARK ENTERPRISES PUBLISHING

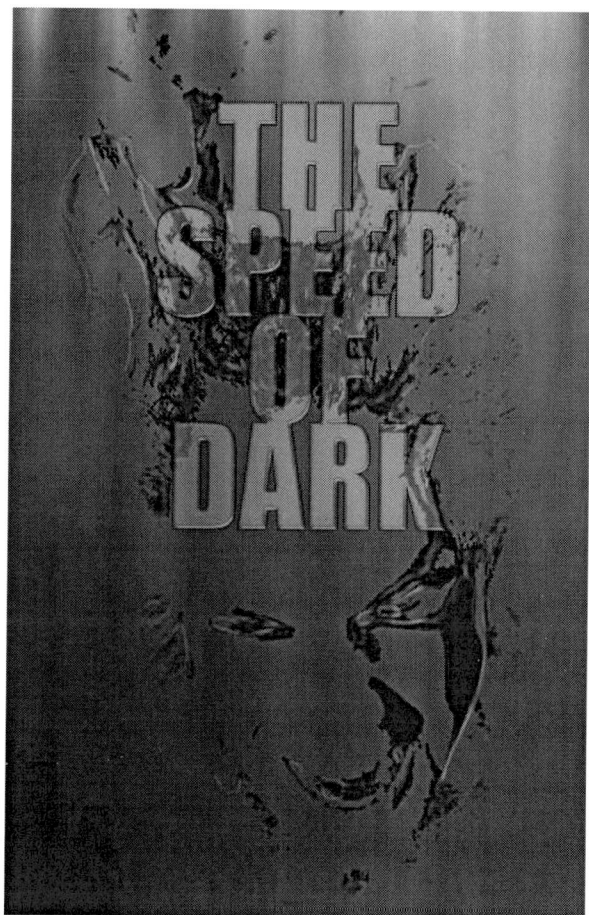

THE
SPEED
OF
DARK

Lightning Source UK Ltd.
Milton Keynes UK
UKOW040038230313

208044UK00001B/35/P